Murder in the Latin Quarter

Murder
in the
Latin Quarter

by
Tony Hays

IRIS PRESS

Bell Buckle, Tennessee

Library of Congress Cataloging-in-Publication Data

Hays, Tony.
    Murder in the Latin Quarter/ by Tony Hays.
      p.   cm.
    ISBN 0-916078-32-9
    1. Hemingway, Ernest, 1899-1961–Fiction. 2. Joyce, James, 1882-1941–
Fiction. 3. Novelists, American–20th century–Fiction. 4. Novelists, Irish–20th
century–Fiction. 5. Latin Quarter (Paris, France)–Fiction.   I. Title.
    PS3558.A877M86 1993
    813' .54—dc20   93-220991
                                                      CIP

This is a work of fiction. All characters, institutions, corporations, or other organizations depicted in this novel are the product of the author's imagination or, if real, are used ficticiously without any attempt or intention to describe their actual conduct.

Cover by Holly Lentz-Hays, Manchester, Tennessee.
Page composition by Cascade, Sewanee, Tennessee.

For
Joe and David
the last of my immediate family
and the best of brothers,

and,

as ever,

Holly,
who is always there for me.

But most especially,
this book is dedicated to
those incredible characters who
made Paris such a magical place to be.

Other Books
By
Tony Hays

Murder On The Twelfth Night

Acknowledgements

Several people assisted me in the research and writing of this book. I would be completely remiss if I didn't acknowledge the support and assistance of Dr. Dorys Grover, Dr. Richard Tuerk, Dr. Brenda Bell, Ms. Sylvia Kibart, Deanna and Neil Maxwell, Dr. Jay Pilzer, and Anjanette Gilley. They read varying drafts of the novel or assisted in the gathering of research materials. Without them, this story could not have been told. And Ms. Amy Foster, whose wishes for my success know no bounds.

One person deserves special mention. Jeannette Palmer read practically every draft of this novel, and she steeped herself in the history and lore of expatriate Paris so that she might be of the most assistance possible. No writer ever had a truer, more loyal, or more devoted friend and supporter. A teacher, editor, and motivator, Jeannette has never failed to give my career the gentle (and sometimes not so gentle) pushes it needs to keep me on track.

One

*S*moke stings my face, filling my nostrils and choking my lungs. I blink through the tears and see the landscape drifting by far below, a huge red, barn standing like Colossus against the emerald fields. Twisting the joystick left and right, I try to bank out of the smoke, try to avoid the Fokker triplane beside me. But the pilot matches my banks and rolls like an expert while fire licks at his goggles.

Then the goggles burst into flames.

And the pilot rips them away, but his eyes are engulfed in fire and they ask me "why" from an already blistering face. It is the face of a child, and as I watch the flesh peel, black and burned, from the blazing, white bone, he cries to me through a gumless mouth, and the face becomes my father's.

I scream.

I woke up, screaming.

Somebody was knocking at the door. Hard. I threw back the thin quilt and crawled out of bed. Not much of a bed, really; the mattress looked like it was Henry VIII's bib, but the squeaky springs had a charm all their own.

The table holding my old Olivetti reached a leg out and tripped me, stubbing my toe. I yanked at the door as a "Goddamnit!" slipped out between my clinched teeth. In the doorway, a mop of brown hair bobbed around at waist level. It was Julien, my landlord's son, nine years old with deceivingly innocent brown eyes to match his hair; he held out a flimsy—an intercity telegram.

"Comment allez vous?" he asked sincerely as I stood there rubbing my toe, a frown the size of Texas covering my face.

"How does it look like I am?" I grunted.

"But I heard a scream, Monsieur." And it was his turn to frown.

"Oh, that." I donned an evil smile. "That was the last little boy who asked too many questions." He rolled his eyes, unimpressed with my implied threat. "Is that for me?" I pointed at the telegram. If the addressee wasn't at home, the delivery boy would leave it with the landlord, or concierge as she was more commonly known. Julien's mother, a hawk-nosed old crone, detested handling my mail—I'd mentioned to her once, purely in jest, that her nose resembled the cowling on a Sopwith Camel—and so she usually sent Julien if there was anything for me.

"It's from Monsieur Hemingway," the little boy offered.

"Mind if I read it for myself," I grumbled.

Julien shrugged and I flipped him a franc. He grimaced.

"It's just a telegram," I countered. "You didn't save my life." We went through this ritual every time.

"You are a rich American," he protested, a firm set to his jaw.

"And you are a French thief. Out!"

He tried looking stern, but the giggle stole out anyway, and he slid back down the hallway, stowing the coin in his pocket.

"What the hell does Hemingway want?" I asked myself, closing the door. The note didn't tell me much, just enough to make me want to go back to bed. But the dreams wouldn't keep their distance, and so I opted for Ernest Hemingway.

• • • •

Finding Hemingway wasn't a problem. I always knew where he'd be—good days, the hotel; bad days, the cafe. One thing about the boy, he was predictable. So, when I got the message from Hem—that's what everybody called him (Ernest seemed . . . wrong)—that he wanted to see me, I swallowed my hangover, shrugged on my one suit and raincoat, and trudged over to the Cafe de la Gare on the Place St-Michel, knowing he would be there instead of the hotel room he rented for writing. If the day was too cold, Hemingway bypassed the room for the cafe. He was too cheap to buy firewood, though he claimed that the flue didn't draw as well in bad weather.

The trip took about fifteen minutes from my flat on the rue des Ecoles. I'd rented it the year before from Max Eastman when he moved. Rain pelted me all the way, not the gentle, slow rain that Parisians love, but a hard, nasty rain that slanted in under the canopies of the streetside cafes and drove even the hardiest of diners indoors. Spring had arrived in force, and I wiped the beginnings of a runny nose as I pushed open the door.

"Jack Barnett!" The voice assaulted me across the dim room.

I squinted and saw a big, hulking figure standing at a table in the back corner. He had broad shoulders, like the boxer he pretended to be, and his dark mustache sat neatly atop a genuine smile. He stuck out a wide, thick hand and I grabbed it in mine.

"Glad you got here so quick, Jack." Hemingway motioned to a chair.

I peeled off my raincoat and tossed it in the corner. "What's up?" I said, dropping finally into a seat and wiping my nose again. "I thought you were in Genoa covering that economic thingamajiggle."

"Sylvia Beach," he said, his mustache twitching. "And the thing in Genoa starts next week."

I frowned. "What about Sylvia?" Sylvia and I had met right after the war, but Sylvia was into books and opened a lending library; I was into forgetting and did anything that focused my mind in the present and away from the past. I tried once to focus on Sylvia, but, well, it couldn't work out that way. We became friends instead. I'd known her longer than Hemingway, but Hem had a knack of quickly getting close to people that I didn't share.

"She's got a problem, Jack." Hemingway ran his hand through his black mop and sipped a rum St. James. "I figured you could help."

"What?" Sometimes Hem could be straight and to the point; sometimes he could be evasive as all hell. I glanced at a French newspaper lying on the table. The headline screamed something about Germany's failure to make reparation payments in accordance with the Versailles Treaty. It was that, among other things, that led to this powwow at Genoa. David Lloyd George, the British Prime Minister, instigated it. Poincaré, the French premier, was raising hell about it. The U.S. Ambassador to France was mad because President Harding had ignored our invitation and didn't want to send anybody. The Commies were sending a delegation, and nobody liked that, including one of Lenin's own little protegés, some guy named Stalin. The U.S. Secretary of Commerce, Herbert Hoover, wanted to go himself. I, personally, didn't give a damn who went or what they did.

Hem looked around furtively. Nobody was there but us and a

bored waiter. "She's got a dead body in the back room of the bookstore, Jack. Found it this morning at seven when she went in."

"Somebody read themselves to death?" I was looking for the joke, but something about Hem's grimace put a rock in my stomach.

When Hemingway smiled, he bared his teeth. When he frowned, his mustache seemed to blow up like a balloon. That hairy thing on his upper lip looked now like it covered his whole face. "No kidding, Jack. This is for real. The guy's been knifed in the back. She's almost frantic. It's been an hour since she found him. I told her I'd meet you here. Sylvia needs some help. We thought of you."

"Great. What made you think I could help?" I motioned for the waiter, and he headed towards us. "And why here instead of the bookshop?"

"Monsieur?" the waiter asked. Hemingway held his reply.

"Un vin, blanc."

Hemingway grinned a little then. "Wine? I thought you were strictly a beer man."

"You're buying, and when somebody else is buying, I don't short myself. You didn't answer. Why me? And why here?"

Hemingway shrugged. "I was on my way over here to write, and it was closer to your flat. As for the 'why you,' you have buddies on the police force. You know about these things."

"No excuse."

He ignored me. "And you're a friend of Sylvia's."

"So are you."

"But you've known her longer."

"This isn't a contest, Hem."

"But one of us is going to win."

"And the other's going to lose," I finished, rolling my eyes and sipping the wine the waiter had just brought. "You need Auguste Dupin."

"Leave Poe out of this. You helped the police find the guy that was killing those people at the whorehouse. You've got experience."

"That was an accident," I grumbled. "Sylvia needs the *police*."

"Sylvia needs *you*. Too much is going on at the shop right now. The police would complicate things."

He was probably right. Sylvia was publishing some book by James Joyce, and it had already been banned in the States and Great Britain. Supposedly, the book was filled with 'immoral' content. The French weren't normally opposed to that kind of thing, but mix it up with murder and things could get sticky.

I sat quietly for a minute or two, trying to think of a way out of it. I'd sent off a story to the *Louisville Courier* on Parisian horse racing the day before, and I didn't have anything else lined up. Horse racing was how I'd met Hemingway. Since I did some newspaper work, the Press Club on the Right Bank let me join. Hem was a member, and since both of us liked horse racing, we fell together, got drunk together, told each other lies, just like the rest of the Americans in Paris.

I wasn't really impressed with him at first. He was just one of probably two dozen young Americans who came to Paris to be writers. A couple were good, some were okay, the rest ended up getting drunk and going back home after a few months. I didn't know much about Hemingway's writing then—he'd only been in Paris a few months—but he was likable, annoying sometimes, but likable. Big and friendly. Back home we would have been friends, and maybe that's why I was drawn to him. In Paris, not much resembled Liberty, Missouri. Probably the biggest difference between Hem and me was that I wrote for money; Hem wrote for love.

Writing wasn't really my thing. Trouble was, I couldn't figure out what my thing was, so I stumbled through newspaper stories and sold them to a half-dozen papers back in the States—anybody that would pay. Luckily, it didn't cost much to live in Paris. A room cost eleven francs a week. Cheap by anybody's standards.

I fingered my wine glass and considered my options. If I said yes, I'd have to put up with Sylvia and her literary friends. If I said no, I'd have to go back to my flat and stare at the four walls. It wasn't much of a choice.

"Okay, Hem. You sold me. Let's go see Sylvia's corpse."

• • • •

"Who is he, Jack?"

I turned around and bumped heads with Hemingway, who thrust his face over my shoulder for a better look. "How the hell should I know, Hem? You want me to ask him? If you haven't noticed, there's a knife in the center of his back, and he's not complaining."

"What am I supposed to do?" Sylvia Beach interjected, pushing brown bangs away from her forehead. Sylvia was thin and wore her hair short. She was a cultured kind of pretty, not beautiful, but she had a backbone of iron and a steel spirit that showed in the angles of her face.

"Keep people out of here until I figure something out." It wasn't a good answer, but it was the best I had. I locked onto the neat hole the knife had sliced in the guy's shirt and didn't say anything for a minute. "The first thing we've got to do is find out who he is. The 'why' and the 'how' will come later. He sure must have pissed somebody off."

I continued to stare at the body, wedged between boxes of books on the floor of Sylvia's shop, Shakespeare and Company. Actually, it was in the backroom, but that didn't keep it from being on Sylvia's property, and it sure didn't keep the guy from being dead. The Paris police were easy going, but not about knife-decorated corpses. My nose started running again, and I wished I were back in bed. I wished Hemingway hadn't sent for me. I wished . . . well, a lot of things.

"I've got to get back up front." Sylvia finally broke the silence. "We open in just a few minutes, and Arlaine will be here."

"Who's Arlaine? What about Myrsine?" Myrsine Moschos took care of the shop for Sylvia. I liked her; she was a good kid.

"I gave her a holiday," Sylvia explained. "Arlaine—Arlaine Watson—just came over from the States. She needed some money. I needed some help."

"Keep her out for the time being," I cautioned. "Does anybody else know." I emphasized the "anybody." Sylvia knew who I meant.

"I haven't talked to Adrienne since I came in this morning." She sent me a half-frown.

Adrienne Monnier was Sylvia's "friend," a relationship I didn't discover until I offered Sylvia the use of my bed for the night. She was polite, but inflexible. Of course, it's not like I could have done much about it if she'd crawled in, but I always hoped.

"What smells?" Hemingway was wrinkling his nose.

I turned away from Sylvia and sniffed. Gasoline. Kneeling beside the body, the scent got stronger. "Give me a hand," I instructed Hemingway.

Shoving a box of books out of the way, I noticed the title on one—*Ulysses*—and the author, James Joyce. So this was the big, controversial novel. Looked too long for me to read. We turned the dead man over with a little effort and put him face up. The man was dressed in a dirty brown, linen shirt and trousers. His feet were covered in pretty standard, black, work shoes, though they were clean and looked new. He had one of those indeterminate faces—could be thirty, could be fifty. His hair was light, almost blonde, and his eyes were greyish-blue. Yeah, his eyes were open and staring up at me reproachfully, like *I'd* shoved the knife in his back.

"Ever seen him before?" I asked Sylvia.

She shook her head.

"Look." Hemingway pointed to the area just vacated by the body.

It was an ordinary looking wine bottle, except for the damp, greasy rag sticking out of the neck and the liquid slowly puddling on the floor. I squatted closer and sniffed. Yeah, gasoline.

"Nice," I said.

"What is it?" The question was really more rhetorical than actual. Hemingway might be young, but he had a good idea what it was.

"Molotov." They started calling them Molotov cocktails back during the late teens. The Bolsheviks over in Russia made them popular when they kicked out the Czar. Back in 1919, I went east looking for John Reed, a crazy journalist who was in love with the Bolsheviks. The Whites and Reds were still skirmishing, and I saw some of those little homemade bombs do their work. It gave me nightmares for a month.

"Great," Sylvia said, unconvincingly. The wrinkles in her forehead were getting deeper by the second.

"Hey, Hem. Look at this." I hefted the bottle and pointed it at him.

He glanced at it. "It sure ain't pretty."

"No, you idiot. Look at the rag."

Hem pulled the rag straight without dislodging it. "It's dry up top, wet down inside. That doesn't make sense. It should be wet all over."

"What are you two talking about?" Sylvia wasn't getting my point.

"You're supposed to dip the rag in gasoline so that when you light it, it burns nice and quick. A dry rag might take too long as a fuse. In a street fight, somebody could just pull the rag out."

"But what's the point, Jack?" Hem asked.

He had me there. "I'm not sure. But it's odd." I avoided looking at the bottle for a minute and saw a bit of paper sticking out of the man's shirt pocket. It was a note written in a tight, cramped hand— "12 rue l'Odeon, 11 ce soir. JJ."

"What is it, Jack?"

I handed it to him and he scanned the scrap for a second.

"'JJ.'? James Joyce?"

"Oh, God no! It can't be Mr. Joyce." Sylvia always called him "Mr. Joyce."

"Who knows. Murder doesn't seem quite his style. All I've seen him do is slurp up food at Michaud's."

"Me, too," Hemingway agreed.

I took the note back and tucked it into my pocket. "What's that?" Another scrap lay on the floor.

I snagged the piece of paper and studied it. Nothing but a funny looking cross, a cross with all its arms broken. Somebody's doodling, I figured. Putting it away, I checked the body again. Something protruded from a hip pocket. "Grab that, will you," I instructed.

Hem reached down and produced a black leather wallet, worn and frayed. He flipped it open and studied a card sticking out. "'Phillipe Jourdan. Voyageur de commerce. Pierre Legrain et fils, fabriquer des machines á ecrire.'"

"What in the hell is a traveling typewriter salesman doing dead in your backroom?" I shook my head. "Look, was there anything unusual about the shop this morning? You know, lights left on that you turned off, anything like that. Books flung around. Papers messed up."

Sylvia thought for a moment. "No. Nothing, besides him," and she pointed down at the body, "was out of place. The lights were off as usual; everything was the same as always. My desk is just as I left it yesterday."

"And you're sure you don't know how a murdered typewriter salesman ended up in your storeroom? Nothing out of the ordinary has happened in the last few days?"

"No," she shook her head. "Nothing. I don't have the slightest idea about any of this. But, if I don't get up front, a dozen people will be back here looking for me." She lightly pressed my hand. "I appreciate this, Jack."

"I'd like to say 'no problem,' but I'd be lying."

She slipped out the door and I started to turn back to the body, but something at the backdoor caught my eye.

The door was shut, but the jamb was cracked. A piece of wood was broken away from the frame, completely at one end, but still attached at the other. I grabbed the knob and pulled without twisting. The door opened, bending back the cracked piece enough to allow the catch free passage. Once the catch had passed, the errant wood sprang back into place in the frame.

A blast of rain and cold air swept in the opening. I glanced outside. The door led out into an alley behind the the bookstore's block of buildings. Nothing and no one was in the alley now, just a couple of empty wooden boxes, streaked dark by the rainwater. Looking down at the entrance, I saw two deep sets of footprints in the mud, one larger than the other. The shelter of the building had kept them from being washed away in the rain.

"Well, this is how he got in. And the murderer, too. Unless, the murderer was already waiting for him."

"Which implies," Hem began, fingering his mustache, "that it was somebody with access to the shop."

"Imply, hell!" I snorted. "It screams it. But there's nothing else to substantiate that kind of conclusion." Through the shop door, I heard loud voices. Probably some customer complaining about a book.

Hem reached over and tapped the pocket where I'd stuffed the note. "That might. Do you know Joyce, other than at Michaud's, I mean?"

I grimaced. "Yeah, I met him once with Sylvia. Sort of an ass, if you ask me."

Hemingway grinned. "He's a genius, Jack."

"He's still an ass. And that still doesn't answer the question of the door. If the murderer was already here waiting on him, why break in the door?" My head was spinning. A body, a bloody knife, notes, broken doors, and *Ulysses* all kaleidoscoping around my brain. It was the way I used to feel when I came out of a simple loop, back when I was just learning how to fly. You know you're still above ground because you haven't crashed, but you're not sure where the earth is; the blood is rushing to your head and back down again; the wind's in your face and your hair, and you can smell your own fear. After a few seconds, though, you level out and everything comes back into focus and you get your bearings. Maybe this would work that way too.

"You all right, Jack?"

I looked up at Hemingway and saw genuine concern. I nodded. "When did it start raining?"

He rubbed his jaw thoughtfully. "I'm not sure, but I think sometime after midnight."

"Then, it's a sure bet that this guy was knifed before twelve.

He's completely dry, and if he was out in this rain without a coat, he'd still be soaked."

"Hey, you're right. I hadn't thought about that. Isn't this great? Wait till I tell Hadley. She won't believe any of it." Sometimes Hem could be like a little boy. And he was totally devoted to his wife, Hadley. She was a good kid. I'd only met her a couple of times, but she seemed to keep Hem straight and God knows, he needed that.

"You're not gonna tell Hadley anything. The best way to help Sylvia is to keep this as quiet as possible. It might be smart to dump this guy out back." I studied the dead man for a minute as I weighed the risks. "If it was dark, we could take him further away, but in the daytime, well, it's too much of a risk. A body in the alley will still implicate Shakespeare and Company, but it won't be as tight a connection as having the body in here."

"No," a new voice sounded. "But it might make you—how do you say it—a prime candidate, that's it, a prime candidate for obstruction of justice charges."

I didn't have to turn around. I knew who it was. "Shit." The word slipped out before I could catch it.

"Very inventive, Mr. Barnett." He was small and dark. A tiny mustache sat on his lip, and a long black coat wrapped around him. His eyes were onyx, deep and probing. He turned those eyes on Hemingway and smiled politely. "I don't believe we've met, Monsieur."

I stood. "Ernest Hemingway, this is Police Inspector Duvall."

Two

uvall continued to smile, but, as two uniformed gen-darmes entered behind the inspector and positioned themselves on his flanks, the look on Hem's face was worth a fortune, like a little boy caught stealing candy. "Long time, no see, Inspector." I smiled at the little policeman.

Duvall hung his head and shook it reproachfully. "I thought we had parted company permanently, Monsieur Barnett. But, here you are, interfering with the police once more."

"I don't remember interfering the last time. Seems like I was able to lend a hand." My voice had more strength than my spine, and I put on a smile to reinforce the facade.

"Oui," Duvall agreed. "But, we would have eventually settled the matter without your assistance." He stuck his hand inside his overcoat, pulled out a cigarette—Lucky Strike—and slipped it into his mouth. Magically, a lit match materialized in his hand, and he touched it lightly to the cigarette, inhaling deeply. Once, I'd asked him how he made matches appear out of thin air. He told me it was of "no consequence." And that ended that.

Duvall brushed past Hemingway and glanced down at the dead body. A frown popped onto his face. "Do cadavers follow you?" he asked me gruffly.

"Not usually. In fact, I try to avoid them, but I could say the same thing about you, Inspector. How did you know about this one?"

A smile replaced the frown, but his eyes never left the corpse. "An anonymous message this morning. Such messages often come to me. It is my job, Monsieur. It is not yours."

"Touché, Inspector, touché."

"Jack. . . ." Hemingway was getting fidgety. He pushed back his hair and smoothed his mustache.

Before I could answer, Sylvia slipped back into the room. She watched Duvall as closely as I did, but she shot a more than meaningful look my way.

"Mademoiselle Beach, do you know this man?" Duvall wasted no time in getting to the point.

"Do you know every dead body in Paris, Inspector?" Sylvia was taking no prisoners.

The French have a gentle smile, a smile that masks a cobra's strike. Duvall turned that smile on Sylvia then. "Sooner or later. But *this* body interests me now. Do you know him," he repeated.

"No. I've never seen him before," Sylvia admitted.

"And why are Monsieur Barnett and this man," he waved off-handedly at Hemingway, "here?"

"I'm a booklover, Inspector. Didn't you know that?" I saved Sylvia the trouble of answering.

"I wasn't sure you could read, Monsieur."

"Jack is a friend of mine," Sylvia intervened.

"And him," Duvall jerked a finger towards an ever nervous Hemingway.

"He's writing the Great American Novel," I answered for her.

"Aren't they all?" Duvall chuckled, but the reply seemed to satisfy him.

Hemingway retreated into a corner, a pout growing on his lips.

"Mademoiselle Sylvia, we are aware of the problems your book— *Ulysses* isn't it—yes, well, we're aware of the controversy in America and England over this book. It is not something that normally troubles us, but this," and he pointed at the corpse, "this troubles us deeply."

"I assure you, Inspector, that this has nothing to do with the bookstore, or *Ulysses*." Sylvia staked out her ground.

"If that is so, then why was Monsieur Barnett speaking of 'dumping the body out back,' I believe he said."

Sylvia swallowed the lump in her throat—I watched it go down— and squared herself on the Inspector. "I guessed that you would immediately assume a connection between this man and the unjustified difficulties with Mr. Joyce's new book. Jack—Monsieur Barnett—is an old friend, and I thought he could help me keep the bookstore out of this. Obviously, I was not thinking clearly. I apologize for our attempt to circumvent the law, but I assure you, once more, that this poor soul has nothing to do with me, the bookstore, or the new book." Her voice barely shook at all.

At this pronouncement, a genuine smile broke across Duvall's lips, relaxing his face. "The truth is always good, if it is the truth." Sylvia tensed again, and the unbearable pause lengthened interminably before Duvall spoke again. "But your words have a sound of sincerity to them. And I will choose to believe them, or rather part of them, for the time being. You don't look like the murdering type." He knelt beside the body, picked up the wallet, and studied the card inside. After a few seconds, he handed it to one of the policemen and muttered something in French that loosely translated to "Check this out."

"However," Duvall turned back to us, "you cannot assume that just because you do not know him, that he has no connection to Monsieur Joyce's book." He hefted the bottle. "This is an incendiary. And these are boxes of the book in question. N'est pas?"

Sylvia nodded.

"Well, then. Let us suppose that this man came here to burn these books. He was surprised by someone and killed in a scuffle. The murderer, frightened, ran away."

"But, that would mean," Hemingway said, moving out of his corner, "that the murderer was already in the bookshop when the victim broke in."

"Broke in?" Duvall questioned.

"Yeah. The back door's been forced," I told him.

Duvall busied himself for a few minutes checking the door and the alley beyond. He studied the fractured wood closely. Suddenly, he pulled back on the separation and wedged his fingers into the split.

"Voila!" he announced, exhibiting a tiny bit of fabric.

"That's cute, Duvall. Do you pull rabbits out of hats, too?" I couldn't resist the jibe, but Sylvia frowned disapprovingly.

"Look at this, Monsieur. Does it match the clothing on the body?"

I glanced at the cloth, a greyish plaid. Nothing like the stuff the corpse was wearing. "Okay, it's different. But we know somebody else was here. The guy didn't kill himself."

"Everything is of note, Monsieur." Duvall seemed a little put off at my lack of appreciation for his detective skills. He was competent enough, don't get me wrong, but I wasn't ready to concede anything.

"Maybe the piece tore off the murderer's clothing," Hemingway offered.

"Exactly, young man." Duvall threw me a knowing look. "Who has access to the shop besides yourself?" He turned to Sylvia.

She thought for a moment. "Myrsine Moschos, my clerk, Adrienne Monnier, and Arlaine Watson, an American girl here on holiday and filling in for Myrsine. That's all."

"Do you have extra keys?"

"Of course. I keep one at my flat and one here in my desk."

"Then, I will collect those, plus the ones held by Mme. Monnier and this American fille. And yours, Mademoiselle." He held out a hand.

Sylvia stared at him confusedly.

"They're closing you down, Sylvia," I told her.

"How quaint." Duvall nodded. "But, he is correct. Until further notice, the bookshop is 'closed down.' You may reenter tomorrow to handle your personal affairs, but no customers may be served until permission is given. The front door will stay locked."

"You can't do this!"

"But of course I can, Mademoiselle. You have a murdered man in your backroom. This is now a crime scene."

"But we have books to mail. Copies of *Ulysses* that have been promised to subscribers!"

Duvall shook his head curtly. "Nothing in the backroom may be touched."

"The harder you argue, the worse it will be, Sylvia," I cautioned.

The angles in her face grew even sharper, and I thought I saw a slight shade of crimson edge across her features. The pause was getting more than awkward, but finally she slipped a ring of keys from a pocket in her dress, selected two, and handed them over to Duvall.

"And the spare you keep here?"

"Follow me." Sylvia was curt.

We went back through the door into the bookshop proper. Wooden shelves lined the walls from floor to ceiling, and the shelves were loaded with books. Shakespeare, or at least a miniature bust of him, sat on a marble mantle against one wall. A half-dozen photographs decorated the walls above the mantle. Huge windows fronted the shop, and the entrance, looking from the back, was to the far left.

The shop was as much a lending library as a place to buy books.

Somewhere, back at my flat, I had a subscriber's card. I bought it back in the days when I hoped Sylvia might provide more than a little diversion. Sylvia had just moved to rue de l'Odeon the summer before.

She started out around the corner on rue Dupuytren, but rue de l'Odeon was a busier avenue, and Adrienne Monnier's bookshop was just across the street. I helped her move some stuff over, but it was about then that I discovered that I had about as much chance of getting close to her as the sun has of rising in the west.

Sylvia's desk sat in a corner. A big poster, screaming **"The Scandal of Ulysses"** in bold black letters, hung on the wall behind the desk. Another one was right below that and it announced, "Arnold Bennett on *Ulysses*." Sylvia went over and opened a drawer. A blank look crossed her face.

"Is there a problem, Mademoiselle?" Duvall asked.

"My spare set of keys is missing." Her forehead wrinkled in concentration.

"Stolen, perhaps," the inspector offered.

"I'm not sure," she said, but then the wrinkles smoothed and the blood drained from her face.

"You remember?" Duvall was no fool.

"I loaned them out yesterday."

"May I ask to whom?"

She turned and looked at me and Hemingway, and when she spoke, it was to us. "Mr. Joyce borrowed them so he could check the copies in the backroom for errors."

Somehow I knew it before she said it.

Hemingway frowned. "Then the note could have been. . . ." He stopped when he realized his goof.

"Note?" Duvall smiled again, the cobra smile.

"Good work, Sherlock," I muttered to Hemingway as I pulled the note from my pocket.

"Jack!" Sylvia exclaimed.

"What do you mean, 'Jack'?" I pointed at Hem. "He's the one that said it. Hiding it only makes it worse, now."

Hemingway hung his head a little as I passed the note to Duvall. "We found it on the dead guy."

The inspector unfolded the slip of paper and read it slowly. "Very interesting. 'J.J.' Could this be James Joyce, perhaps?"

"Absolutely not!" Sylvia was blunt and to the point.

"But, Mademoiselle Sylvia, look at the facts," Duvall began. "A man with an incendiary device is murdered in your backroom among boxes of a book written by your Mr. Joyce. The dead man has a note on him with the initials 'J.J.' (I'll ignore the fact that Monsieur Barnett and his companion intended to conceal it.) And, Monsieur Joyce had access to the room at the time. How can I help but be swayed by this evidence?"

"By not jumping to the most convenient conclusion," I interrupted. "You're assuming that the murderer was already in the backroom. Why couldn't both men have entered from the rear door? Didn't you see the two sets of footsteps back there? And you're also assuming that the Molotov was intended to destroy the books. It could just as well have been intended to destroy the Eiffel Tower. There may have been two conspirators. They argued. One murdered the other in the alley and broke in here to dump the body and make his getaway," I rattled on, talking off the top of my head.

Duvall held a thin hand up. "Enough! You have made one or two interesting points, I concede, but that does not eliminate the possible connection of Monsieur Joyce to this murder. I will want to talk with him at length."

"Talk to who! What the hell's going on here? Sylvia, Jack, Hem, speak up. What's going on? A man can't even read in peace anymore."

I looked up and saw a man approaching from a corner of the shop. His red mane was long and brushed back, looking more like a cock's comb than a head of hair, and he sported sideburns and a neatly-trimmed, pointed beard. His forehead was round and protruded just a bit, lending him an intellectual look and giving him a vague resemblance to old Vladimir Lenin. His suit was rumpled, and he waved a cane around as he walked towards us.

"Good morning, Ezra." Only Ezra Pound could walk, brazenly, enthusiastically, into a totally unknown situation and try to take command.

"Jack, what the hell's going on here?"

"Inspector Duvall thinks that James Joyce murdered somebody." Duvall frowned at me.

"Balderdash. Joyce murders words, not men." Pound's bushy eyebrows moved up and down with each word.

"Be that as it may, Monsieur, but this shop is closing. You'll have to leave." Duvall was insistent.

Ezra drew his head back in amazement. "This is outrageous. Sylvia, are you going to allow this?"

"I can't stop it, Mr. Pound. And I'd very much like to." Sylvia smiled tiredly.

Pound looked incredulous. "Well, of all things." He turned and stomped towards the door, pausing only long enough for a "Come by later, Hem, Jack, for a drink," and then he was gone.

"You Americans make for, how do you say it, an interesting day."

"It's our gift. The French are so boring."

"Jack!" Sylvia groaned. "You'll just make matters worse."

Duvall waved her off absently. "Monsieur Barnett and I are old friends. Half that passes between us is immediately forgiven."

"And the other half?" I prodded.

". . . is stored away for the future," Duvall finished with a gentle laugh, and even Sylvia tried to grin. "Come now, Mademoiselle Beach; surely you know that I must do my job. Even Jack knows that. I didn't kill the man in the back of your shop. But someone did. And it is my unpleasant job to find out who."

"You speak very strong, eloquent English, Inspector," Sylvia said graciously.

Duvall gave a little bow. "I'm not certain that I deserve the compliment."

"Enough of the false modesty, Duvall." I couldn't take it anymore. "He's got a degree from Columbia."

"Really! And you're just a. . . ." Sylvia faltered.

"I did not like the life academic," he explained politely. "It lacked . . . how shall I put it . . . zest, yes, that's it, zest. So I chose a job with more variety."

One of the gendarmes had been on the telephone, and he came over to Duvall finally, mumbling something in his ear. The inspector nodded and, with a whisk of his hand, sent the officer on some unknown errand. "And now, Mademoiselle Beach, I really must insist that you close the doors."

A couple of young guys had wandered in and were browsing through the bookshelves. I looked at Hemingway and jerked my head towards the customers. He nodded, squared his shoulders, and headed over to the pair, whispering something almost fraternally in their ears. They both turned, looked at Duvall, and scurried out the door.

"The photographer will be here in a moment, and then the . . .

25

how do you say it, Jack? . . . 'meat wagon,' that's it, meat wagon will arrive to pick up your unwanted guest," Duvall continued.

"Mind if I see the photos when you get them?" I asked.

"Jack . . ." Duvall began, the warning already in his tone. "There's no reason for you to become involved in this."

Now, that was the first logical thing anybody had said all day. With any sense, I should have walked away and gone back to bed to nurse my cold. But, as much as I liked Duvall, he tended to have a one track mind. Once he got fixed on something, he was set for life. And he'd already decided that James Joyce killed the man in the backroom. Sylvia didn't believe it; Hemingway had an open mind about it. I wasn't convinced. Too many ifs wandering around. Too much circumstantial evidence. I wanted things tied up in neater bundles than this. Guilt and innocence were important matters to me, things that occupied a great deal of my time.

While I didn't like Joyce, I had to agree with Ezra Pound. He just didn't seem like a murderer. The Molotov, the note, the footprints in the mud, and the funny cross were like reference points on the map. But, right now, all they did was lead in a circle. Sylvia did need my help, or at least it made me feel good to think she did, and that—feeling good I mean—didn't happen much. And thoughts of going back to my apartment, of going back to sleep, weren't very pleasant.

"You're right," I told him. "There may not be any reason, but Americans are an irrational people. I'll just hang around the edges and stay out of your way."

Duvall started to say something, but then he closed his mouth, threw up his hands, and shrugged. He knew it wouldn't do any good to argue. He found that out the last time. Besides, though he'd never admit it, he valued my opinion. "The first time you make a nuisance of yourself," he warned, "you're out."

"Whatever you say," I assured him.

As I finished, a young guy, late twenties, with dark hair and heavy eyebrows, whispered something to the policemen at the front door and then slipped between them and into the shop. He wiped his hands nervously on his dirty overalls. "Mademoiselle Sylvia?" His voice was soft.

Sylvia turned around. "Oh, Paul." She looked back to Duvall. "Can he clean up the gasoline yet?"

"Who is he?"

"Paul Dounat. He makes deliveries and keeps the place clean. Odd jobs, mostly."

"No, he'll have to wait. I want nothing disturbed until the photographer gets here."

"But the stench might ruin some of the books!" Sylvia protested.

Duvall shrugged. "The price of having a dead body in your storeroom, Mademoiselle. He may clean up later."

The young man moved off towards a corner.

"Wait!" Duvall marched over to him. "Does he have access to the shop after hours?"

"No," Sylvia shook her head impatiently. "He works only in the day, and only part time. But the books, Inspector. I can't afford to lose any of them."

A shout at the front door interrupted her.

"What the hell is that?" I craned my head for a better look, but all I could see was flailing arms and a cane wrapped around one of the gendarmes.

"Oh, no!" Sylvia moaned.

"Uh, oh!" Hemingway added.

"Jesus H. Christ," I said to myself.

"This must be Monsieur Joyce," remarked Duvall.

It was Joyce, doing his damndest to get past the gendarme at the door.

"You don't understand, my good man. I am James Joyce. I use this as my mailing address. I have business here."

Joyce was medium height and thin. His dark suit, just a little threadbare, hung loosely from his frame. He was long-jawed with small, watery, blue eyes—I could really only see one; the other, the left eye, had this big dark leather patch—and circular pince-nez glasses sat on his nose. He wore a polka-dotted bow tie, a white shirt, and, believe it or not, dirty white tennis shoes. The eyepatch and his little goatee and upturned mustache lent him a swashbuckler air, but that wasn't quite it either. Schoolmasterly, yeah, that hit closer to the mark, and it was pretty close to the truth since that's what he'd been before his writing career took off. I say took off, but from everything I understood at the time, he was making his living mooching off friends, like Sylvia. But right now, he was hung up between two polite, but insistent, gendarmes.

"Miss Beach! I must protest this treatment!" Joyce's voice was softly aggravated.

"Mr. Joyce, I—"

"Arrêtez-vous!" Duvall snapped, interrupting Sylvia. The gendarmes slowly released Joyce, and he straightened his clothes before approaching us. "Monsieur Joyce. How good to meet you at last." Charm oozed out of Duvall's mouth, but it was charm tainted with a cobra's poison.

Joyce finally made it over to the desk where he plopped down, uninvited, into a chair. "Miss Beach, I don't understand all this. Please, explain."

"We discovered a corpse in the backroom this morning, Monsieur Joyce," Duvall answered for Sylvia. "Were you in the shop last evening?"

"Of course." Joyce stared intently at Duvall. "I checked the copies of *Ulysses* that had come from the printer. After the Huddleston review in England last week, we have secured a number of orders. I hoped to send more review copies out to boost orders even further. But sending misprinted or badly bound books to reviewers would not be wise. I told Miss Beach I would be here; indeed I borrowed her key."

"What time did you arrive?"

"About eight."

"And you left at what time?"

"Just before eleven. I had finished about half of the books."

"Did you see anyone? Did anyone try to enter the shop while you were here?"

"No," Joyce said after a moment, shaking his head. "All was quiet when I left."

"May I have the key Mademoiselle Beach loaned you?" Duvall asked politely.

Joyce didn't move. "No, you may not."

"Mr. Joyce!"

"You do have a way with words, Joyce," I admitted, shaking my head at his audacity. "A real bad way." I glanced at Hemingway, and a new look was growing on his face, doubt laced with a heavy dose of rising suspicion.

"Do you have an explanation, Monsieur Joyce?" Duvall pronounced "explanation" the French way.

Joyce blinked at Duvall with his one watery eye. "Very simple, Inspector. I was robbed of it last night, not to mention the thirty francs I had with me."

"Can you describe the thief?"

"Hardly. He approached me from the rear and put a pistol to my back."

"And then," I prodded him along.

Joyce paused and studied me for a long second. "And then, he went through my pockets, taking the key and my money. And then, he left me."

"Where did the theft occur?" Duvall asked, his face blank.

"A block down the street. Towards my flat."

"You saw nothing?"

"No."

"You heard nothing? The thief never spoke?"

"No. Just a grumbled threat as to what might happen if I didn't remain still and silent. But it was an experience of some aggravation. Those were the last francs I had. Miss Beach." He turned to Sylvia. "I must have more. My family must be fed."

"Don't worry, Mr. Joyce." Sylvia comforted him as she would a small child.

"Come with me, please." Duvall ignored Sylvia's disapproving look and pointed towards the backroom.

Joyce blinked at the circle of faces around him and then followed the inspector. I fell in behind them—no way I was going to miss this—and Hemingway was right with me. Sylvia stayed back. Maybe she was afraid of what she might see in Joyce's face. Who knows.

They hadn't moved him. He was still lying face up, staring blindly at the ceiling. The Molotov was on the floor, just where I'd left it. Duvall stood off to one side and pointed down at the corpse.

"Do you know this man, Monsieur?"

Joyce glanced quickly at Duvall, like he was trying to understand the question; then he knelt beside the body and studied the pale, unmoving face. He looked almost like a cop himself, leaning down that way, but when he turned back towards Duvall, his face was unreadable, indescribably blank.

"I have never seen him before in my life."

"Hardly an original line, Monsieur."

"I wasn't striving for originality. This man is as unknown to me as," and he turned and looked at me, "as he is."

He stood and sniffed the air. "Is that petrol?"

"Yeah," I grunted and pointed at the Molotov.

"Gia! This is outrageous! Miss Beach! Miss Beach, come here this instant!"

Sylvia appeared in the doorway, a look of pure fright on her face. "What? What is it, Mr. Joyce?"

"It's an abomination, Miss Beach! Someone has obviously tried to burn my books. My subscribers must get their copies. This kind of outrage cannot be allowed! Something must be done!" And he glared meaningfully at Duvall.

I have to admit; it was a great performance, and I couldn't see a glint of insincerity. Skilled liars can be pretty genuine in appearance, but if Joyce was lying, he was damned good. Easily the best I'd ever seen. That one, weeping, blue eye of his was as honestly outraged as I'd seen in a while.

"Something will be done, Monsieur. Strange that you would assume that this man intended to destroy your books."

Joyce turned a look of curiosity on Duvall. "Nothing strange about it. Many people would like to see my book destroyed. Even now, it is banned in the United States."

"But," Duvall began. "Would that not give you a motive to kill this man?"

"Possibly. If I had killed him. But I have already told you that I didn't."

"You had both motive and opportunity, Monsieur Joyce. Strong evidence in such a case."

"That is incorrect, Inspector. I may have had motive, but there was no opportunity. I was not here at the same time as this man." He said the last word like there was some question about the guy's qualifications for being human.

"We have only your word for that," Duvall reminded him.

"And we have only your assumption that he had opportunity, Duvall." I jumped in. This was getting us no where. Joyce wasn't going to confess, and Duvall wasn't going to let up.

"Yeah, Inspector." Hemingway rumbled up beside me. "He says he wasn't here when this guy was. You say he was. It's your word against his."

Duvall eyed both of us through narrowing slits. "For the moment, you are right. Time, however, may tell a different story." He turned back to Joyce and held his hand out. "Your passport please."

Joyce's eye flickered confusedly.

"So you won't leave the country," I explained to him.

He looked at me again, really seeing me for the first time I think. "Have we met?"

"Sylvia introduced us once," I reminded him.

"Oh." He reached into his breast pocket and produced an Irish passport. Staring at it for a few seconds, he finally handed it over to Duvall with a sigh. "Please don't lose it. Getting a replacement can be such a bother."

"Brother," I muttered and Hemingway poked me in the side while Sylvia glared at me.

"But, of course, Monsieur." A slight grin lit up Duvall's face. "And, later, could you come to my office to answer some further questions, this afternoon, perhaps?"

Joyce squinted and wrinkles appeared. "I don't really have the time," he began.

"Mr. Joyce!" Sylvia exclaimed.

He looked at her as his squint became a full-fledged frown. "But, if you insist."

"A necessity, Monsieur."

"Could we go back up front now?" Joyce pulled his collar away from his neck. "It's intolerable in here."

"I fully understand," the inspector replied.

And so did I. The dead guy kept looking at me, reminding me of other times—times I'd been trying to forget. Joyce wasn't the only one getting sweaty around the collar. And there was this cock-eyed kind of noise going on up front. I kept hearing familiar phrases, words from Missouri, words from the pulpit, words from home.

We all trooped back into the bookshop, where a bright-eyed, very attractive blond was entrenched behind the desk, holding at bay an overweight, red-faced, blustering man with curly brown hair and a twitch in his right eye. One of the gendarmes had abandoned his post at the door and was leaning over, or maybe I should say leering over, the desktop and trying to look down the blond's blouse, attempting to appear interested in the controversy at hand.

It took about a half a second to figure out why the fat guy was there.

"God's vengeance is at hand! We must condemn James Joyce's obscene filth to the fiery pits of hell where it was conceived! I *will* see Miss Sylvia Beach now!"

It was a hell of a morning in Paris.

Three

I liked the blond behind the desk as soon as I saw her. And I wanted to stay away from her, far away. She looked wholesome, clean; you know the kind, and she immediately drew my attention away from her Bible-thumping assailant. Her blue eyes twinkled, and I sensed that it came from innocence, not mischief, and I couldn't meet her gaze.

"Miss Beach." The voice wasn't sultry either, unsure, but no seductive qualities at all. Jesus, I thought, she must squeak when she walks.

"Arlaine," Sylvia speedwalked over to the desk, focusing on the blond.

"Miss Beach, what's going on? Reverend Karper *insists* on seeing you again." She didn't get up, and she didn't take her eyes off the leering gendarme. A smart move on her part.

"Arlaine, there's been a . . . , well, a murder here."

"Murder! Have you Heathens struck down a Servant of God as you do the Devil's Work!" Two short sentences and the fat guy was already sweating.

He made me incredibly uncomfortable. Shrink him by a hundred pounds, deepen the whiny voice by an octave, and it could be my father belting out Old Testament epithets.

"Oh," Arlaine said, and the brightness in her eyes dulled just a little. A helplessness tinted her face; she started to say something, stopped, and hesitantly gestured toward the Bible-thumper.

"There's really no time to explain now, but the shop is being closed by the police, as you can see." Sylvia ignored her gentleman caller to his obvious irritation.

Duvall didn't make the same mistake. He snapped something in French to the gendarme, basically telling him to drag his ass back to the door and keep people out, and then he turned to this guy. "Who are you, Monsieur?"

"I am the Servant of God Almighty!" he blustered. "And I have come to keep this woman from blaspheming God's name by publishing this piece of wanton perversion known as *Ulysses!*"

"Oh, Jesus!" I muttered, and God's Servant sent a lightning bolt look in my direction.

Duvall had more patience than me. "Beyond being a heavenly agent, do you represent a more worldly organization?"

Sylvia wore a pained look on her face. She didn't want, or need, to deal with this guy, and she was putting it off as long as she could, obviously satisfied to let Duvall run interference.

The man stopped blustering for a second, and some of the red creeped out of his cheeks and back down into his neck. "I am the Reverend Quintin Karper of the Society Against Immoral Literature. After our recent court battle in which, through God's blessings, we were triumphant in preventing this work of iniquity from being published in the United States, rumors reached us that a Miss Sylvia Beach intended to publish this book here in Paris. I came here to do battle with Satan for Miss Beach's immortal soul and to prevent the spreading of such perversion." The Reverend Quintin Karper paused for a second, and a dark light sparked in his pig-eyes. "Are you with the police? And am I to understand that a murder has been committed here?"

"Oui," Duvall answered. "I am Inspector Duvall. The mademoiselle said you had come 'again.' Have you been here before?"

"Yes. I came to see Miss Beach yesterday, but she *refused* to discuss the matter with me." Obviously, he couldn't understand why anyone would refuse to talk to him.

Sylvia didn't look happy, but she held her ground. "I was busy."

Duvall raised both eyebrows. "So, your visit to Paris is connected with Monsieur Joyce's new book?"

"I seek to prevent his heathen book from seeing the light of day. Such blasphemy should not be allowed to exist under God's heaven."

"You seem pretty determined to stop it," I said, making sure my Missouri drawl came through loud and clear.

"In any way you can," Hem nodded.

Karper had a round face, and it grew plumper and more pleased with each passing second. "God's servants are not restricted in this world. His Will be done."

"Would you burn copies of the book to prevent distribution?" Duvall asked.

"I sense more than the simple question in your voice." You've got to give him that; Karper wasn't stupid.

"We have reason to believe that the victim was trying to burn Monsieur Joyce's books." Duvall gestured towards Joyce, who stood in a shadowed corner.

Karper spun around and targeted Joyce. "You are the Blasphemer James Joyce?"

"I am James Joyce." Joyce's voice was flat, and his one visible eye blinked.

Something in Joyce's tone took Karper back, and the preacher was silent for a second. Duvall watched the pair study each other. I was disappointed. Joyce was supposed to be so damned good with words and the best he could do was "I am James Joyce." As far as I was concerned, his reputation was going down in flames.

"Do you realize the sin against God that your book represents?" Karper finally found his tongue again.

"No. Do you?"

"Well, I never—" Karper went back to blustering, fumbling for words, and his twitching eye vibrated in a frenzy.

"Oh," Joyce said softly. "I'd be a bit surprised if you hadn't."

"Enough!" Duvall ordered. "Come with me, Monsieur Karper. I wish to show you something." He motioned towards the back room.

The two men—Duvall and Karper—headed through the door, but Duvall stopped and turned back. "Are you coming, Jack?"

"I'll sit this one out, Inspector. I've seen him before."

Duvall shrugged. "It is your decision." And they disappeared.

"Sylvia," Hem whispered. "You better put this whole *Ulysses* thing on hold."

She pushed an unruly lock of brown hair from her forehead. "I think Duvall just did that for me."

"You told me nothing out of the ordinary had happened the last couple of days," I reminded her. "Do you normally get visits from the Society Against Immoral Literature?"

"It didn't seem important," she said, hanging her head just a little.

"Miss Beach," Joyce began, striding forward. "Those copies must be delivered to our subscribers. They have been paid for."

"Joyce." I broke my silence. "You just aren't getting the picture, are you? Duvall is going to hang your Irish ass out to dry. And this Karper character is sure to give him every assistance."

"What do you think, Jack?" Hem said, and somehow I knew exactly what he was talking about.

"Yeah. Karper's appearance seems pretty coincidental. And he seems deadset on shooting your book out of the air, Joyce." The more I thought about it, the more logical it became. "Could be that maybe he had a little to do with that corpse being back there."

"But a preacher?" Arlaine's face looked as confused as her voice sounded.

"The ends, my dear Miss Watson, always justify the means," I told her, speaking without benefit of a formal introduction. But, I figured that unusual circumstances overrode formalities. "Besides," I continued. "I've seen his kind before. Anything for God and the Holy Crusade."

Sylvia smiled at me with already tired eyes. "You've always had an incredibly blunt way with words, Jack. That's one of the reasons I like you."

Duvall and Karper emerged from the back room about then; Duvall had a questioning look on his face, and Karper was slowly, hesitantly shaking his head.

"How much longer do you plan to stay in Paris?" Duvall asked.

Karper's little eyes focused on James Joyce. "Until I'm assured that James Joyce's soul has been returned to the bosom of the Lord."

"Or?" I couldn't resist the question.

Karper turned to me then. "Or, until I'm assured that his book will never see the light of day."

I didn't like the way he said it, and he knew that and didn't care.

"It is possible that I may have more questions for you. Where are you staying?" Duvall cut the argument off at its root.

"The Hotel Jacob. I'm available at your request. God's Servants always assist the Law. Miss Beach," he looked to Sylvia, "I'll be talking to you later."

"I will look forward to it," Sylvia said politely, far more politely than she felt.

Karper spun on his pudgy legs and waddled out of the bookshop.

"So?" I asked Duvall.

The inspector shrugged. "He said he did not know the man."

"Fascinating," Hem said.

"Don't count Brother Karper out yet," I warned. "His kind have a peculiar way of popping up when you least want them."

"Inspector?" Joyce said. "Do you have a need for me?"

"Not at present, but do not stray too far, Monsieur. We *will* be talking further." Duvall dismissed him with the flick of a hand.

Joyce said his goodbyes and disappeared out the door.

Arlaine turned to Sylvia again. "Miss Beach. I'm terribly confused. This just doesn't seem real."

"Jack and Hem will explain it to you." She grabbed my elbow and pulled me towards the desk.

"Yes, Jack will explain it, I'm sure," Duvall appeared beside me.

"But, Duvall, I wanted to. . . ." it came out more sputtered than spoken.

"I'll call you when I know something else. Go now, there's nothing more here." Duvall shoved me from behind.

The girl was confused.

"I'm sorry, dear. This is Jack Barnett, an old friend of mine. And you know Ernest," Sylvia explained. "Please, Arlaine, they'll tell you everything you need to know."

"She's right, Miss . . . ?" Duvall hesitated.

"Watson."

". . . Watson," Duvall continued. "We must clear the shop. The investigation must proceed."

"Come on, Hem," I finally grunted. "Let's get some coffee." Duvall wouldn't pass up an opportunity to get rid of me for a while. A wet stream was trying to get away from my nose; my chest was starting to feel heavy, and my headache was beating out a Latin rhythm. Between the cold railroading its way through my system, Sylvia's dead body, James Joyce, the Reverend Quintin Karper, and being sent to babysit some American tourist, the day was definitely turning to crap.

I checked my watch—only ten in the morning.

• • • •

"I'm really confused." When Arlaine Watson shook her head, blond hair went everywhere.

I plucked three strands out of my coffee and laid them on the table. Hemingway grinned at me and wrote something in a little notebook he had. "Jerk," I muttered.

"What?" Arlaine leaned over the table.

"Nothing. Look, I'm just as confused as you are," I admitted with a sniffle, trying to stop the growing stream. "Sylvia went into the backroom this morning and found a dead body back there. She panicked. Hem happened to come by early and she sent him to get me. I showed up, we checked the situation out, figured it looked bad for Joyce but that he probably didn't have anything to do with it, and were about to dump the body out back when Duvall appeared. Somebody tipped him."

"Why would you want to move the body?" The innocence on her face was too much. It reminded me of other times.

"Because, Sylvia has enough problems with this book of Joyce's. She doesn't need a dead body, one that probably has nothing to do with the shop, complicating her life. The Right Reverend Karper is just one example of how complicated her life can get."

"But it might have something to do with the shop."

"Yeah, Jack. What about that? What if it does?"

"I guess, then, that Duvall will find out and old Jim Joyce may find himself behind bars. And the great *Ulysses* will no longer be published in France, or probably anywhere else either. And the Society Against Immoral Literature will rejoice."

Hemingway chuckled. "'Jim Joyce', I'll have to try that sometime." He stroked his mustache for a second as his eyebrows came together in a nosedive. "What *is* going on, Jack? Have you got a feel for it, yet?"

I shook my head. "No more than you do. The whole thing stinks of a set-up. The door bashed in from the outside. Joyce's key stolen. Somebody tipping the police that the body's there. The note signed 'J.J.'. This guy, Karper, coming out of the woodwork at just the wrong moment. It's tied up too neat for Joyce to be the murderer. There's got to be more to it than that."

"Joyce sure doesn't help matters any," Hem pointed out, taking a sip of pernod. He could drink all day long and never really show it. It was his gift, I suppose. Though, I heard that Hadley could match him drink for drink.

"What did Mr. Joyce do?" Arlaine asked. "And why shouldn't you just let the police handle it?" Her veil of innocence grated on me like sandpaper, and it drew me to her as surely as my dreams came at night.

"Where are you from?" I couldn't help asking.

Her eyelashes flickered at me a couple of times. "A little town in Iowa."

"Jesus, I should have known. Well, other than act like the pompous ass he is, Joyce hasn't done anything." I turned back to Hem. "I've got to be honest with you. He may be a genius, but son of a bitch ranks up there somewhere too. And he's about as cooperative as a stone statue. God! I wish this cold would go away." I pulled my handkerchief out to stop the flood from my nose. "To answer your second question, Duvall is a great guy, but he's singularly narrow-minded."

"You're not too damn accepting of other people, Jack."

"I don't have to be," I grumbled, stuffing the damp handkerchief back in my pocket. "But, the truth is, I don't think Joyce killed anybody."

"Things sure do point in that direction," Hem argued.

"That's the problem. Too many things point at Joyce. Like I said, it's too damn neat. He's in the shop at the approximate time of the meeting. We have a note signed with his initials. The dead man is lying on top of a Molotov cocktail capable of making this book of Joyce's—a book half the world has banned—go up in smoke. Somebody, obviously, wants us to think Joyce did it. But it doesn't make sense to me. Joyce might stab somebody with an ink pen to defend his books, but not a knife. He just doesn't strike me as the type. He's too wrapped up in his work. Yeah," I laughed to myself. "So wrapped up he's forgotten what working for a living is."

"Hey!" Hem turned defensive. "There's nothing wrong with writing."

I remembered, then, something about Hadley, Hem's wife, having some money that supported them or helped support them. He did some articles for the *Toronto Star*, I knew, but that couldn't bring in much. But, like I said, it didn't cost much to live in Paris. Even if you rented a second room just for writing, I guess.

"Yeah." I let it go. No use making Hem mad. "But try this on for size. Karper tries to preach to Sylvia yesterday about all this. She refuses to listen. He figures God will forgive him for anything he does, so he plants the dead body in the backroom, frames Joyce, and tips Duvall. God's Will be done."

"But he said he didn't know the guy," Hem argued.

"Jesus, Hem, he wouldn't admit it. At least, not until he had to. If Duvall arrests Joyce based on the frame, without Karper getting personally involved, so much the better for Karper. Later, if things aren't going the way he wants them to, he can always come out with some new information to jerk Duvall's chain. Believe me, I've seen Karper's kind." I turned back to Arlaine. "Do you know Joyce very well?"

"Just for a few days. Since I started working at the shop. He comes in every day and talks to Sylvia. Sometimes he has mail there. I've noticed that several people use the bookshop as a mailing address. His wife came by one day looking for him. She's something else."

"How so?" I asked. You never knew in a deal like this who was gonna pop up out of the woodpile.

Arlaine flipped her hair again. "She has all the emotion that Mr. Joyce lacks. He's Irish, too, but she acts it."

I nodded. That could explain a lot. I filed it away for future reference. "Anybody else looking for him?"

She thought for a minute with her eyes closed. I noticed the veins in her eyelids and the length of her lashes, and the color of her hair, and. . . .

"Hey, Jack."

I shook myself. "What?"

"What was that other piece of paper you found?" Hem was looking at me with almost a smile on his face.

"I'll tell you later. One question at a time." I looked again at Arlaine. "So, did anybody else come looking for him?"

She'd opened her eyes during my exchange with Hemingway. "No, no one that I can recall. A lot of people come around the shop every day, so I can't say for sure. Sometimes there are so many I can't keep track of them all."

"Yeah. I could see that this morning. Place was like the Gare de Lyon. Well, that answers that." I reached into my pocket and retrieved the piece of paper. "Here." I flipped it onto the table.

The broken arms of the "X" looked even stranger against the wood. Whoever drew it had done so in a hurry; the edges of the design were uneven, and the arms weren't really in alignment with each other.

"That's a funny looking thing," Hem said, picking up the paper and studying it. "It's sort of familiar, though." He frowned, and it pulled the mustache down at the corners of his mouth.

"Really? I've never seen anything like it." But, my denial didn't kill this nagging feeling I had, a feeling that somewhere, recently, I *had* seen it.

"What's the next step?" Hem got straight to the point.

I reached for my handkerchief one more time and wiped my

nose. "If Karper or somebody is trying to implicate Joyce, they have to have a motive, a reason. Why would anyone want to get Joyce out of the way?"

Hem stroked his mustache. "Well, if Joyce was arrested, Sylvia might have to stop publishing *Ulysses*. If a murder was tied to it, the authorities might confiscate the whole inventory of books. And with Joyce in prison, he wouldn't be doing a hell of a lot of writing, I don't think."

"Okay," I agreed. "Any other reasons?"

"Maybe somebody just doesn't like Joyce," Arlaine said. "And, maybe, the police are better suited to handle this. I don't want to sound like an old harpy, but you two are writers, not detectives."

I harrumphed. "Excuse me, lady, but you're confusing me with my friend here."

"Whatever," she smiled. "But, if it isn't Joyce, then why not somebody who just doesn't like him? Does it have to be Reverend Karper? I mean, it's been my observation that a lot of these writers are pretty fragile. Couldn't somebody be jealous?"

"Not much of a reason to frame somebody for murder." Didn't sound like much of a possibility to me either.

"Who the hell knows," Hem answered, shaking his head. "Is there a good reason for something like this?"

"Probably not," I nodded. "Probably just strong reasons and weak reasons."

"So, who's to say that whoever framed Joyce didn't do it for a really weak reason? Answer that one."

I didn't want to. Nobody wants to think that a crime doesn't have a good reason, but the truth is hard to take sometimes, and I remembered the murders at the brothel the month before. No reason there. That's what kept me flying loops for so long.

"But," I said, "we still can't say that Joyce is definitely innocent. Maybe Joyce owed this Phillipe Jourdan some money? God knows he's borrowed from everybody else in Paris."

"And London, too, I hear," Hem added. "There is, still, the note. As far as I know, he's the only 'J.J.' that has anything to do with the shop."

"What about it, Arlaine?" I asked. "Seen anybody else with the initials J.J. since you've been there?"

She closed her blues eyes again, a habit I'd come to associate with deep thought. "Well, I have been through the subscription list a couple of times. I . . . I don't remember anybody else with those initials." Her eyes flew open again. "But that doesn't mean anything. I haven't got the file memorized." Concern wrinkled her face. She wanted so much to do the right thing. Reminded me of myself five years before.

"No, I don't guess you have, but it sure doesn't help Joyce right now, does it? Yeah, Joyce *could* have killed this guy." I said it. But it still didn't sound right. "Looks like our job, whether we want it or not, is to find out if he did. Quick. So if he's guilty, Sylvia can dump this book of his before she takes a real bath on it."

"And, if he didn't?" Hem asked.

"If he didn't," I said, "well, then, I guess we'll have to help Duvall figure out who really did."

Hemingway got that excited little kid look again, and I wiped my runny nose. He rolled his shoulders like he was getting ready to box. Arlaine pushed a handkerchief at me, and I gratefully took it.

"What can I do?" She flashed her blues at me again.

"Go over to Sylvia's flat and find out about this J.J. business," I directed. "See if anybody else on the subscription list had those initials. Or anybody else that even hangs out at the shop. And ask Monnier about it." I always thought of Adrienne Monnier in the masculine.

"What about me?" Hemingway frowned, afraid I was going to leave him out, I guess.

"You'll come with me. I need an introduction to some of these people like Gertrude Stein and the others. I've met Stein before— hell, I know her brother Leo pretty well—but, Ezra Pound's the only one I've spent any time with." Ezra was a great drinking buddy, and God knows I had enough of those.

The duties divided, I tossed some coins on the table for the wine and started to rise.

"Wait a minute," Arlaine began, still sitting at the table with a pout growing on her pale face. "When will I see you again?"

I don't know what kind of look crossed my face, but she raised her eyebrows when she saw it.

"I mean when I've talked to Sylvia, and I have something to tell you."

My normal hemorrhoidal look returned, and I glanced at Hemingway for a little help. "What do you think?"

Hem scratched his head for a second. "It's Friday. Let's meet over at Gertrude's. She always has a bunch of people in on Fridays.

Tomorrow night the other crew will be at Nathalie Barney's. Tonight they'll be at Gertrude's."

"Sounds good." I turned and walked out, not waiting for Arlaine and knowing that Hemingway would be on my heels.

• • • •

Parts of Paris were incredibly beautiful in those days. The Seine was lovely. The streets were lovely. Everybody loved Paris in springtime. Everybody except me. I always caught a stinking cold, and it usually lasted until summer finally hit. By the time Hem and I got a block away from the cafe, I had already flooded another handkerchief and was heading from mild annoyance to major aggravation. Passing a fish market, I bent down, stared into the horde of glazed fish eyes, and sniffed. Nothing.

"Cold really bothering you, huh?" Hemingway asked.

"You're perceptive, buddy. I've always said that."

"Why don't you drink some milk and brandy? I hear that's supposed to be good for a cold."

A shiver started in my belly and radiated from my toes to my head. Milk and brandy. Just the memory of that taste turned my stomach and put me back in the cockpit of a Spad 13.

"No thanks, Hem."

"Sure." He looked a little hurt and didn't say anything for a block or two. We moved further up into the Latin Quarter, and I began to feel guilty.

"Look," I explained. "I used to drink milk and brandy to settle my nerves during the war. It, well, it gives me bad memories."

Hemingway's eyes lit up. "Really. I hadn't heard about that. Rough time, huh?"

"You might say that." I forced a smile.

The big guy nodded gravely. "I know what you mean. I was wounded in Italy, you know."

"I've never been to Italy." Changing the subject was top priority with me.

"Well, you ought to go," Hem took the bait and spent the next ten minutes telling me about some love affair he'd had with a nurse there and how pretty the countryside was, none of which I wanted to hear, but it kept me from having to answer more questions.

He finally stopped in front of an old apartment building on rue du Cardinal-Lemoine, next to a dance hall called the Bal du

Printemps. The door to Number 7, a heavy wooden affair with a single large plate of glass, sat in the corner of an angle in the street.

"What's this?"

"Home," Hem grinned. "I need to check in with Hadley for a minute."

"You live in a dance hall?" Hem and I drank a lot together, but I'd never been to his flat.

"Up above it." He pointed to a row of windows. "Come on up."

"No, thanks." Domestic scenes didn't interest me. In fact, nothing was more disinteresting. And the couple of times that I'd seen Hem and Hadley together they spent a lot of time calling each other by pet names. I couldn't stomach that kind of love. A thought struck me. "Didn't Joyce used to live around here somewhere?"

"Yeah, down the street at 71."

I nodded and Hemingway bounced up the stairs and into the building. When he opened and closed the door, a strong smell of stale urine engulfed me; it had to be strong to get past the roadblock in my nose. Most of these French apartment buildings had bathrooms—pissoirs they called them—on each landing and they always smelled. I took a couple of steps further away, but it started sprinkling again. That was my choice, flirting with pneumonia or smelling piss. I decided on pneumonia.

The break from Hem gave me a chance to do some thinking about the whole business. I needed to separate emotion from the thing. Sure, I didn't want Joyce to be involved because that might involve Sylvia. And I really liked Sylvia. She was a good friend, Monnier aside. But the fact was, Joyce was weird. He could have done it and then forgot that he did it. No. I stopped myself. Joyce wasn't that weird. I kept picturing his face in my mind's eye, and the tag "murderer" just didn't seem to fit. It was a gut instinct, a hunch.

I used to play those sometimes when I went up on patrol. Something would tell me that I'd find a Hun scout over a particular segment of the patrol sector, and sure enough, there he'd be, just ripe for the picking, floating along without a care in the world. The feeling I had just then was exactly the same. Only this time it was telling me that there was a lot more to this than I realized.

Duvall was smart; I knew that. But he had a decent circumstantial case against Joyce, and he wasn't seeing past that. Karper was a wild card, and I needed more information before I could figure him out. It was getting pretty clear that to get Duvall off Joyce, I'd have to have the whole thing sewn up tight. The thing with the hookers had been easy in the final analysis, after all the pieces came together. Just simple addition. Convincing Duvall had been the tough part. But this one was going to take some fast footwork.

Hemingway appeared back on the street about then, and I broke off my train of thought. He had a big grin on his face, but I knew he hadn't been gone long enough to do more than get a kiss.

"Where to first?" he asked.

I wiped my nose again. "Let's head over to the typewriter company the dead guy worked for. Finding out something about him should be a priority."

"Won't the police already be doing that?"

"Yeah. But that doesn't cut us out. People don't like to talk to the police. Sometimes, in fact, they just clam up."

Four

Pierre Legrain et fils occupied the lower floor of a three story building in the heart of Paris' manufacturers' district. The storefront was dingy; the windows needed a hard cleaning, and the company name was written across the glass in peeling gold paint. Our boy Phillipe hadn't been doing much of a job from the looks of things. The only thing visible through the dirt on the window was a desk and a bored-looking secretary who kept studying her fingernails and crossing and uncrossing her legs.

"There's one for you, Jack." Hem poked me in the side.

I looked at him and sniffed back a stream running the hundred yard dash down my upper lip. "I prefer women whose ability for conversation isn't limited to 'do you like my nails red or blue?'" As if I could do anything if I had one. But I didn't tell Hemingway that. It wasn't something you went around talking about. "Let's go."

We went across the sidewalk and into the store. The girl looked just as bored inside as out, and I saw then that she had a huge mole on the side of her face, and her teeth could pass for the Black Hole of Calcutta.

"Bonjour, mademoiselle," I started in my best French, which was never very good. Hemingway just smiled.

"Bonjour." Silence. End of statement. She continued to study her nails.

"Nous sommes en information cherchant." I figured I'd let her in on the secret of our visit. A convenient "searching for information" should do it.

A careless nod and flip of her brown hair.

"Ou est la directeur?" If she wasn't gonna help me, at least I could ask to see the manager. And Hemingway was beginning to snicker.

"He is in the back repairing a typewriter." Her accent was barely noticeable.

"You speak English very well," I told her, just a little pissed off that she hadn't said so before.

"You speak French like a street whore," she replied with a smile.

Hemingway's snicker had turned into a chuckle. I looked down at her and wiped my nose. "Just trying to judge my audience."

"Pig," she answered without losing her smile.

I walked past her, and she resumed studying her nails.

"You do this well with women all the time?" Hem asked as we passed a couple of junky looking typewriters, their guts ripped apart and lying spread across a table top.

"If you only knew," I grunted.

Pierre Legrain looked like he'd seen better days, maybe even a better life. The hair on his head was almost non-existent—what little covered his balding pate was a dirty gray. He wore a workman's apron, and it was marked with holes from hours and hours of la-bor. He was hunched over a typewriter perched on its side on top of a long work table. A dozen similar tables covered the cavernous backroom of Pierre Legrain et fils. But only Pierre—pere it looked like—was at work. No one else could be seen, and the clicking sounds of his labors echoed through the room in a lonely, barren rhythm. I felt like I'd invaded a tomb.

"Monsieur Legrain?" I asked.

The old gray head didn't rise. His concentration was fixed on the typewriter before him, and the creases at his eyes told me that he was having a hell of a problem.

"The platen, it will not turn," he said in only slightly accented English. "This is not right."

"Maybe it's stuck on something," Hem offered, fidgeting a little.

"The owner must have done something to cause this," he de-cided.

"Pourquoi?"

At that the old head did rise and irises sparkled from eyes set deep in a heavily wrinkled face. "Because, Monsieur, I myself built this machine. It would not dare to . . . ," he searched for the right word, "act badly."

"Sometimes machines do not act as we would wish."

Pierre Legrain turned away from the recalcitrant typewriter and nodded slowly and sadly. "Is it not the way with everything?"

"Business doesn't look good," Hemingway said taking a look around.

"These tables once were filled with working men." The old man waved at the empty seats, his voice bouncing off the distant walls.

"Where's your son? Doesn't he help?"

"The Ardennes."

I nodded. "And the girl?"

"His wife. She has a child and must work. She answers the telephone and keeps my books."

"You don't make your own typewriters anymore?"

He looked at me with tired laughter in his eyes and studied the ink stains beneath his fingernails. "Once I made the finest typewriters in France. My typewriters were in all the government offices, all the embassies. The name Pierre Legrain and quality, they were the same thing. But now, no Monsieur; I only repair typewriters. There have been no new machines produced here since before the war. How may I help you?"

"I am looking for a man named Phillipe Jourdan."

Pierre Legrain thought for a minute and silently shook his head. "No. I know no one by that name. He is a friend of yours?"

"No. Just someone I need to find. You are sure you have never heard of Monsieur Jourdan? Perhaps an old employee?"

Again, the old man paused in thought. "No. I know only Henri Jourdan, who I drink wine with every day at five. He is a good friend, a good companion. And for the last four years there has been only the girl and I."

I nodded. "Do you charge much for repairing typewriters?"

"Only what I must."

"Then I will bring you mine to be cleaned."

"Merci," the old man said, bowing just slightly.

"De rien," I waved his thanks off. The old man went back to his repair job, and I turned to Hemingway. "Come on. Let's get out of here."

"Aren't you going to—," Hem began, but I smacked him in the stomach with the back of my hand, and he got the message.

I didn't bother to insult the wart-faced girl this time, the girl who answered the telephone that never rang. She sneered at me, but I understood a part of her now, and so I didn't look at her. Once on the street, I broke it all down for Hem.

"Come on. He's all that's left of Pierre Legrain et fils. No other workmen. No new machines produced. No need for traveling salesmen. And, finally, no knowledge of Phillipe Jourdan. The guy was obviously using a phony business card. Why tell the old fellow that some dead man was running around claiming to be his employee? I'd say he's got enough to worry about."

"Yeah, okay, but what about Duvall?"

"We'll let Duvall be the bearer of confusing tidings."

"I guess. Where to now, Sherlock?"

"Your sense of humor is frightening," I snarled. My nose started running yet again, and the thought of damming the flow with one of my soggy, sticky handkerchiefs was less than appealing, so I wiped the stream with my jacket sleeve. In the process, I got a glimpse at my watch, eleven thirty. Half the day shot and nothing accomplished. That's one from my father.

He said it every day, usually more towards sundown, when darkness started closing around us. I asked him once why, if life was so lacking in accomplishment, he didn't just end it all. He washed my mouth out with lye soap and made me copy "Thou shalt honor thy father and mother" twenty times, but he didn't repeat his favorite slogan that day, or the next.

I reached into my pocket and pulled out the piece of paper with the broken-armed cross on it. "Let's check this thing out. I've got a feeling I've seen it before, but I'm not sure where. Something tells me that it's got some religious significance. There's a guy I know on the Boulevard St. Germain who might be able to help. If Phillipe Jourdan wasn't a typewriter salesman, maybe tracking this down will tell us what he really was. Sylvia's not gonna get off the hook if we don't keep going. And this is all we've got to go on right now."

The rain had let up, but a stiff breeze seemed like it might be blowing in more wet weather, a line of evil, grayish-blue clouds edged the skyline to the west. I noticed Hem staring at me.

"What?"

He shook his big head. "You're a strange kind of guy, Jack. I know about you and Sylvia."

A nasty warmth coursed through me. "What do you know about me and Sylvia?"

"That you made a play for her. That she turned you down, because she. . . ." He didn't finish; he didn't have to, and the pause was more than awkward.

"So she told you," I said finally.

"No, Gertrude told me."

"I've met Gertrude Stein maybe once! How in the hell did she know?"

"Sylvia told her, I'm pretty sure." It seemed natural to Hemingway. I'm not sure why it didn't to me.

"What? Do they have some kind of club where they sit around and talk about all the idiots that have made doomed passes at them?"

Hem grinned. "Naw. If they did, Gertrude wouldn't have too many stories to tell, and she couldn't stand being out of the spotlight for that long."

I had to laugh. From what I'd seen of Gertrude Stein, he was right. "I made a mistake. I've made a lot of mistakes. That's one of the more minor ones. Besides, it doesn't matter anyway."

"But it's interesting. You don't dislike her or anything, do you? I mean, you're not repulsed by her because of—"

"No." We were walking back towards the Latin Quarter and clouds, thick and heavy, still scudded across the sky, but breaks appeared here and there and sunlight tried to stream through. Seemed like my earlier prediction was off the mark. My nose was clearing out some, too. I inhaled and, despite the little pain that comes with congested lungs, I enjoyed the newly fresh air. Paris always seemed cleaner after a rain, like every once in a while God had to wash down everything and everybody in the city. "What right have I got to be repulsed? She's my friend. She does what she wants to and that's okay. If she was in Liberty, Missouri, she'd have real problems, but she's in Paris, and that makes it okay. Hell, if she was in Liberty, Missouri, she probably *couldn't* be my friend. She probably wouldn't want to be." I looked over at him, and he was furiously scribbling in a notepad as we walked. "You're making notes. Why?"

He stopped and turned a little red. "I'm trying to understand some things. That's all. I think I see what you're saying, though. Paris is a woman you make love to often, comfortably, but without marriage getting in the way. No one cares if you make love to her, because they're making love to her too. *Everyone* makes love to her. And none of the rules apply here, because everyone ignores the rules. Yeah, I know what you mean."

I sniffed. "I'm glad you do, cause I sure as hell don't." But, down deep, I did.

We walked along quietly for a little while. More clear blue than clouds showed in the sky by then, and it looked like the rain really was over. Despite my clogged nose, I smelled fresh, baking bread. Paris always smelled like food to me, rich, delicate foods. I took another deep breath and luxuriated in the scent.

"Liberty, Missouri," Hem said after a minute.

"What about it?"

"Is that where you're from?"

I thought about the question before answering. "Yeah, that's where I was born and raised. I'm from Paris now. Paris is the only place to be now."

"Yeah," Hem said with a soft, gentle smile and taking a deep breath of his own. "I know what you mean." But he really didn't know what I meant, and neither did I.

We crossed back over the Seine and reentered the Latin Quarter. Our part of Paris was waking up. It was well past noon, and shopkeepers were finally getting some customers. I saw Robert McAlmon, another one of the hundreds of American journalists in Paris, staggering along towards a cafe. Hemingway waved to him; McAlmon squinted, recognized Hem, and waved torturedly.

"What's his problem?"

Hem laughed. "He probably stayed out all night with Joyce drinking. Both of them are bad about that kind of thing."

"Not last night he didn't," I reminded Hemingway.

"Yeah, you're right."

"Does Joyce spend a lot of time out late?"

"Some. His eyes bother him a lot and that keeps him in part of the time, but he loves to go out drinking. I'm not sure how those guys do it. They drink till four in the morning and then write masterpieces all day."

"Sure," I grunted. "But that gives me an idea. When we get the photo from Duvall, we need to show it to some of Joyce's drinking buddies. If Joyce is being framed, then there's a chance that the murderer saw the victim hanging around Joyce at some bar. I mean, it doesn't make sense that Joyce would simply kill a total stranger. Even Duvall won't buy that story for long."

"No. But maybe," Hem began, stroking his mustache slowly, "the killer doesn't care if the frame-up works forever. Maybe, he's just buying time."

"Buying time for what though? Till he can get away. I've thought of that, but, hell, he could already be in the states by now. I'm not saying you're not right; I'm just saying it's not likely."

"Maybe."

An old man stumbled down the street in front of us. His ragged clothes were hardly more than strips of linen, and one sleeve dangled empty. Thick streaks of gray ran through his hair, but his face said thirty. He didn't seem to see us as he rambled past, but I caught his arm and turned him towards me.

"Alors!" he shouted. His eyes were filmy and red, but not bloodshot, and fear quickly covered them. Part of his shirt ripped away in my hand and felt oily, greasy, dirty.

"Taissez-vous, mon ami," I silenced him softly. "Bois de Belleau?"

The fear subsided, and his reddened eyes searched for my face. He ran a still nervous hand over his unshaven, shadowed jaw and nodded.

I reached in my pocket, retrieved a bill and shoved it into his hand. "Dix francs, mon ami."

His fingers gripped mine before I could pull away. "Merci." Then he let go and staggered on down the street.

Hemingway watched him long after I had stopped. He turned back to me and pushed an errant lock of hair out of his face. "Belleau Wood?"

"Mustard gas."

"Poor bastard. I didn't have to see any of that."

"I didn't either, from ground level that is." I remembered staring down, though, as I flew over, and it lay over the forest like a blue blanket. Sometimes the blanket would be peeled away by the wash of a low-flying plane, and the soldiers lay like little stickmen on the broken ground.

"You were a pilot, weren't you, Jack. I'd forgotten. How many did you shoot down?"

"One too many," I told him.

Hemingway didn't ask any more questions for a minute, but I could feel him staring at me.

"How are the stories going?" I asked, anything to make him quit staring.

"Some days good; some days not so good. I always try to leave off when I know what's gonna happen next. That way I don't have any trouble getting back into it. Getting cranked up on the new ones is tough sometimes, though." Hemingway's eyes smiled when he talked about writing. "But, hell, when it's going good there's nothing like it except making love. Don't you think?"

"I don't write the kind of stuff you do, pal, so I wouldn't know." If only feeling good came that easy. "You must really like it here, Hem. I never hear you talk about home."

The big head drooped a little. "I don't always get along with them, Jack. My mother and I, we, well . . . we don't get along. Let's just leave it at that."

"That's better than I'm doing. Not only don't we get along, but they don't understand me and I don't understand them. Why did you come to Paris?" I shifted gears.

"Paris is great. You can live cheap and get some writing done. It's like you said a minute ago, there's no place to be except Paris. You can be with other writers here and learn from them."

"That's real important to you, isn't it?" I was beginning to see something more than a big, friendly, puppy dog.

Hemingway's eyes sparkled. "Yeah, Jack, it is."

We stopped in front of an antique store on the Boulevard Saint Germain, a place called "Bon Tresures," and I pushed the heavy, wooden door open. It fell back with the jingle of a small bell, and Hem and I went in.

"Jack Barnett! You sorry son of a bitch! Where have you been keeping yourself? No, don't tell me. Probably laid up with a whore somewhere." The words tumbled out of Francis P. O'Connor as he lumbered towards us. That was one of his endearing qualities; he could talk a hundred miles a minute and walk only a mile an hour. Frank O'Connor had grown three sizes since I'd seen him last. But he was dressed in the latest suit, tailored to make him look his best. Or at least as good as he could with that massive expanse of pink crowning his skull. I'm not sure Frank had ever known hair.

"Bless me father, for I have sinned." I recited solemnly and crossed myself in the approved manner. Hem just stared.

A grin spread across Frank's plump face. "You've sinned a hell of a lot more than I could ever forgive. And, besides, I sold the confessional."

"What a bastard! How can I receive absolution?"

Frank turned around and trundled towards a table in the back of the shop. He tipped a vase as he wedged himself down the aisle. Hem dashed up and caught it before it fell.

"Good catch," I muttered to Hem, sniffling again and getting a full snout of a musty, stale odor.

Frank twisted around and grunted nonchalantly. "Ming. A missionary sold it to me last week. Robbed me blind on the deal.

Come, have a seat." He motioned to a trio of chairs, circling a low, highly polished, wooden table, as he lowered himself into one.

"Frank, this is Ernest Hemingway, a friend of mine."

Hem stuck his hand out, and Frank took it in his big paw.

"What's with all the Catholic hocus-pocus?" Hem asked.

"Frank's a retired priest."

"You are too kind, Jack." Frank bowed politely at the lie. He turned to Hem. "I am, legally speaking, a defrocked priest. They stripped me of my rank and vestments. You see before you a man bereft of his religion."

"But not forsaken by his God," I stuck in, knowing it was coming anyway. Frank threw me a nasty look.

"God forsakes only those who are stupid enough to believe that he has forsaken them."

"Any particular reason they kicked you out?" Hem asked.

"Jack, I'm not sure I like your young friend. He's too inquisitive."

Hem turned red in embarrassment. "Sorry, I—"

"I was a chaplain for the American Expeditionary Force. Indeed, I often ministered to Black Jack Pershing himself, when one of my more protestant brethren wasn't around." Frank enjoyed telling the story himself so much that I had to let him tell it, lies and all. "But I was not always the mountain of flesh you see before you. Nay, young man, just a few years ago I was a sleek, handsome, youthful, though somewhat bald, priest. However, my seminary training had not been fully assimilated and I found myself falling prey to certain pleasures of the flesh at a certain chateau near the German border. In other words, I was discovered fornicating with the lady of the house by a very self-righteous Baptist chaplain (who, I happen to know, wanted in her pants as well and was only acting out of jealousy)."

"Surely they didn't kick you out just because of that." I had to give Hem one thing; he didn't always buy things hook, line, and sinker.

"There were other trifles," Frank admitted, waving his hand in dismissal.

"Yeah, two Rembrandts and a Van Gogh that Frank 'liberated' from this same French dame."

"So you're a thief too," Hem nodded in understanding.

I chuckled. "It wasn't so much the thievery either. The Catholics are very forgiving by nature. Other factors came into play. See, he had taken—"

"A vow of poverty, Jack," Frank interrupted. "Just spit it out." His cheeks turned a healthy red again, and he grinned at Hem. Frank loved to shock and confuse people. And he spent several minutes feeding pornographic crumbs to Hemingway who lapped them up like a hungry dog.

"Your sinful ways aren't why we're here, Frank," I interrupted. "We've got a little mystery to solve." I pulled the piece of paper out of my pocket and tossed it on the table. "You see, Hem, Frank is not only a degenerate; he's also an expert on religious symbols and artifacts."

"Part of my priestly training," Frank explained to Hem. "A part, I might add, that often comes in handy when some holy relic passes through my door. It affords me, shall we say, something of an advantage in dealing with less educated people. But what good is arcane knowledge if you can't profit from it. Let's see what you've got." He leaned forward with a loud grunt and snatched the scrap with his pudgy fingers.

No one spoke as Frank studied the broken-armed cross on the piece of paper. Two or three clocks ticked in the background in an obvious conspiracy to drive me crazy.

"Well, Frank," I said finally. "Do you know what it is or not?"

"You are an impatient man, Jack. Someday you'll pay for your impatience." He heaved a sigh and dropped the scrap back on the tabletop, leaning back as the chair's joints groaned in protest. "I know something about it, but this one is an oddity. It's called a fylfot. The oldest religious symbol known to man, or, rather, known to have been created by man. Still in use in India, China, Japan, and by some native tribes of North America. At first, I believe, it represented the sun gods of the various religions. Of course, while *I* still hold with certain tenets of sun worship such as nude sunbathing, that religion has woefully fallen by the wayside."

"What's so odd about this one?" I asked, trying to get him back on track.

"You pose questions which require more physical activity than I care to undertake," Frank grunted. "However, because it's you, I'll seek to satiate your curiosity."

He pulled himself up and waddled over to a wall lined with books of all sizes, shapes, and colors. Some looked pretty old, and I'd seen Hemingway drooling at them earlier. Frank passed a hand over the spines as he looked for the one he wanted. Finally, he pulled a ragged volume down, one with dark green, tattered covers.

Easing back into his seat, which groaned even louder this time, Frank turned the pages with one finger until he hit what he was looking for. Finally, he turned the book around so Hem and I could see.

"Here, look."

It was a picture of a broken-armed cross like ours, except it wasn't like ours. Something was different. I laid the scrap of paper down next to the book.

"Hey, its arms go the wrong way," Hem said.

Frank nodded solemnly. "One must assume that since the picture in this volume was selected by experts, it is accurate. And, since your doodle is handmade, its self-proclaimed artist obviously got it wrong."

None of this made a hell of a lot of sense to me. They were right. The arms of the cross in the book went counter-clockwise, while the broken arms of our cross pointed clockwise. But now I had two questions. Why were they different? And what was an ancient symbol for sun gods doing on a dead man's body in Sylvia Beach's bookstore?

"I wish I could help you further, Jack. You always bring me such interesting questions. But, unless you know something more about where this drawing came from, there's really nothing else I can tell you." Frank seemed genuinely sorry, which wasn't a customary condition for him.

"Found it on a dead traveling typewriter salesman," I grunted out of the corner of my mouth.

A frown slinked across Frank's chubby face. "You don't have to be nasty about it, Jack. If you don't want to tell me, just say so."

"No, really Father . . . , I mean, Mister O'Connor. He ain't lying," Hem said hurriedly. "Well, not really, anyway."

"Truly? How fascinating. Tell me more." Frank leaned forward, a gleam growing in his eyes. For a minute, I thought he was going to tumble over onto the table.

"Later," I said, standing up. Aggravation was setting in heavier by the minute. Every little lead seemed to evaporate. "We've got work to do."

"You're being incredibly rude, Jack. I've always said your social skills were woefully inadequate." Frank put on a wounded look.

"No time for your insults today, Frank. But I do appreciate your help. And I won't forget it."

Frank lounged back in his chair. "Don't worry. I won't let you forget." He smiled mischievously. "Debts must always be paid, sooner or later."

Hem scrambled to his feet, and we made our way back towards the front of the shop. "I'll come by tomorrow or the next day, Frank. Maybe sooner, if I find out anything new about this thing." A lot sooner, if I came up with something solid on the stupid-looking cross.

With Frank waving goodbye behind us, I opened the front door and started out, Hemingway close on my heels. About then, a crack sounded, like a backfiring car. Or a gunshot.

And the little glass window in the door next to my head shattered to pieces.

Five

‘D own, Jack! Get down!"

I stood there looking at the gaping hole in the door. What the hell? Somebody had been following us. And then I crashed down on the floor next to Hem.

"Jesus, Hem. Give me some warning before you jerk me around."

His eyes were on fire, but it was a sick kind of excited flame. "I *did* warn you. We sure must be rubbing somebody one helluva wrong way." Hem's mustache was twitching.

A car sped off in the distance, and suddenly everything got darker.

But it was just Frank looming over us and blocking out the light. "I wouldn't do this for just anyone," he grunted as he leaned over and helped us to our feet. "Jack, you owe me for a window."

"Frank, you're a self-centered asshole." I brushed at my suit, cutting myself a little on a piece of glass clinging to the fabric. I brushed again before I realized I was bleeding. It was my one decent suit, a conservative brown, and now it had this dark streak. The day had gone completely to hell.

"Jack." Frank put on his you've-hurt-me-so-much look. "Please. If I knew who had shot the glass out, don't you think I'd be sending them the bill? But," and he shrugged and grinned an embarrassed grin, "since I don't, I only have you to blame. Besides, you're okay."

Hemingway had jumped up and was brushing himself off. An excited gleam still danced around in his eyes.

"You're sick," I told him.

"You need to learn to loosen up a little bit," Hem advised. "Maybe we should go a few rounds. You know, get the old machine perking." He shadow-boxed a jab or two.

"You need a head doctor. Like that Freud guy in Vienna."

"Maybe, but it proves that we're on the right track."

"No kidding. But the question remains, which is the right track? Hell, we're still as lost as we were this morning. All we have are negatives. Phillipe Jourdan was not a traveling typewriter salesman. This is not a flyfloat."

"Fylfot," Frank reminded me.

"Fylfot," I corrected myself, "but it's almost exactly like one. And somebody *is* taking potshots at us. We're hardly a threat right now, except to James Joyce. And Duvall is going to be real excited over this turn of events." Jesus, this was getting to be a nightmare. "Watch your ass, Frank. If they, whoever 'they' are, think you know something, you could be in for trouble. Obviously," I flicked the last sliver of glass off my suit, "they don't mess around."

Frank rested his hands on his enormous stomach and looked thoughtfully at the door. "My posterior is my concern, but I will watch it, though to do so requires an inordinate amount of time. I will tell you, however, that as you and your friend wallowed on the shop floor, I observed a slick, black Model T, the kind favored by the embassy crowd, driving away at a high rate of speed."

"Now, what the hell does that mean?" I asked no one in particular.

"Trouble, my good friend," Frank said solemnly. "Nothing but trouble."

• • • •

After giving the Model T time to get far, far away, Hem and I left Frank's shop.

The streets were busy. A few cars, a few horse-drawn wagons, a lot of people. The automobiles made a chug-a-lug kind of sound. The horses clunked along and occasionally made a plop-plop kind of sound. The people filled the rest of the void, babbling in Norman French, Parisienne French, German, and a little English. A drunk staggered out of a bar, and I checked my watch—3:00 p.m. God, I loved Paris. It made me feel normal.

"Where to next?" Hem asked.

I thought for a minute before answering. "I want to see Joyce again. Not," I hurried to add, "that his presence is so exciting, but because to be honest with you, I'm at a loss. Phillipe Jourdan hasn't panned out. We've got Karper and Joyce to look at. Maybe if we can pin down Joyce's exact movements we'll have a clearer idea of the sequence of events. Besides, it's too early to go to Stein's apartment. And Duvall hasn't had time to get the photographs developed or the autopsy report in."

"Fine by me," Hem said, and we headed off. After a few minutes of silent mustache twitching, Hem spoke up again. "I still don't see how we're gonna find out much more about this fylfot thing. Maybe it is a symbol for a sun god or something and the guy that drew it didn't know he was putting the arms backwards."

"Good point. But, I'd think that anybody that believed in that hocus-pocus enough to carry around something like that would be careful enough to draw it right." It'd been my experience that religious people were always incredibly picky about their symbols, but less careful about following all their rules. Karper's comment about "God's servants are not restricted in this world" kept coming back to me. And I couldn't say his attitude was a big surprise. "Where's Joyce hanging his well-fed hat these days?"

"He's living in a hotel over on the rue de l'Universitie just down the street—number 9, I think. Nora keeps bugging him to get something better, but they just don't have the money right now."

I grunted. "No, probably not, with him feeding their faces at Michaud's all the time. Hell, I work semi-regular and I can't afford Michaud's much at all."

A couple of Citroens passed and I flinched in reflex and Hemingway laughed at me. "You're awfully skittish, Jack."

I straightened myself and gave him a "go-to-hell" look. "It's been a long time since I've been shot at. And it was never one of my favorite things."

"You don't have much of a sense of adventure. Besides, you were up in the air, with nothing to hide behind. It was different down on the ground."

"You lack common sense. And I don't care if you're behind a concrete wall, getting shot at is about as much fun as the bloody flux."

"This way." Hem laughed at me and motioned to the right at the next corner.

In a couple of minutes we were standing in front of No. 9, an okay looking private hotel. It had rows of long, narrow double windows and narrow white shutters to match. At the base of each window was a fancy black iron grill. A sign hung on the wall at the corner—"7th Arr. RUE DE L'UNIVERSITE." Hemingway led the way in and up, past the unmistakable smelly pissoirs on each landing, and to a door on the third floor. I knocked, hard. A woman's scream burst out of the door as it flew open, slamming against the wall with a bang.

If James Joyce was of average height for a man, then his red-headed wife was tall for a woman. Nora Joyce stood in the doorway, her eyes blazing. "What will you two be wanting? And say it in English; I don't speak this heathen French." Her Irish accent was thick.

Hemingway stepped forward. "Uh, Mrs. Joyce, I'm Ernest Hemingway. This is Jack Barnett. We wanted to see Mr. Joyce, if we could."

She looked us up and down, her red curls shaking with every movement of her head. "Am I supposed to be knowing either one of you?"

Hem started to answer, and I shut him up with a hand against his chest. "No. But your husband does. We came to talk to him about the murder at Shakespeare and Company last night."

At the mention of murder, those Irish eyes quit smiling, and I knew that I'd goofed.

"Murder! What in the name of St. Patrick does my good-for-nothing husband have to do with a murder! James Joyce! Quit your infernal, eternal, writing and get in here." She stomped back through the flat, leaving the door open, and I took that for an invitation to enter.

The familiar figure of James Joyce emerged from one of the backrooms. A kid, about seventeen, lounged on a sofa reading a book. "Georgio, have you finished your studies yet?" Joyce ignored us and looked down at the boy. A cat was curled up beside the kid and seemed as interested in the book as he was.

The boy glanced up like he was bored as hell. He shrugged. Joyce frowned and motioned for a bedroom. George Joyce climbed up off the couch slowly and headed for his homework. The cat stood, stretched, and padded softly after him. It was hell being seventeen.

James Joyce was still wearing the same clothes we'd seen on him earlier. I told myself to remember to ask Hemingway if Joyce dressed the same all the time. "Please, gentlemen, sit." He waved at the couch.

I plopped down without a lot of ceremony, and Hem sat next to me. Joyce found another chair and lowered himself into it. Nora stood in a doorway, leaning against the frame, her arms crossed sternly over her apron front.

"We wanted to ask you some more questions about this business at Shakespeare and Company last night," I began, sitting up and leaning forward.

Joyce pulled the glasses away from his face and rubbed a hand across his eyes. "This is becoming tiresome, gentlemen."

"That's really too bad, Mr. Joyce." I used the accepted manner of address since I didn't want to piss him off yet. "But it's become a real problem for Sylvia and the bookstore. And if you didn't catch the drift earlier, Inspector Duvall is sort of set on hanging this around your neck."

"What murder is this sniffling idiot talking about, Mr. Joyce? I expect an answer!"

"You haven't told her?" I was a little surprised.

He rubbed his eyes again. "I didn't think it was worthy of repeating."

"You made a mistake."

"Mr. Joyce," Hem began. "These guys are serious. They think you killed that guy because he was about to torch those copies of *Ulysses*. Jack and I don't think you did it, and we're trying to keep you out of jail. The only way to do that is to figure out who the real murderer is."

Nora Joyce's eyes just kept getting bigger and bigger as she dropped her arms and stood ramrod straight. "You good for nothing! Is this what your infernal writing has brought you to—murder?"

To Joyce's credit, he just laughed a small laugh and seemed unmoved by her explosion. I, on the other hand, was looking for shelter. Her face was almost as red as her hair, and, since I'd already been shot at once that day, I didn't fancy getting caught in the path of an Irish tornado.

"You heard the gentlemen, Nora; they don't think I did it." He cleaned his glasses, slowly and methodically, squinting at Nora with his one, visible eye as he wiped.

"Then, why do the police think you did?"

"Because," Hem started, "the guy was found dead on top of a bunch of copies of *Ulysses* and it looked like he was trying to burn them up."

"Ridiculous. James Joyce is no murderer. He's worthless and

spends all his days doing nothing but writing his silly books, books, I might add, that I've no interest in reading. But a murderer? No, he's no murderer." And, her decision made, Nora turned and tramped off to the kitchen.

"How about telling us a few things if you could?" I asked.

Joyce replaced his glasses over his eyepatch and leaned back in the chair. "I'll try."

"What time did you go to Shakespeare and Company last night?"

"About eight o'clock. I had a drink with Robert McAlmon and then went over to check the copies. I wanted McAlmon to go with me—my eyes aren't very good—but he wanted to stay and drink."

"Where did you have the drink?"

"At the Brasserie Lipp, just west of rue de l'Odeon on the Boulevard St. Germain."

"Yeah, I know where it is." Everybody in Paris did. They had great sauerkraut and wieners. "And then?"

"I walked over, let myself in, and tried to check the books. It was difficult."

"Why?"

Joyce fidgeted in his chair. "I recently had eye surgery. I have glaucoma."

"So, how did you check the books?"

"I used a magnifying glass and looked for errors in the text."

"A little bit late for that, isn't it. I mean, it's already been printed."

"Yes," Joyce grunted. "But if there were errors in this printing, I could catch them and ensure they don't reappear in the second printing. And, as I told you this morning, I have no wish to send badly bound or misprinted copies to my subscribers or reviewers." I felt like a schoolboy getting a lesson. "But, as I said," Joyce continued, "it took me an inordinate amount of time. My eyes are just not strong enough."

"Must be tough to write like that." I was sympathetic.

"I adjust. You see, I am forced to—"

"Okay, okay, then what happened?" He was getting off the subject and I was sympathetic, yeah, but not really interested.

"I did as many as I could and then left, about 10:30 I think."

"Did anyone come into the shop while you were there?"

"Not that I recall."

"Who knew you were going to be there?"

That one took him a minute. He squinted his eyes, and the pain was obvious in his frown. "When I asked Miss Beach for the key,

Miss Watson, the errand boy, and a few customers—Kopfmann, the German, and others—were there."

"Who's Kopfmann?" I looked to both Joyce and Hem.

Joyce answered first. "He's a German writer just recently come to Paris. I met him briefly at Shakespeare and Company yesterday."

"Was the good Reverend Karper around?"

Joyce sighed. "No, he wasn't."

"Did you talk to any of them about it? Did you talk to anyone after you left the shop yesterday afternoon?"

"No," he shook his head. "No, I came home and worked here until I went out with McAlmon after supper."

"What about him? You told him, didn't you?"

"Of course I did." And that schoolmaster look grew on his face. "I've already told you that. I tried to get him to help me."

"Did anyone see you leave?"

"There were some people across the street, but I couldn't see them well enough to know who they were."

"Where did the guy steal the key from you?"

"Just a block away from the bookstore."

"What did he say?"

Joyce thought for a minute, rubbing at the manicured beard on his chin. "He spoke in a rough, gravelly voice, what little he did say. It seemed to me that he was intentionally distorting his voice. He simply searched my pockets, took the keys, my money, and then he was gone."

"As simple as that?"

"As simple as that indeed," Joyce replied.

"And what did you do then?"

"I came home. What else was there to be done?"

"You could have called the police."

Joyce frowned. "Gia! My good man, do you realize how many robberies there are every night in Paris?"

I did, but I was surprised that Joyce did. And what the hell did "Gia" mean? He'd said that a couple of times. I sniffled for a minute and stood up to pace. I do my best thinking pacing. But the closer I paced to Joyce the more fidgety he got.

"Is something wrong?"

"You have a cold."

"Thanks for the diagnosis." The last thing I needed was an amateur doctor.

"Please stay a reasonable distance from me. I detest colds and other infections." The words sounded pompous, but they came out kind of pitiful and the quiver in his cheeks added to the effect.

"Okay, okay." I paced in the other direction as a young red-haired girl, in her early teenage years but tall for her age, ran yelling into the room.

"Babboo! Babboo!" She dove into Joyce's lap and buried her plump cheeks into his stomach.

"What is it, Lucia?" Joyce's voice was soft and gentle.

"Georgio is teasing me!"

"Then, we'll have to deal with him, won't we?"

She looked up and stared at Joyce fiercely. "Yes. Right now!"

"No, my dear, later. I have to speak with these gentlemen."

Lucia disentangled herself and headed back to the bedroom and another assault on Georgio, I figured.

"My children are normal children, Mr. Barnett, but I'm afraid I spoil them."

I stopped pacing. "Better to spoil them, I think, than to preach at them. But get back to this robbery. What did he take?"

"The keys to Miss Beach's shop, the key to the flat here, and my thirty francs." He stood quickly. "I must write a letter to a friend of mine in England. I need more money."

"You need to get a grip on reality! The Paris police have their eye on you as the number one suspect in this thing. Doesn't that bother you at all?"

Joyce blinked at me with that one, watery eye. "But I didn't kill anyone. Why should I be concerned?"

Hem shook his head at Joyce and spoke for the first time. "Mr. Joyce, I don't know how it works in Ireland, but in America, and probably France, sometimes they arrest innocent people."

Joyce sighed and was quiet for a few minutes. I started pacing again, keeping my distance so I wouldn't infect him. "But you gentlemen," he began, "are trying to find out who did kill that man, correct?"

"Yeah."

And Joyce sighed again and headed back towards the bedroom. "Then, I leave it in your hands. If Miss Beach trusts you, I shall as well."

James Joyce was gone. Back to his "infernal" writing, I figured. I could hear Nora Joyce in the kitchen, humming a tune. The two kids were giggling in a bedroom. My nose was running again. Hem and I left.

Seconds later found us back down the stairs, out the door, and on the street. If I had thought Joyce was innocent before, I was doubly sure now. I checked my watch. We were closing in on four o'clock. My stomach was growling.

"Does Gertrude serve food at these wingdings?"

"Sort of, but not really," Hem admitted.

"Then, let's get something to eat."

• • • •

The Cafe aux Deux Magots of St. Germain des Pres has always been a pretty well known joint for Americans. Sitting on the Boulevard Saint Germain, one of the major avenues on that side of the Seine, it has never had the popularity of the Brasserie Lipp across the street, or even the good wieners. But you could get a decent meal, the waiters didn't hover over you, and Hemingway always liked the tables in the quiet back corner where we could see the black-jacketed waiters, their white aprons extending down below their knees, gossiping in front of the banks of empty, orderly glasses. We both tended to avoid the terrace, covered with its little round tables and wicker-backed chairs.

I liked the food and the booze. You could get pleasantly, quietly, perfectly drunk. And there would always be somebody around like Hem or Bob McAlmon or Ezra Pound to see you home if they were sober enough to be any help. That was an important question. If there was anything we Americans did in Paris, it was drink— whiskey, pernod, rum, wine, especially wine, champagne, you name it. Drinking was good. Forgetting was better. I did a lot of one and not enough of the other.

I let Hem lead the way to his favorite corner, and we plopped down with our backs to the wall. It made me feel more comfortable to be able to see who was coming in. Especially after somebody decided to use my head for target practice. Surprisingly, the only other person I recognized was Pablo Picasso who sat quietly eating by himself, a thoughtful look on his face, chewing each bite carefully before swallowing.

"How long before Duvall arrests Joyce, do you think?" Hem motioned for a waiter as he spoke.

"Tomorrow, or the next day. It depends on what he finds. Anything else that points to Joyce, and your friend is gonna be behind bars quick. You can count on it."

"And that'll finish *Ulysses*," Hem mumbled.

"What is all this crap? What is *Ulysses?*" I'd heard stuff floating around in the expatriate community, in Montparnasse, for months about this scandalous novel Joyce had written, but that's about it.

Hem's eyes lit up. "It's great, Jack. You've got to read it. It's gonna revolutionize literature."

"Then, why the hell's it banned all over the world."

"Not everywhere, just in the United States and England," Hem said defensively. "And only because they've got a bunch of conservative bastards in charge of things."

"Well, yeah, but the states and England pretty well cover the English-speaking world. There's *something* about it that somebody's objecting to."

"Yeah, well," Hem looked almost uncomfortable. "Some of the scenes are pretty sexual."

I understood then. "Maybe I oughta read it. Sounds good."

"They had a lawsuit in the states over it. The Society against Sin and all that Crap filed against letting *The Little Review* publish it in serial form and they won. Some guy named John Quinn did a helluva job defending them, but it didn't work. I think he owns the original manuscript. Do you really think the book has something to do with this?"

"If Karper's involved, it almost certainly does."

"Come on, Jack. It's just a book. People don't kill each other over books."

"You don't know the members of the 'Society against Sin and all that Crap,' as you so refreshingly dubbed them. Don't forget that gleam in the right Reverend Quintin Karper's eye when he proclaimed himself God's Agent. People like Karper would slit their own grandmother's throat to make a point. Believe me; I know." My father was one of those. He believed in all the great sins; violations of anything in the Old or New testaments were inexcusable. Hellfire and damnation were the only reasonable punishments. I pulled the little drawing out of my pocket and flattened it out on the table.

"What the hell have you got there, Jack?"

I jumped half out of my seat. "Goddamn you, Ezra! Haven't you ever heard it's not polite to sneak up on somebody?"

Ezra Pound sat down with us, his cock's comb standing straight up, and snatched the piece of paper out of my hands. I started to grab it back, but a look of surprise showed up in Ezra's face, and I let him keep it.

"Well, isn't this a piece of something. How'd you happen on to this, boys?"

"You know what it is?" Hem asked.

"Sure," he answered, tossing the drawing on the table and leaning back.

"You wouldn't mind telling us, would you?" I showed a quick flash of aggravation.

"You mean you don't know?"

"Ezra," I explained patiently, "if I knew, would I be asking you?"

Those bright eyes of his went back and forth between me and Hem, and a line of concern crossed his face. "You don't know, do you? And this has something to do with whatever happened at Shakespeare and Company this morning, doesn't it?"

I nodded. What the hell, Ezra sure as hell didn't kill anybody, and if he could help clear it up, I needed him.

"It's a swastika."

"No it's not. It's a fylfot."

"A swastika *is* a kind of fylfot, Jack. I'm surprised you didn't know that."

"Don't be surprised, Ezra. Just tell me what you know." I liked Ezra Pound a lot, but he could really get on my nerves.

Ezra's eyebrows started doing dances as he picked up the slip of paper and looked at it again. "See how the arms go clockwise. Regular fylfots don't do that."

"We know, Ezra." Hem was getting as aggravated as I was. Somebody had told me that Hem was giving Ezra boxing lessons. From the look in Hem's eyes, I'd hate to be Ezra at their next bout.

"Only one group that I know of is using this as a symbol, and they just started using it within the last year or two. The NSDAP in Germany. They're called Nazis." Ezra tossed it back on the table, and the broken cross stared at me.

"The Nazis? You mean that bunch of Germans that run around Paris chasing Communists?" Hem was confused, and I was running right behind him.

"They're a political party, too, Hem," I said, my mind already churning. This whole thing felt like a spin I wasn't going to conquer. First it was Joyce, *Ulysses,* the typewriter salesman who wasn't a typewriter salesman, mysterious notes, God's Agent, and now

Nazis, some lunatic fringe political group in Germany. The French hookers were beginning to look like a cakewalk, and this thing with Joyce was beginning to defy belief. "Tell me, Ezra, do they drive black Model Ts?"

"What?"

"Just a question. What else do you know about them?"

Ezra shrugged. "They've got some radical ideas—anti-Bolshevik, anti-Semitic—but all in all, they seem to be okay."

"Being anti-Bolshevik I can deal with, but anti-Semitism is another thing."

"Well," Ezra said. "Sometimes you've got to take the bad with the good. As long as they don't let it get out of hand. I mean, Germany is full of political groups fighting for control. Hindenburg, the Nazis, the Communists, hell, most people over there belong to at least two parties just in case one goes defunct. They're long on ideas and short on cash to finance any kind of long-term movement. So, does this mean the Nazis are involved in this business at Sylvia's?"

"Maybe." I half-ignored the question. I knew enough about the Nazis to know that Hemingway was right. They did have a bunch of people in Paris, and they did seem to spend a lot of their time spying on the Communists. But what could the Nazis possibly have to do with James Joyce, the bookstore, or *Ulysses?* It wasn't making any sense. Jesus, I thought to myself, I'm sounding like an echo chamber. But, it wasn't making sense. And the problem was, somebody was shooting at me, and I still couldn't figure out who or exactly why.

And while I was thinking about that, a small figure in a trenchcoat appeared beside our table and from the half-smile on his face, I knew that he wasn't going to make me happy.

Six

ou are a busy man, Jack Barnett." Duvall sat down without being invited. "First the typewriter factory, then a window shot out, and finally Monsieur Joyce's flat. Would it not be better for you if you went back to writing your articles on horse racing?"

"Probably," I grunted. "Did you have me followed?" I knew he hadn't, but what the hell.

Duvall looked hurt. "Jack. Why should I have you followed when you make so much noise as you move through my city? One just has to step outside and listen for the sound of gunshots."

"Duvall, Ezra Pound." I ignored his joke and made the introductions.

"What is this, Jack?" Duvall grabbed the swastika before I could cover it up.

"Some of my artwork. You see why I avoid artists. I'm afraid they'd be jealous."

"Picasso has nothing to fear." Duvall tossed it back on the table, gesturing across the room at Pablo. "But I am beginning to see this symbol more and more. And it is troubling."

"Yeah, how's that?" I leaned forward, a little too eagerly, and Duvall's eyes narrowed just a bit.

The inspector opened his trenchcoat and relaxed in his chair. He lit a cigarette, another match appearing out of nowhere, and inhaled deeply. "This new German party, the Nazis, they have adopted it for their symbol, but it has been used in Germany for longer than that."

"Really," Hem moved closer.

"Oui," Duvall said, nodding his head sadly. "Just after the war, some radicals in Berlin began using it as a symbol of Anti-Semitism. They think Germany is being ruined by Jews."

"You said you'd been seeing it more and more," I prompted.

"The Nazis have agents here, and they are quite concerned with the growth of Communism in Germany and France. Unfortunately, some of these agents are very young, and they succumb to childish impulses and paint this symbol on alley walls."

"You don't seem too fond of the Nazis. Seems to me that they might inject some life into Germany. The current president over there sure as hell isn't doing anything." Ezra was argumentative; his beard-covered, pointed chin stuck out defiantly.

Duvall smiled. "I distrust any group who adopts as their symbol one of hatred. Hatred only seems to breed hatred."

"Perhaps," Ezra said grudgingly, "perhaps."

"Excuse me for interrupting your political debate," I injected, "but you didn't come here for intellectual stimulation, Duvall. What do you want?"

Duvall turned away from Ezra. "To tell you that my case against Monsieur Joyce grew immeasurably stronger late this afternoon."

"How so?"

"Do you remember this piece of fabric," and he laid the little bit of cloth from the backdoor of Shakespeare and Company on the table.

I swallowed hard and nodded. A nasty, clammy fist grabbed my stomach. Something inside was telling me where this was going, and I thought I was gonna be sick.

"We searched Monsieur Joyce's flat this afternoon, shortly after you were there, and we found a coat which matches this piece." He stopped talking and puffed on his cigarette. "Which," he resumed after a second, "was missing a piece of this size."

Yeah, I was gonna be sick. And not just from my cold. But I couldn't give up. "Let me ask you a question, Duvall. If Joyce stabbed this guy, why did he bust out the backdoor when he had a key?"

"To throw us off the trail, mais certainment. He was attempting to create confusion. It might have worked but for this," and he grinned like a Missouri possum, "mistake."

"Yeah, let's forget for the moment that the door was busted from the outside in."

The inspector shrugged. "Monsieur Joyce is not stupid. He could not be respected by so many were he not gifted in some way. Naturally, it would have been very suspect if the door had been broken from the inside to the out. He knew this and, so, did not do it."

"Why didn't you arrest him?"

"How do you know that I have not?"

"You didn't come here to tell me that you've got him locked up." I was guessing, but it seemed like a good hunch. Something in his posture told me that he wasn't finished yet.

Duvall inhaled deeply on the cigarette again, flicking the ashes into a glass tray on the table. "The American preacher, Karper, came to see me this afternoon, my friend."

"Why doesn't that surprise me?" I asked Hem. He smiled and shook his head. "And what did God's Agent have to say?"

Duvall leaned forward on his elbows, and I swear his eyes softened, reached out to me in sympathy. "He made a fascinating confession, Jack. He said that the dead man, this Jourdan, was working for him. He said that he had hired Jourdan to burn Monsieur Joyce's books. Only after much prayer did he realize that, and I quote, 'God wanted me to come clean.' And that, my friend, that combined with these other details brings James Joyce closer and closer to the guillotine. I have motive and opportunity. Mademoiselle Beach recognized the knife as one which was used around the shop. Voilà. There is the means. Three strikes, as you Americans say, and you are soon out."

That cold fist gripping my stomach tightened down harder. James Joyce had about as much chance of getting out of this as Custer did at Little Bighorn. But something about Duvall's pronouncements didn't seem right. "Why *haven't* you arrested him yet?"

"I wanted to see if you could give me some reason to avoid suspecting him."

"You don't think he did it either, do you?"

He smiled again, and little crow's feet deepened at the corner of his eyes. "Let us say I am skeptical. Our typewriter salesman is not what he says he was. We cannot discover, yet, who he really was. (I find Monsieur Karper's confessions, shall we say, terribly convenient at best). Some anonymous person calls me to tell me of this murder. You are shot at while investigating the affair. A bit of cloth from a suit, that Joyce *and* his femme claim he never owned, appears in his closet mysteriously. It smells strongly of a deception. More than that, Jack Barnett, it screams of a deception."

"We've been trying to tell you that," Hem said.

Duvall waved him off. "But, I am being pressured to wrap this up. People of power are interested. The evidence, circumstantial or not, is stacking up against your friend. I will be forced to arrest him unless I have solid evidence that clears him. Share with me, mon ami. What do you have?"

"Nothing I can afford to share right now." I needed time to sort all of this out. I needed to line it up and see where it led. I needed another drink. I waved for the waiter. "But give me another forty-eight hours."

"I do not donate to charity."

"Call it a favor. Look," and I got serious with him, "Joyce isn't going anywhere. He does well to find his way from Michaud's to his flat to Sylvia's bookstore. Why don't you arrest Karper for attempted arson?" I thought it was a reasonable idea.

"Arresting your major witness for attempted anything seems bad etiquette. And, if I wait forty-eight hours more, you may be dead," Duvall pointed out.

"So? At least he'd die with some dignity." I knew Ezra couldn't keep silent for long. His eyebrows were working in conjunction with his red cock's comb, and the effect was, well, indescribable. "I'm not Joyce's best friend, Inspector, but I tell you that he's not a murderer. It is inconceivable. . . ."

Duvall stood to leave as Ezra ranted on, overriding Duvall's words. "Forty-eight hours, Jack. That is all. [*This is unspeakable, Inspector. You have no evidence worthy of the name. . . .]* I'll send you a flimsy when I find out who our voyageur de commerce really was. [*I'll write an immediate denunciation of your actions. . . .]*" And he was gone, with Ezra hot on his heels, and I swear that Duvall clapped his hands over his ears by the time they made it to the door, and Ezra was still talking.

Hem was chuckling softly. "He's something, isn't he?"

"Duvall or Ezra?"

"Both."

And we laughed together.

After a minute of staring into our wine glasses, Hem stroked his mustache a little awkwardly. "Why didn't you tell him about this swastika thing?"

"I can't lay all my cards out yet. Anyway, Duvall's a fool if he doesn't know that it's involved, but there's no use confirming it for him now. Too many odd things are going on. Think about it, Hem. If Karper hired Jourdan to burn Joyce's books, then why is somebody shooting at us from big black automobiles? But if Jourdan was a Nazi, maybe the Communists are involved. And, if that's so, then surely Shakespeare and Company was just a convenient place to dump the body. Or was it?" A new thought struck me. "We've got to look for connections between the bookshop and these fanatics. I wonder if any of Sylvia's customers are particular friends or enemies of any or all of these groups?"

"Maybe. Writers come in a couple of different breeds—those who claim to be anti-political and those who are completely political. Few, if any, are likely to be part of Karper's crowd. But writers can be very passionate people. Hell," he grunted. "Just look at that Montparnasse crowd. Passion is their middle name."

Hem never thought much of Montparnasse and the expatriates who lived there. It was fun watching him dissect his own brethren. Unfortunately, that didn't get this thing solved.

"Look," I began, "we've got to get logical about this thing. Duvall is going to lock Joyce up in two nights if we haven't got something more to give him. And this little swastika sketch isn't going to be enough. We know what it is now. But we still don't know who Phillipe Jourdan was, nor do we know who robbed Joyce. Obviously, that's how the coat got into Joyce's apartment. And we've got to deal with the right Reverend Quintin Karper. He may be just an opportunist, or he may be up to his eyeballs in this thing."

"Yeah," Hem said. "Looks like we've got some legwork to do. Maybe Arlaine has got something for us. It's just about time to meet her over at Gertrude's."

I put off thinking about Arlaine. "Legwork is right. Somebody is building a damn good case against James Joyce. One more bit of evidence tagged on him and it's all over. And if they hang him with this murder, the only place you'll be seeing *Ulysses* is in the incinerator."

• • • •

Gertrude Stein had to be one of the ugliest women I'd ever known. She and her brother Leo came to Paris back around 1903 and got a flat on the rue de Fleurus. Gertrude wrote. Leo was sort of a jack-of-all-trades in the art business. He collected and studied art. And he had some of Gertrude's ego, but he was a nice enough guy with a big, thick black beard. He got tired of Gertrude and her companion, Alice Toklas, before I ever came to Paris and moved to a place over on the Boulevard Raspail. I'd have gotten tired of them long before that. Leo had some nice paintings, if you're into that kind of thing. I liked him. He was a pretty good guy to talk to, and I used to stop by and say hello when I was in the neighborhood.

Gertrude, on the other hand, I only visited when I absolutely had to, which meant never. I didn't care for her; the feeling was mutual. She liked to have writers sitting around her feet falling for every cliché that drifted out of her mouth. For one thing, I never liked clichés; second, I only wrote to keep a minimal amount of roof over my head. I guess Gertrude had some nice paintings too. But that didn't excuse her arrogance. She could only exist someplace like Paris. And since there was nowhere else like Paris, that's where she was.

She and Alice were . . . well, together, always. Alice Toklas was a small, dark woman. I never thought of her as particularly attractive either. She had this little mustache, faint but obvious enough so you couldn't help but notice it. Match that with Gertrude's gargantuan ugliness, and maybe the two of them deserved each other. Hem told me once that he and Hadley went to see the great Gertrude (and I mean that in a couple of different ways) and Alice commandeered Hadley. "Wives," Hemingway told me, "were to be seen and not heard." Something about that bothered me way down deep, but, like I said, it was Paris, and anything could be excused in Paris. And if there was anything *I* was into, it was excuses.

"This, of course, is one of Picasso's. He has learned so much from me. He paints with the skill of a master, but his poetry, well, I told him to paint." Gertrude was pontificating. She was showing a small group her collection of paintings. Cezanne, Picasso, and the rest. When Hem brought me in, she sneered, shot me a dirty look, and promptly ignored me. Ezra always liked her, and I couldn't see why. But Gertrude didn't have the patience for Ezra's nonstop mouth, and she found excuses (so Ezra told me) for not inviting him—like some chair that he supposedly sat in and broke. Like I said, excuses.

I obediently followed along behind her. The living room area of the flat was actually a pretty good size. A huge, finely detailed rug covered the floor. Two chairs flanked the fireplace. One, large and overstuffed for Gertrude, and a smaller seat, with a finely-detailed wooden frame, for Alice. The center table was a giant, marble-topped affair. Above the fireplace were more of Gertrude's treasures, her paintings.

I'd always liked Gertrude's mantle. It reminded me of the one at our house back in Missouri, ornate and elegant. Apparently, French designs had been the thing back in the late 1890s at home. Wooden tables sat along the walls and all carried vases, statuettes, or some other kind of bric-a-brac. The browns and greens in the room didn't really help the sterile feeling I got when I was there. And it made me feel uncomfortable.

Gertrude's little group contained five people—Arlaine (looking suitably impressed), some big guy with a monocle, a skinny kid who barely looked old enough to tie his own shoe laces, Winnie Ellerman, and Sylvia, who looked about as depressed as I'd ever seen her. Alice was out of sight, which suited me just fine. I'd never been really fond of her.

"Leo and I split our collection when he left. I kept the Picassos of course, and he took those Matisses." She said Matisse like it was a disease, and from the looks of some of his paintings I tended to agree with her. Gertrude was heavy and square. Hem told me her face was "strong and German." I would have called it "arrogant and aboriginal." When the light hit her face just right, two black holes appeared where her eyes were supposed to be, and the vision moved from the realm of faces to that of skulls. But her skin was smooth, and in repose an innate softness emerged.

Hem confided to me once that he wanted to sleep with her. I never knew if he was telling the truth or not. If so, Hem's taste in women was open to serious questions. That particular night she wore this long robe-looking thing. Sometimes she sported a flower basket kind of thing for a hat. That little decoration was missing.

Hem went up and joined the group, and Arlaine slipped away. I liked watching her walk. It almost made me feel like old times, almost. She was wearing a conservative, blousy kind of dress. Her eyes were dancing and smiling, still caught, I figured, in that Gertrude Stein trance.

"What did you find?" I didn't want to waste any time.

She leaned in close, and I could feel her warmth. "Nothing that we didn't know before. No one else on the subscription list has the initials J.J., but I do know that the police questioned everybody on the street. And before you ask, I don't know what they found out."

"I do. At least part of it," I admitted. Keeping my voice low, I briefed her on what Duvall found in Joyce's apartment and the Reverend Karper's confessions. Gertrude was still busy showing off her paintings, so she didn't notice us whispering. Alice, on the other hand, had stepped back into the room and was staring a hole through us. Sylvia once told me that she thought Alice was gypsy-looking; I thought she was scary-looking and told Sylvia that; she just laughed.

Arlaine's blue eyes grew a look of deep worry. "I've heard through the grapevine that Duvall found some other things out later."

"Like what?"

"Like that Joyce didn't leave when he said he did. That someone saw him leaving an hour later."

"So Joyce can't tell time."

"But that would put him there at the time of the murder."

"Maybe. But all we have to set the time of the murder is that note, which may or may not be genuine, and the body, which is yet to be heard from."

"Except for that preacher," she pointed out, and I saw a look of complete understanding in her eyes. She was quick.

"That's true. What about these guys?" I asked.

"The guy with the monocle is Helmut Kopfmann. He just got in from Berlin. Supposed to be an emerging new German writer." She was whispering in short bursts, keeping her back turned to Gertrude and the rest.

"German, huh? That's right." I remembered it then. Joyce had said that Kopfmann was in the bookshop when he borrowed the keys from Sylvia. "Anybody saying anything about Joyce or this book?"

She was silent for a minute. "Gertrude made a passing kind of comment, but nothing of consequence."

"Don't let Gertrude hear you say that. Everything she says is of consequence. Just ask her."

Arlaine giggled. "Shush! She'll hear you."

"I hope she does. Tell me more about this German." I took her by the elbow and steered her away from the crowd.

Stuck off in a corner with her was sort of stifling, though pleasant in a way I hadn't felt in years. Her lips had just the right fullness and her complexion was light and smooth.

"Not much more to tell. He's written some criticism and is working on a new novel."

"Could he be jealous of Joyce and all this crap about *Ulysses?*"

"Maybe." She looked skeptical. "He hasn't had anything good to say about anything written in English, that's for sure."

"Who's the kid?"

"Another American. He's been making googoo eyes at me all evening."

"Not your speed, huh?"

"A little young for me. I've always preferred older men." When she said that, she moved closer to me, slightly, almost casually, but I didn't miss it, and I don't think she intended me to.

"What's his name?" I ignored the gesture for the moment.

"Wilder. Thornton Wilder, I think they said. He writes, of course. Does everybody in Paris write?"

"Just the Americans, but most of them do more talking and drinking than writing. Not many people here," I observed.

"The big party is always Saturday night at Nathalie Barney's. At least that's what Sylvia said. Apparently, invitations to Gertrude's are more restricted. Nathalie's sounds more like a free-for-all."

"Yeah, in more ways than you could imagine. I've heard about Nathalie's parties. They're not for the weak-stomached."

"What's that supposed to mean?"

"Later," I whispered as Gertrude finished her tour.

"Bryher. Won't you read for us?" Gertrude made her way over to the big chair. She spoke to a pretty girl, with a serious hair cut—or more appropriately hack job. "Bryher" was the artistic name of Winnie Ellermann. I'd known Winnie for a long time. She married Bob McAlmon for propriety's sake. I was never really sure what good that did, or why they cared about propriety. Bob wasn't really taken with women, if you catch my drift. And Winnie didn't really fancy men. Sometimes it seemed like everybody I knew had something against heterosexuality. But Paris inspired that, tolerated it, and maybe that's why so many "liberated" people flocked there. And maybe watching all of them is why I felt so good about Paris then.

Bryher's poetry was skillful. She read with a soft, lilting tone and said some revealing things, not that I paid a lot of attention; it was the rhythms that made poetry palatable to me and it was to those I listened. Every once in a while, Gertrude would smile and nod. In fact, Gertrude's smiles kept getting bigger and her nods deeper and more satisfied with each of Bryher's verses.

"**Crash!**"

The explosion rocked the mood, and dishes and a tray ended up scattered across the floor.

Alice stood over the broken cups lying uselessly against the carpet. "I'm so very sorry," she said, her mouth tightening into an embarrassed smile. But, from the way her eyes narrowed at Gertrude, I got the distinct feeling that Gertrude's smiles at Bryher would fetch her more than broken dishes if she didn't stop.

The message must have been received because Gertrude sat stonefaced through the rest of Winnie's reading. Winnie didn't seem surprised, or bothered for that matter. We all dutifully applauded as she finished.

"Mr. Barnett," Gertrude's voice rang across the room. "Have you written any *horse* articles lately?"

"No, but thanks for asking." I looked back to Arlaine who smiled a little uncertainly.

The chair creaked, and I knew Gertrude was shifting herself. Here it comes, I thought.

"I invite Mr. Barnett in occasionally," she explained to her other guests, "so that he might keep me informed on the animal kingdom. He spends so much time with them."

"You're too kind," I nodded and smiled without turning around.

"Mr. Barnett, Ernest and I have been having a disagreement. Perhaps you could be of assistance."

Nothing I could do to avoid it, so I swiveled back towards Gertrude and walked across the room. Hem seemed perturbed about something. Bryher retreated to the shadows, looking more than a little bored. This Wilder kid was standing by the mantle looking half-frightened, half-amazed. The German (and I kept a close eye on him) leaned against the wall, his monocle bobbing up and down. Sylvia had disappeared into the kitchen with Alice.

"I wouldn't be surprised." I smiled pleasantly.

She ignored my comment. "Ernest, who writes well for a youngster, has written a story I consider *inaccrochable*. He claims it must be written in the way he has done it. And while that may be true, I doubt that many readers will agree with him. Rather they will be repelled."

I spotted Hem flinching at the word "youngster," but that served him right for being so buddy-buddy with Gertrude. "And how did he write it?"

"He wrote a story concerning a young man and young woman and what they did on a dock one night. It was—"

"I know what young men and young women do on a dock at night," I interrupted her. I knew where she was going, and I wanted her to get to the point. Hem had already filled me in on this minor controversy.

Gertrude's face wrinkled up more than it was already wrinkled. "Then you agree that such is not suitable?"

"It depends, I guess, on who's doing the telling. Does Hem tell you what to write?"

"Of course not," and it was obvious she considered the idea ludicrous.

Hem looked at me with this "please don't" expression, but Gertrude aggravated me.

"Then, I don't see why you should tell him anything. Let the boy write what he wants, how he wants."

"But, what's wrong with her offering her advice and experience?" Sylvia asked, breezing back into the room with Alice and quickly noting the stormclouds boiling across Gertrude's face.

I started to tell her exactly what I thought, but Arlaine kicked me very quietly and very painfully. "Anyway, what's *inaccroachable* about that subject?"

Gertrude rolled her eyes. "It is not for pleasant viewing, reading. Such things are not to be written of, just as such paintings should not be hung. It is like what two male homosexuals do together. Pitiful. Surely, Mr. Barnett, you wouldn't argue that what two men do together is in anyway wholesome or clean. It is disgusting, animalistic, pitiful."

"I, personally, don't really pursue *that* kind of activity, but who can call that anymore repulsive than what two women do with each other." If there was a prize for the most dirty looks given to one man at one time, I won it hands down. Arlaine kicked me again. Sylvia frowned. Alice narrowed her eyes, and her dark features grew a shade darker. Gertrude glared. Hem, on the other hand, seemed tickled.

"Mr. Barnett, the two are wholly dissimilar! What two women do is beautiful, natural. There can be no comparison. Women stay together a lifetime. Men change partners randomly. The emotions are of the basest sort."

"I don't know, Gertrude." I shifted into my best Missouri drawl. "I can remember my daddy preaching against all such activities. You can't tell me that you have any Biblical defense for homosexuality?"

Well, I might have said that France had run out of wine. It certainly would have sparked more of a response. At the mention of the Bible, everybody fell silent. I felt like I'd walked into Heaven's Gates wearing an "Elect Lucifer" button.

"Aww, that's alright, Jack. There's some of my stuff she likes." Hem tried to lighten the mood. "And she's been a real help." If Hem's nose got any browner, he wouldn't be able to smell through it.

"I find that there is a certain simplicity to his writing. He may be doing something very new." Gertrude tried to recoup some semblance of control.

"I haven't read any of his stories," I said. "And I probably won't."

"That doesn't surprise me," Gertrude replied, taking the opportunity to giggle at my expense.

I smiled appropriately and turned towards the German. "Herr Kopfmann. How do you like Paris?"

The monocle wiggled. "It is a pleasant city. I was here a great amount of time before the war."

Funny, when we say the War, we use the capital letter. Hell, you can hear it booming out loud and large. When a German says war, it's always with the little "w."

"Here on business, or just for fun?" I tried to sound friendly, light.

"I have been working on a new *roman*. Part of its setting is here in Paris and I thought I would come and do research."

"When did you get in?"

The monocle wiggled again. "Three days ago."

"And how's it going?"

A look of thoughtful consideration curved the mouth below the monocle. "Sehr gut. Very good."

"Enough of your pedestrian banter. What is your *roman*, your novel, to be about?" Gertrude cut off my interrogation.

"I'm writing about the war, and how it affected my people."

"And you have come *here* to do research?" Sylvia was a little confused. She brushed that perpetual lock of wavy brown hair off her forehead.

"If I do not understand the minds of our former enemies, then my *roman* will be incomplete. It will have holes."

"That's an interesting idea. What do you mean, exactly?" Hem moved in closer to the circle.

Kopfmann readjusted his monocle and took on a schoolmasterly look. Parts of the German psychology left me in a mood to laugh. "If you know something and leave it out, it may be inferred by the reader, Ja? But if you leave something out of your work because you don't know what that emotion or feeling is, then you have created a gap, a hole that can never be filled. The reader senses these things."

Hem's mustache swelled across his face. "I like that."

Gertrude readjusted her lumpy body in her seat. "I've always thought that writing was telling what you know."

The Wilder kid sort of sprang to attention on that note. "But obviously," he began, "there are different ways to tell what you know."

"True," Gertrude nodded, looking at the kid for the first time. "And there are different ways to look at people. Some consider Communists as idealistic revolutionaries; I see them as people who fancy that they had unhappy childhoods. Therefore, I would paint them in that light."

I hated conversations like this. "So, Herr Kopfmann, what else would you like to do in Paris?" Anything to get away from all this philosophical claptrap about writing.

"I had also hoped," Kopfmann said smiling, (like most Germans once he got the floor he didn't want to give it up) "to spend time with Mr. James Joyce while I was here in Paris. I have read several of his stories and consider him a fine writer. I met him briefly yesterday."

If Sylvia had brought Kopfmann to Gertrude's, she had forgotten to warn him about the one, major, cardinal sin. Even I knew this one—Never, ever, praise James Joyce in front of Gertrude Stein. Silence wrapped itself around that room like a cast around a broken leg. The angles of Gertrude's square face grew even sharper, completely destroying any hint of that softness I mentioned earlier, and she sunk lower in her chair. Alice, who had sat quietly until then, leaned forward and spoke for the first time.

"And I'm sure that Mr. Joyce would be pleased to talk with you. He enjoys talking to everyone, I understand, even the taxi drivers. How was Berlin when you left?" The intended slight was clear to everybody but Kopfmann.

But, that brought the conversation back out of the spiralling dive Kopfmann had sent it in. I'd heard what I wanted. A German was in Paris, anxious to spend time with Joyce, two days before the murder at Shakespeare and Company. And, he was privy to Joyce's plans for the night of the murder. I glanced at Hem and Arlaine and from the looks they gave me, I knew the connection wasn't lost on them either.

Kopfmann kept talking; Wilder started loosening up some; Hem,

Arlaine, and I slipped off toward a corner. Gertrude didn't notice, but Alice watched us with those dark, almost haunting eyes. Sometimes she sent shivers down my spine.

"Interesting, ain't it," Hem began.

"I'd say fascinating," I agreed.

"This could explain a lot of things." The gleam in Arlaine's eye was unmistakable. Obviously, detective work appealed to her.

"So," Hem began, "we watch Kopfmann?"

"Right. We need to find out where he goes and who he sees. And," I cautioned, "if it is him, we have to make sure that we've got all our bases covered."

"I'll follow him," Hem decided.

He wasn't my first choice, but I'd run out of other options. I had to make do with what I had. "Fine."

"What about the Reverend Karper?" Arlaine asked.

"We're running short of manpower," I pointed out. I mulled over the problem for a second, and a thought occurred to me. It wasn't the greatest idea. But it might work. "I think I can take care of Karper. Let me worry about him. Now, Arlaine, you—"

Sylvia waltzed over into our little semi-circle before I could finish.

"You're not being very sociable," she reminded us.

"We're busy working. For you, I might add," I reminded her. "And listen. Watch yourself, Sylvia. Something strange is going on." I explained to her about Frank O'Connor and the potshot somebody took at me.

A streak of worry crossed her pretty brown eyes. "Maybe I should cancel the smuggling operation," she said, pursing her lips. "That would be best, I think, until this matter is resolved."

"Smuggling!"

Arlaine kicked me again as I frowned at Sylvia.

"What the hell are you talking about?"

Her pursed lips broke into a half-smile. "Oh, Jack. It's not what you think. We were going to have some copies of *Ulysses* smuggled across the Great Lakes into the States. There have been several subscribers there and we needed to figure a way to get their copies to them. I've been working on arrangements with a friend in Chicago."

"Jesus, Sylvia. It doesn't matter whether it's booze or books. Smuggling is smuggling. Karper would love to hear about this little operation. Just wait a while and let's get this thing settled."

I could tell that Sylvia was a bit put off with me, but she nodded reluctantly and looked back towards Gertrude, Kopfmann, and Wilder. Somebody else had wandered in; I thought it was Bob McAlmon, but I wasn't sure.

"I better go back over there," she said finally.

"Yeah, I'm gonna hit the road." My nose was running like the Orient Express, and I was bone-tired. It'd been a long day. "Hem, you keep an eye on our friend."

He nodded and followed Sylvia towards Gertrude and the rest, a big, mustache-spreading smile on his face.

"What about me?"

I turned and looked at Arlaine. Her hair fell just to shoulder length and the blue in her eyes reflected the fire in the fireplace. A little shiver ran through me, but I shook myself and decided it was my cold. "Meet me tomorrow at the Brasserie Lipp. We've got some fast legwork to do. Duvall gave me forty-eight hours to clear Joyce and I've blown three already without any progress."

She crossed her hands, pulling them to her shoulders and hugging like she was cold. "Two days. Not much time."

"You're not kidding. We'll start by talking to anybody and everybody along the rue de l'Odeon. Then, . . . **AAAHHH CHOOOOOO!**" Then, I sneezed. Blinking through teary eyes, I saw a soft, motherly look hit Arlaine's pretty face.

She pushed an outlaw strand of hair off my forehead and laid the back of one hand against my skin. "Jack, you're not well. You've got a fever."

I wiped my nose. "No kidding." My ears were ringing and my heart pounding, and at least half of that had to do with the cold.

"I'll get you home," she began, with a nasty gleam in her eye. "Somebody has to see that you're properly tucked in."

Then she slipped her arm through mine, pressing her full, incredibly soft breast against my arm, and led me out into the cool Paris night. I didn't bother to say goodbye to Gertrude. She'd understand, and appreciate, my bad manners.

We took a right on rue de Fleurus and walked thirty steps or so, threading through the usual street traffic, when I noticed a black Model T following behind us at a snail's pace.

Seven

I put my arm around Arlaine's waist and hugged her tight against me. She didn't argue.

"Listen. When we cross Guynemer, instead of going around the Luxembourg Gardens, let's try to go through." I usually avoided the gardens—I hated pigeons—but, right then, I was damn glad they were there.

"How romantic." She squeezed in tighter. "I wasn't sure if you were getting my hints."

"Pretty tough to avoid a fast ball. Christy Mathewson could learn a thing or two from you," I grunted. She began to pull away, but I held on tight. "Just listen. There's a Model T back about ten yards on our right. It's acting strange, like the one that Frank O'Connor said tossed a bullet at my head earlier today." I glanced around at the street crowd. "Too many people right here, but if they're gonna try it again, it will probably be on that loop around the palace."

"But," Arlaine began, "if we go through the garden, they won't be able to follow."

"Right. At least not until they've gotten out of their automobile, and then we'll have too much of a headstart. If we can get into the garden. They may have the gates locked."

I felt this tug at my sleeve; it was Arlaine twisting around. "What are you doing?"

"What kind of automobile is it? A Model T?"

"Are you crazy? Don't let 'em know we saw them!"

But it was too late. Arlaine had let go and spun around to get a better look, raising a hand to her brow. And we were standing right under a streetlamp.

I heard it before I saw it. The Model T lurched out of its half-crawl and sped down the street towards us. I looked around frantically for cover, but there were no convenient alleys to duck in.

The auto was getting closer with each thump of my heart. Jesus! It was almost on top of us.

Grabbing Arlaine by the arm, I spun her back against the streetlamp, mashed her against the pole, and braced for the bullets.

The roar got louder.

And louder.

And then it was gone.

Nothing happened. No bullets, hell, not even any shots.

I twisted around just in time to see the Model T fly round the corner of Guynemer and out of sight. "Well, I'll be a son of a bitch."

"Uh, Jack?"

Turning back, I found my lips less than an inch from hers. "Yeah?"

"I like you a lot, but could you let me breathe a little?" Her voice was cramped and choked.

"Oh, yeah, sorry." I backed away from her, and she sort of peeled herself off the streetlamp. People passing on the street stared at us, and I heard a couple of comments about crazy Americans.

"You didn't have to go to all that trouble to get close to me. I think you're cute."

My heart was still jumping a mile a minute, and I was pretty sure it was because of the Model T. "Yeah, well, I'm afraid I wouldn't be your type."

"You are a little impulsive," she admitted, straightening her clothes. "But I could learn to like that."

"That's not quite what I meant." I started off down the street, and she hurried to catch up. The Model T had vanished from sight. What had that been about? Why did they suddenly zoom away? Was I too jumpy? Arlaine wasn't worried about the Model T; she had her mind on something else it looked like, or she figured I was trying to get close to her.

"What do you mean? Just who are you? Why are you mixed up in all this? Hemingway said you were a pilot during the War. Sylvia said you were from Missouri."

"You've been asking a lot of questions." The frown on my face grew stronger by the second. My heart was coming down off its race, and I tried to relax. Wherever the Model T had gone, it didn't seem to be coming back, but my eyes were glued to every auto that came in sight.

"Sylvia, I asked. Hemingway didn't have to be asked."

My frown broke into a chuckle. I couldn't help it. "Hem likes to talk."

She slipped her arm back into mine. "So, which are you, Jack Barnett, a Missourian or a soldier?"

"Both, I guess." The temperature had picked up a degree or two, and it was pleasant out. The rain had deserted the sky, and stars were everywhere. The burble of contented pigeons echoed from beneath the eaves of buildings. If I could have smelled the air, I knew I'd get a hint of springtime in Paris. "Missourian first, soldier second."

"Tell me about the soldier. Tell me what you did in the Great War."

"You're not one of those are you?"

We turned the corner onto Guynemer and headed around the Luxembourg Palace. Traffic was pretty heavy; a wagon or two still plied the streets, and you could hear the horses snorting and clicking their shoes on the pavement. The occasional Bugatti, Hispano, or Citroen puttered along the street. The fence beside us, around the gardens, looked like a series of spears, gold-tipped points up, protecting the palace. We passed the gate and I glanced in and, through the moonlight, could see the giant avenue leading up to the palace, lined with little benches and chairs.

"One of those what?" she asked.

"One of those girls who find war glamorous and exciting." I purposefully avoided looking at her.

"You and Hemingway don't seem to have the same attitude about it. He talks about the war a lot, every time he comes into the bookshop it seems like. But you seem to never talk about it."

I shrugged. "Hem saw some things, but he didn't see what I saw. At least not in the way I saw them."

"But you were a pilot, right? I mean that wasn't like being down in the trenches, was it?"

"In its own way." A little defensive edge was creeping into my voice, and I tried to head it off. "Tell me about Arlaine. Why is she here?"

"Avoiding the issue, huh?" she teased.

"No. I just don't have any great and wonderful stories to tell. I was a pilot. I flew a lot of patrols. I survived. End of story." Partly anyway.

"Did you shoot down any of their planes?"

"A few."

"How many's a few?"

"Jesus!" I couldn't keep the annoyance out of my voice. "Are you keeping score?"

She stuck her lower lip out and pretended to pout, but her eyes were still smiling. "No, I was just curious. The less you talk about it, the more curious I become."

"Twenty-one." It was easier just to tell her.

"That's a lot," she said, the lip slipping back into place.

"Twenty-one too many," I agreed.

"You're not proud of what you did?"

I couldn't help but chuckle a little. "Pride is a virtue I had in plenty."

"You say it in the past tense."

"I meant it in the past tense."

"What happened?"

"Too much to tell."

"Even to me?" She lay her head over on my shoulder as we walked, and I could feel her hair against my chin.

I wanted to talk, but something slipped up my throat and held my tongue. Maybe it was congestion. Whatever it was, I just couldn't, wouldn't say it. "No," I said simply. "Not even to you." We walked on in silence for a few minutes. Other couples moved along the sidewalk, talking in quiet whispers. "What about Arlaine?"

She pulled her head from my shoulder and kept staring straight ahead. "Arlaine is just Arlaine. Just what she appears to be. No secrets."

"Then why Paris?"

"I'm from a small town in Iowa, but I went to college in New York. A lot of my friends came here, said it was a great place to be. I thought I'd see what was so great."

"What have you found?"

"Nothing very surprising. People here just sin out in the open. Back home they hide their sins behind closed doors and brown paper bags."

"And Arlaine?"

She looked at me then and laughed. "Arlaine doesn't sin. She doesn't believe in sin."

"Then how can you believe in Paris?"

The smile stayed on her face. "I don't. None of this exists. You don't exist. I don't exist. Gertrude doesn't. We're all just dreaming."

I winced at the word "dream." She didn't catch it, and I was glad. Something about her made me comfortable, more comfortable with a woman than I'd been in four years, but at the same time uneasy, in a way that I blamed on myself. One thing was certain, though; I knew I preferred this kind of dream to the ones I'd been having.

"No comment?" she asked.

"No comment."

"Then you're an avoider."

"A what?"

"An avoider. You avoid the realities of things."

"You just said we weren't real. We're all dreams," I reminded her with a frown. She was getting too damn close for my own good. "Let's talk about something else."

She cupped her free hand around her chin and acted like she was in heavy concentration. "Well, let's see. You've cut out the war and Paris as topics. What's left?"

"Not much." We circled the palace and headed towards the rue des Ecoles and my flat. "Where are you staying?" I said it short and blunt.

Her hand fell away from her chin, and she got a little nervous, jerky. "Uh, a hotel. Number 1, Place de la Sorbonne. Hotel Select."

"Great. It's on our way. I'll just drop you off and go on home. I tell you, this cold is getting the better of me." I made the logical excuse. We had turned onto rue de Vaugirard and really were headed towards her hotel. That little bit of uneasiness began to shroud the comfort I'd felt with her. It more than shrouded it; the uneasiness crushed the comfort and left me uncertain and afraid. Maybe she could help me; maybe she couldn't. I think, most of all, the fear of finding out was too much.

She pulled her arm out of mine and put about a foot between us. In the lamplight, as we walked, I saw that her face had hardened. "Okay." Her voice was brittle. "It's just across the Boulevard St. Michel and then up a block or so."

Nothing else was said until we got in front of the hotel. She didn't seem as innocent then as she did in the bookstore that morning. But there were still some things she didn't understand, and I wasn't in a mood to show her.

Suddenly, she turned towards me. "Have I misread some signals somewhere?"

I started sweating again, but I told myself it was the cold. "Maybe. Maybe not. I'm sort of confused about it, too. Look, there's some things about me you don't know, some things nobody knows. It's gonna take some time to work through all this, and we don't have a lot of time right now. But, even if we find time, you've got to understand that nothing may come of it anyway."

She smiled again. "As long as I wasn't barking up the wrong tree."

"Just the wrong time of year." I crossed my fingers hoping that I was right.

I looked away for a second and when I turned back, her lips were there. You've got to give her one thing; she knew how to kiss. And she gave me one long one. Things started beginning that hadn't begun in a long time, but I pulled away, and with a sniffled, "See you tomorrow," I trudged off down the street towards the rue des Ecoles and my dreams. I didn't look back.

• • • •

"Two francs! You deserve less than a franc." Julien and I negotiated again. He had met me with a stack of mail as I dragged my tired butt back from Arlaine's hotel. "This looks like nothing but junk. Quality counts, Julien."

"But, Monsieur, I am not responsible for what the mail contains. It is only my job to deliver it to you." He was standing firm, as firm as a nine year old can.

"I'll give you ten francs—"

"Dix francs!"

"Dix francs, if," I held up a hand to put his excitement on hold. "If you will do me a favor."

The gleam sped away and caution crept in. "And what favor do you need, Monsieur?" God, for a nine year old, he was cagey.

"I need a special message delivered."

"To whom?"

"To Madame Mariette Lanier at the Le Panier Fleuri on rue de la Huchette."

Julien raised his eyebrows. "Ma mere would not like me going to such places." But his voice held no fear, and I knew it was just a negotiating tactic.

"You have been to such places before, standing around outside until you are run off." An embarrassed red slipped into Julien's face, and I knew I'd hit home. "Madame Lanier has some men who work for her. I need to see one, immediately."

The raised eyebrows went even higher. "Monsieur means a woman, not a man, n'est pas?"

"No," I said, shaking my head. "Madame has a few men who do odd jobs for her. I need a special job performed. She will send one. Tell her I sent you, and you will be well-treated. Madame owes me a great debt."

"That is a long way, Monsieur," Julien answered doubtfully. "Fifteen francs."

"Okay," I agreed. "But five now, ten when Madame's servant comes to see me."

"Ten now, five then."

"No." I trusted Julien, but I wanted the end prize bigger than the teaser. He was, after all, a little French thief.

His brown eyes narrowed, and the little forehead wrinkled for a second before smoothing. "Oui."

I gave him five francs, and he disappeared down the hall. Throwing the stack of mail on the table, I fixed myself a drink while I waited. And another, and then another.

I knew that Madame Mariette would help me. Monique was one of her girls. And it was Madame's brothel that I'd saved. One murdered customer is bad for business; three dead patrons meant closing your doors for good, especially when one of your girls is accused of the murders. Yeah, Madame Mariette owed me.

And, late that night, her man came to the flat. He was just the kind I wanted, vaguely unkempt and more than vaguely immoral. His skin gleamed with a thin sheen of oil, and he smelled of whiskey and cigarette smoke. Standing before me, he shifted nervously from foot to foot and fondled his hat with rough, time-scarred hands. He was unsure of himself with me, and I was glad. That was the only way to keep a man like him under control, that and treating him like a human.

I explained what I wanted, and I described the Reverend Karper. "He's staying at the Hotel Jacob. I want to know where he goes and who he sees. Can you do this?"

"Yes, Monsieur." He wouldn't look at me, just kept fidgeting with his hat. "Do you want anything done to him?"

"No," I said, though the idea of disposing of the Reverend Karper appealed to me. "Just keep track of him for me. Let me know if anything suspicious happens. Is twenty francs enough?" I reached into my pocket.

He held up a hand, finally looking at me. "It is . . . not necessary," he said. "Madame Mariette, I owe her much. She has been kind to me."

"But—"

"No, Monsieur. I owe her and she owes you. So I will do this job to repay part of my debt as she sent me to repay part of hers. It is the way of the world. I will find you when I have something to tell." And he was gone.

Tossing down the last of the drink, I collapsed on my squeaky bed. For a farm boy from Missouri, I had come a long way. If my father could have only seen me then, drunk, disgusted, and hiring bouncers from Parisian whorehouses to follow preachers. I was a sterling example to the kids back home. And that's what I was thinking as the alcohol worked its magic and a heavy stupor robbed my consciousness.

• • • •

The Fokker triplane winds into a red and orange spin, the flames licking back at me. I circle above and watch the fire consume the fuselage and the wings, and still the heat-cleansed bones, the face of my father burned now beyond recognition, are stark against the blaze, and the skull watches me from its spin. It grows closer and closer to the red barn. I scream for him to stop but nothing comes out; the words lock in the back of my throat.

And then the fiery missile hits the barn and the explosive crack stings my eardrums and rattles my bones. Smoke and flame whirl together, spiralling into a face, and I see my father once more. And he mouths my name as his face again disappears in a ball of cleansing fire.

Jesus! I woke up in a sweat, cold and chilling. Throwing the covers back, I jerked upright. Good money, I would have paid good money for a decent night's sleep. But nothing stopped the dreams. Nothing.

With a lot of effort, I staggered to my feet and stumbled into the front room. It was cold. My naked legs started growing goosebumps and so did my arms. I always slept in just my under-wear, a habit that even the cold winters of Paris couldn't break. But within a couple of minutes, I had a fire going in the stove, the coffee brewing, and a pair of pants on.

Sitting at my table, I glimpsed something on the floor, just underneath the door. It was a telegram and I retrieved it.

> Jack Barnett, 51 rue des Ecoles, Paris, France: Need correspondent for Genoa Conference. Will pay $75 plus expenses. Interested? Guy Johnson, Editor, *Cinncinnati Post.*

I tossed it on the table. Jesus, I had to get through this week first. The Genoa Conference was next week. The idea was appealing, though. First, I needed the money. Second, Hem was going and if Hadley wasn't with him, he could be a hell of a lot of fun on a trip. Besides, it was supposed to be a hot meeting, and I always liked to see politicians act outraged in public while they cut dirty deals in backrooms. And this one promised to have a lot of dirty deals. At least one major faction in each participating country didn't want to see their country in attendance. David Lloyd George, the instigator, was both the most respected and the most hated politician on the planet. It was going to be a great vaudeville act; every politician there would perfect his ability to talk out of both sides of his mouth at once. And that made it even more appealing since observing hypocrisy in action was my favorite hobby.

I glanced at the stack of mail lying next to my arm that Julien had brought up the night before. Waiting for the man from Madame Mariette's, I couldn't bring myself to go through it, so, while the coffee pot perked, I started. A letter from an editor in New York wanting a piece on French horse racing. Two bills from a hotel in Chicago I'd never stayed at. A request from *Liberty Magazine* to subscribe. A request from my mother to come home, or at least write.

> Dear Jack: We haven't heard from you in so long I thought I'd write and see if you are well. We are all well tho I've been getting some bad headaches of late. Your father has been preaching at two different churches each Sunday. It sure is hard on him to do that, but he feels like the people need him and so he goes on and does it.

The Women's Auxiliary meets right regular. All the ladies ask about you. There was a time when some of them thought you'd follow your father into the pulpit. I tell them not to give up hope yet.

Just trust in the Lord, Jack, and he will bring you home safe. I'm not sure why you stay over there. It would sure be good to see you. Your mother and father both love you. Please come home. Write when you can.

Your Mother

My mother's letters always put a frown on my face. But she was just doing what she knew how to do, what she thought she was supposed to do. Never, ever, did my father write to me. It was as if he knew what I had done; of course, he couldn't. Only I knew. But, maybe he sensed it. Or, maybe he just didn't give a damn. I laughed at that line about the people needing him. They were supposed to need God. Maybe the truth was that he needed the people.

"Brother Jack Barnett," I said the words aloud as I tossed the letter back onto the table. My mother always had dreams of me being a preacher, but she could never understand that that was the last place I belonged, especially after the war. But even I recognized, beneath my chuckle, that the idea hurt, caused me physical pain, and I didn't understand why.

The more mundane tasks out of the way, I tried to focus on this James Joyce business. And everytime I did, that weird note and the swastika kept coming back to haunt me. I knew they were my aces in the hole, but I couldn't figure out why. Somebody was going way out of his way to frame James Joyce, and for the life of me, I couldn't figure out who or why. Karper was the first and most obvious culprit, but his claims might just be a case of johnny-come-lately opportunism.

The why seemed obvious—to protect somebody else. But the who, that was a real tough one. And something Frank O'Connor said to me came floating back too. The auto was the kind "the embassy crowd favors." Was it from an embassy? Which embassy? That whole idea seemed too idiotic to believe, but at the very least it led away from Karper. Or did it? Maybe Karper had connections at the embassy. Maybe it was friends of Karper's who were pressuring Duvall to end the thing quickly.

Arlaine had said that Duvall ran across a witness that saw Joyce leaving later than he said he did. I made a mental note to track Duvall down and ask who that witness was. Maybe they saw something else too.

And then, there was this Kopfmann guy. First we find the swastika on the dead man, and then this German shows up at Gertrude Stein's. Coincidence? Maybe. But I didn't put anything past the Germans. The little I'd heard about these Nazis put them in a class by themselves. They were supposed to be a radical, right wing bunch, championing such noble causes as anti-semitism and racial purity. Not that I was against the right wing, but what I knew about this den of right wingers told me that they wouldn't exactly be gentle about accomplishing their goals.

But what purpose could killing the guy at Shakespeare and Company, and then framing James Joyce, serve the Nazis? None, that I could see. Everything pointed to a conspiracy to shut down Joyce. And that meant a personal vendetta. Somebody had obviously gone to a lot of trouble just to shut down an obscure Irish writer. Why? That question *did* lead to Karper. The idea that one writer could be so jealous of another that he'd murder somebody and frame the object of his jealousy didn't work. But a Bible-thumper trying to prevent the publication of pornography (or what he saw as pornography) would leave no stone unturned in his Christian quest.

Adding it up just put me into another spin, headed for a complete nosedive, the kind you can't escape from. I needed information that only Duvall could give me. I needed to know who this new witness was, and I needed to know who the dead man really was. If I could just figure that out, I'd be a couple of steps closer to wrapping up the whole thing.

Joyce's exact movements that night had to be determined, just as I had to figure out Kopfmann's whereabouts. Had Kopfmann faked the meeting at Shakespeare and Company after Joyce left? Had he killed the guy and left him to implicate Joyce? Was Joyce's key stolen to give the murderer access to the shop? Did the dead guy really work for Karper? Did Joyce kill him so he wouldn't burn the books? Then why invite him to the shop? Did any of this make any sense?

The only logical explanation for the whole thing still seemed to be that Joyce arranged to meet this guy. But even that defied logic. The man wanted to torch *Ulysses*. Joyce knifed him, and then set it up to look like the guy broke in. He neglected to get his note, arranging the meeting, therefore committing the one mistake that Sherlock Holmes says the murderer always makes. But why ask for the meeting in the first place? Or did Karper arrange that as well? Was Karper the stage manager and director of this little drama?

I poured myself a cup of coffee, dumped my requisite half a pound of sugar into it, and went back to the table. James Joyce just wasn't a murderer. I wasn't convinced of it and neither was Duvall. If Duvall truly believed that Joyce was guilty, he'd have arrested him the day before. When Duvall was sure of something, he moved; he didn't hand out forty-eight hour reprieves. He said he was under pressure to put the thing to rest. Where was the pressure coming from? Official pressure, obviously. Was there some governmental interest in the dead man at Sylvia's bookshop? Could that be connected with Frank O'Connor's description of the auto as the kind the embassy crowd used? Was I making any sense? Probably not. But, if I didn't get off my butt and get to work soon, James Joyce was going to jail.

Still a quarter asleep, I pushed my coffee cup back, stood, and headed for my shoes. The unmade bed brought back visions of Arlaine Watson, and I remembered the night before, not without a little regret. She sure had fooled me. I figured her for squeaky clean, and there was a hint of innocence even after that night. But just a hint. Her actions did nothing to mask her intentions. And for a college girl from Iowa, she seemed awfully eager to jump in bed. Fear held her plans at bay. Not her fear, mine. Fear is a powerful motivator, and it was fear that made me dump her at the Hotel Select. Fear that I wouldn't be able to finish what I started.

I'd tried to solve my problem with a half-dozen prostitutes, and they considered it a professional challenge. But even they failed miserably. In fact, it was because I knew so many of them so well, that I got mixed up in the murders at Madame Mariette's. Duvall was following all the right evidence in all the wrong directions for all the right reasons. The girls knew it, and they came to me. Fortunately for Monique Trudeau, Duvall's prime suspect, I was better at helping them than they were at helping me.

Tugging my shoes on, I realized that Arlaine had gotten further with me just holding my arm than the hookers had no matter what they held. Maybe that's what scared me so bad. Maybe there was hope for me yet. And maybe not.

95

• • • •

The Cafe de Floré was my favorite spot for breakfast. They served a good All-American plate of ham, eggs, and toast, the kind of breakfast my mother would have stood up and applauded. It didn't open real early, but then again, I didn't get out and about very early either. I tried to find rest in the daylight hours, hoping the dreams would leave me alone. Usually, I was mistaken.

The cafe was next door to the Brasserie Lipp and across the street from the Cafe aux Deux Magots. Back in those days, you could find just about any foreigner you wanted in one of those three. And if they weren't there, check the Dome or Gypsy's. Montparnasse was our district, but we were all over the place. The French loved our money and hated our arrogance, and I can't say I blamed them.

But the food wasn't what brought me to the cafe that morning. Duvall loved American breakfasts, and he rarely missed a day of eating at the Cafe de Floré. I needed to know what he knew, and so I trudged over and found him at a back table, wolfing down the obligatory ham, eggs, and toast.

"Jack! Sit, sit." He motioned to a chair between bites, and I nodded at the waiter, who marched off to get my food.

"You're a creature of habit, Duvall. I knew I'd find you here."

Duvall smiled and chewed for a second. "So are you, Jack, a man of habits. You make a habit to interfere in my investigations." He paused and looked around. "Where is your puppy dog? This American, Hemingway. Did you leave him at home today?"

"Hemingway's okay. He's a little young and eager, but he's a good guy."

"Whatever pleases you. I guess you are here to plead for more time, n'est pas?"

"No. I'm looking for information, Inspector."

Duvall showed his mock surprise with a pair of raised eyebrows. "Just information? My, my, Jack. You must be— how do you say it—on to something." He skewered the last piece of ham and shoveled it in his mouth, pushing back his plate at the same time. "Ask, Jack Barnett, ask."

"Who told you that they saw Joyce outside Shakespeare and Company at 11:30 that night?"

Now Duvall's eyebrows raised in real surprise. "How did you

know that? We found a witness only late yesterday afternoon, after I saw you at the Brasserie Lipp."

"I have my sources." I grinned at him, loving his look of confusion.

Duvall studied me for a minute; then he burst into laughter, produced the magical match, and lit a cigarette. "But, of course, the woman, this girl, Mademoiselle Watson. She was there when we questioned the boy." He sank back into his chair and puffed heavily, satisfied that his mystery was solved.

"What boy?" I ignored the fact that he was absolutely right.

"Paul Dounat, the young man who works at the bookshop part time." Duvall doused his match in a lonely little clump of scrambled eggs. "He was across the street the night of the murder between 11:30 and 11:45, headed home to the rue Dupuytren, number 8, I believe."

"Number Eight, that's where Sylvia's bookshop used to be. That can't be where he lives."

"He lives in a flat above the old bookshop. Mademoiselle Beach arranged it, I believe." Duvall continued to puff on his cigarette while I digested this new information.

"Where was he when he said he saw Joyce?"

"In front of La Maison des Amis des Livres, Mademoiselle Monnier's shop, which as you know is across the street and a slight bit north of Shakespeare and Company."

"What's the distance?"

"Insignificant."

"How about lighting?"

"A street lamp outside the bookshop. No, Jack, he could not have mistaken Monsieur Joyce. Dounat not only had a clear view of him, but he knew him, saw him on a daily basis at the bookshop. Whether James Joyce killed the victim or not, Dounat could not be mistaken. James Joyce left the bookshop one hour later than he has said."

Aggravation set in. "But why would Joyce lie if he didn't kill this guy?"

Duvall's black eyes sank a little lower, and his tiny mustache twitched a time or two. "Maybe he did kill him. Jack, I have seen stranger murderers than James Joyce. And this Quintin Karper swears on his mother's grave that he hired Phillipe Jourdan to burn these books. How can I ignore that?"

"But. . . ."

He waved a hand and stopped me. "But, you are correct; I do not believe his story completely. Something about him does not fit. And, mon ami, I do not feel James Joyce's guilt strongly. I tell you, Jack, this affair does not sit well with me. It has a strange texture to it, a sour smell. We received an identification on our victim late last night; did I tell you?"

"No, and it's about damn time you did."

Duvall paused and inhaled deeply on his cigarette, the smoke wreathing his head. "His name was Pfeiffer, Karl Pfeiffer, from Munich. He was a member of this new Nazi party in Germany, one of the thugs who chase Communists through our streets."

"I'll be damned." A pattern was beginning to emerge, and I was glad. "Why the typewriter salesman papers?"

"To keep people from asking questions, I suppose. But he is just the sort that Quintin Karper might have hired to do this job. They are all criminals." Duvall leaned across the table and smiled like he was about to share some big secret. "Funny, Jack, that he should be a member of a group whose symbol you carried just yesterday. Are you withholding evidence from me, old friend?"

I avoided looking in Duvall's eyes. It wasn't time yet. I needed to hold everything I had for maximum impact. "Just something I picked up on the streets. Nothing important."

"I think it is, but I shall let you play out your game for now. Jack, I am not sure that I will be able to fulfill our agreement. Powerful people are anxious that the murder at Shakespeare and Company be quickly settled."

"Duvall, you've got to! It's all beginning to come together." I lied through my teeth. "You don't believe he's guilty any more than I do."

He nodded and sighed deeply. "Enough. I suppose if I do not give in, you will begin crying. All right, Jack Barnett, I will hold off my superiors until tomorrow night. If you cannot convince me by that time that Monsieur Joyce is innocent, I will be forced to arrest him. And he will stay arrested, Jack. The autopsy report came back. Time of death marked at between 11:00 p.m. and 1:00 a.m. I have motive, means, and opportunity. I have a case."

My fingers drummed on the tabletop. "Don't count on it. I think this thing's pretty twisted, more twisted than you or I know. Can you do me a favor?"

"If I can."

"Find out where Karper supposedly met this Pfeiffer guy. That might help."

"I will question him later this morning."

"And, secondly, have you gotten the photographs developed?"

"I expect them this morning."

"Send a set over, will you?"

Duvall nodded and took a heavy pull on the cigarette, releasing the smoke through his mouth and nose.

My mind was doing S-curves and Immelmans. I stood up and stepped away from the table. "Thanks, pal. See you later."

"Jack." His voice called at my back.

"Yeah," I said half-turning.

"The Model T from which the shot was fired at you, it was black and new, n'est pas?"

"Yeah, that's what Frank O'Connor said."

"One of our gendarmes saw a Model T of that description turn a corner a block from Monsieur O'Connor's antique shop at a high rate of speed just seconds after hearing a gunshot, at almost exactly the time you were fired upon."

"Get to the point." I had that sinking feeling in my gut again.

"You are right, my friend; this affair is very twisted. The Model T, it is registered to the U.S. Embassy."

I sighed. "I forgot to tell you, Duvall. That same Model T?"

"Yes?"

"It was following me last night."

"Be careful, Jack. I do not want to find you in my morgue."

Eight

'The U.S. Embassy! What the hell's going on, Jack?" Hem's mustache twitched like he had St. Vitus' dance. "That doesn't make any sense at all. Something ain't right."

I'd left Duvall sitting at his table and stumbled across the street to the Cafe aux Deux Magots, where Hemingway waited patiently, drinking his usual rum St. James at a back table. For some reason, he'd decided to wear a Godawful beret. Otherwise, he was dressed pretty normally—V-necked, knit sweater, tie, and dark jacket. But his eyes weren't bloodshot, they were solid red. And he had this unnatural, green pallor. He looked like hell.

"Jack. Jack!"

"Yeah, Hem, I'm sorry. This whole thing sort of hit me rough." I shook my head to clear it. "Yeah, the American Embassy."

"Well, ain't that a good goddamn? You want to hear about this German, Kopfmann?" Hemingway was more than a little grumpy. Big, black, half circles seemed to hold his eyes in place.

"Yeah. Are you all right?"

"Hell, no, I'm not all right. I tagged along with our friend when we left Gertrude's and he insisted on a late supper at Michaud's."

"Was he paying?"

"Of course. Hell, I can't afford to eat there when I'm working for the newspapers steady."

"Lucky you."

"Right," Hem grumbled. "Anyway, after Michaud's, he wanted to meet more of us 'gut Amerikanische writers.' So, I took him to Gypsy's. Bob McAlmon was there."

"Oh."

Hemingway shook his head, slowly and surely. "Oh, is right. I drank more goddamn schnapps last night than I ever knew existed. I toasted more fallen comrades and more old enemies than I ever actually had. And I heard more Teutonic bullshit than the average American ought to have to listen to in three lifetimes. I didn't get home until four this morning, after singing 'The Marseillaise,' 'The Star Spangled Banner,' and some German song I don't remember, on the Champs Elysees. I think Ezra was there too; I just don't remember. Hadley won't speak to me. Hell, it's a wonder I'm still married."

"Use it in a book. So what's the deal with Herr Kopfmann?"

"Nothing. He didn't go anywhere suspicious. He didn't talk to anybody suspicious. He didn't say anything suspicious. He didn't do anything suspicious, except once he told McAlmon he'd like to sleep with Alice Toklas. Thought she was dark and mysterious. Hell, we must have morted a dozen bottles." Hem rubbed his head between both hands. "Mort" was Hem's way of mixing French and English to say they killed/drank a dozen bottles. He did that a lot.

"No hint of anything having to do with Joyce or the Nazis?"

"Absolutely none." He pulled his hands away from his head. "I don't see any reason to waste any more time on him."

"I'm not so sure, Hem." I told him what Duvall said about our Phillipe Jourdan, the fake typewriter salesman. "This German connection is getting pretty strong. I don't see how we can ignore our only living, breathing German. Besides, you've been drunk with McAlmon and Pound before."

"They don't drink like this guy, Jack. And besides, I didn't see a damn thing that would arouse suspicion. Nothing. Zero. This embassy thing seems more like what we should be looking at. That and this Karper guy. What do you think it's all about?"

"Hell, I don't know. It does throw a whole new wrinkle on this thing. It's some kind of international goulash. You know, sprinkle in a few Germans, add a dash of Irish, mix in both diplomatic and religious Americans, and season with sadistic French humor. Cook it up and you've got . . . what? All I can tell you for sure is that this thing is about more than just James Joyce and his book. The U.S. Embassy doesn't send killers out over a morally destitute novel."

"Even if the Reverend Quintin Karper asks them to?"

"That is the unanswered question."

"You gonna keep going? I mean, getting shot at can get to be annoying."

I thought about it a second. "No choice now. I'm sunk up to my knees and I can't go back. Sylvia needs us. You saw her back room. She's got tons of this *Ulysses* book stacked up in there. Unless I miss my guess, she's tied up a bunch of money in this thing. And, dammit, Joyce didn't kill anybody!" I was sure of that. And I couldn't just let it rest.

"Maybe you should carry a gun, Jack." Hem was serious. I could see it in his eyes.

"No. Not yet. If they had wanted me, they'd have killed me yesterday." I briefed him on the business with Arlaine the night before.

"Whatever you say." It didn't sit well with Hem, and it showed in the tightness around his mouth. "What about Kopfmann? You really don't want me to keep trailing him, do you?"

"Maybe. We'll have to decide that when we know more."

"What about Karper? What did you do about him?"

"I called in a favor from a friend. Karper suddenly developed a new shadow."

"Good goddamn idea."

"We'll worry about Karper and Kopfmann later. From your description of last night, Kopfmann probably won't roll out until late this afternoon. And Karper is covered whenever he gets up." I studied the hungover Hemingway for a long second. "Hadley really that pissed off at you?"

"More than you know. I've been complaining to her for a while about money, and then I go and spend all night drinking with the guys. What do you think?"

Having never been married, I could only have a vague picture, but the smart thing to do just then was to nod in agreement. I did. "You up for another round of questioning? This Paul Dounat, the kid who does the handyman business at Shakespeare and Company, he supposedly saw Joyce in front of the shop an hour after Joyce said that he left. I'm going over to see him."

A pale grin broke across his face. "What the hell. Hadley thinks I'm at the Cafe de Gare writing. Just be careful I don't get sick on you. This hair of the dog," and he pointed at the rum St. James, "isn't doing a hell of a lot of good."

"I'll stay upwind."

We headed for the door, and Hem cleared his throat. "Say, Jack."

I looked at him.

"Did you and Arlaine . . . ?" He raised his eyebrows.

"Hardly." I left him standing there and walked out the door. He hurried to keep up.

• • • •

A cool breeze marked the mid-morning air, remnant of the weather front that moved through the day and evening before. My cold seemed to be the shortlived kind (for once in my life), and all I had left of last night's fever was a slight sniffle. Hem and I hustled through the crowd on the street—the Boulevard St. Germain— headed for rue de l'Odeon.

"You know what woke me up this morning?" Hem asked.

"Hadley complaining about you being late?"

"No," he replied, his face wrinkling into a frown.

"It was just a guess."

"This goatwoman was in the street selling goat's milk. It was incredible. She was old and stooped-over and she led a goat around on a rope." Hem almost danced beside me as he painted the picture. "Someone would stop her and she would fill their pail right from the goat's teat. Then, off she'd go looking for another customer."

"That's Paris," I answered, shrugging one of those c'est-la-vie kind of shrugs.

But Hem's eyes were glowing, some of the hangover forgotten. "No, that's truth."

A gendarme was whistling and directing traffic up ahead as we got closer to the intersection with rue de l'Odeon. The autos were backed up, and people milled around. "What's going on?" I tried to look, but at five feet ten, I didn't see much.

Hem used his bulk to muscle up for a better view. "One of those horse-drawn honey wagons turned over," he grinned.

And about that time, the wind shifted and I got a strong whiff. Jesus! Just about every apartment building had these toilets on the landing, and at night the honey wagons would come along and empty them. Apparently, this one had been a little late in making its rounds.

We got a little closer, and I could see the black and tan horses snorting and stomping, a wild burst of fear in their eyes. The driver, a bandage around his head, tried his best to calm them, but all the autos, the people, and the gendarme's whistling defeated the old guy's attempts. And the horses' stomping grew more fierce, until one snapped its leather reins with a loud pop that echoed off the buildings.

A gendarme rushed forward to recapture the horse, but he slipped in the muck that escaped from the wagon. The horse reared, neighed, and pointed its shod hooves at the helpless officer on the ground.

My breath caught as I watched six hundred pounds of horse descend on the man.

But, just as the iron hooves fell, the old man snagged the gendarme by the collar and yanked him out of the way. The horse clattered sharply against the pavement, stumbled, awkwardly reclaimed its stance, and stood uncertainly for a minute, its eyes flickering back and forth, frightened and confused. The driver quickly gathered the short half-reins dangling beneath the horse's neck.

I pushed at Hem's back, hurrying him through the crowd. The smell of human manure squatted in my nose and added to my uneasiness. Something in the horse's eyes bothered me, made me feel like I was looking in a mirror. As far as I was concerned, it was time to move on. But Hem was as captivated with the scene as I had been, and he ignored my shove and watched intently until the wagon, half its brownish-green load spilling into the street, was righted, and the driver restored some semblance of calm to his animals.

"C'mon, Hem. We've got to get going," I urged.

"Yeah, Jack. Yeah." He turned away then, reluctantly, and we crossed the street at the gendarme's nod and headed down rue de l'Odeon.

A block in front of us a tall blonde, wrapped in a light coat and wearing a triangle of scarf over her hair, appeared in the sidewalk traffic. She was facing sort of northeast, almost into rue Dupuytren, but not quite either. Her stance looked familiar, and as we got closer, I saw that it was Arlaine, apparently coming from Shakespeare and Company which lay further on down the street. I sucked in my breath involuntarily.

"Arlaine!" Hem yelled first.

She turned slightly and looked at us, and it didn't seem like she was real pleased to see me. A hint of a frown crossed her face and then changed into a smile as recognition set in.

"Where you headed?" Hem continued.

We joined her on the corner.

"Shakespeare and Company. I thought I'd see if Sylvia needed me." She didn't really look at me, and I guessed I could understand why.

"Oh," I said, stupidly looking for something to say. "Looked like you were coming from there."

"No." She shook her head quickly, casting her eyes down and holding her voice soft. "I was looking at the commotion up the street."

Hemingway, to his credit, stood off to the side and left us alone, but he had this sickeningly paternalistic look on his face. "Listen, Arlaine," he began. "We're going over to question this Dounat fellow. Want to come along?"

"Yeah," I said quickly. "Why don't you?" It made some kind of sense anyway. Besides, she had been working at Shakespeare and Company too; maybe having her there would make Dounat more comfortable. And I found myself really wanting her around, regardless of the way I acted the night before. I couldn't forget the tingle when she touched me.

She looked at me then, and it was one of the most incredible looks I'd ever been given. Her blue eyes seemed to bore a hole right through me. A little smile broke across her face, but a hardness lingered around the edges. Maybe I'd hurt her more than I thought. Right then, I just didn't know, and I don't remember my heart beating while I waited for her answer. Finally, she nodded.

"Okay," I said, trying to regain some control. "Let's go."

We trooped around the corner on rue Dupuytren and came abreast of Number 8 very quickly. The front of the old Shakespeare and Company looked pretty much as it had when Sylvia had the shop there, not as big a place as the rue de l'Odeon spot, but not bad either. A long metal hook, where Shakespeare's face had once hung, still shuddered a little in the breeze. One window, fronted by a fancy iron grill, was centered above the shop. I figured that for our destination. We stopped, and, consciously or not, all three of us raised our heads and looked at the window.

"Do you know this Dounat guy very well?" I asked Arlaine.

"No," she answered with a quick shake of her head. "He keeps pretty much to himself. From the little I've seen of him, he seems very serious and quiet. Intense. Yeah, that's the word. Intense. Attends classes at the Sorbonne."

I rolled my eyes. Intense, young French student-types gave me a headache. If you stopped in at one of their hangouts, you'd be inundated with Communist philosophy or Sartre or Proust or whatever they were championing that week. I wasn't excited.

We went in the side door and climbed to the second floor. I motioned for Hemingway to knock on the door, and he did, loud and hard.

Nothing. I nodded to Hem again.

Again he knocked.

This time, from the deep recesses of the apartment, we heard a voice. "Que est-ce que c'est?" What is it?

"Je m'appelle Jack Barnett. Parlez-vous anglais? Pouvez-vous parler à nous?" I sure as hell didn't want to talk to him in French. Mine stunk, and from what I'd heard of Hem's it was passable, but not what we needed for down and dirty questioning. I didn't know about Arlaine.

The door sprung open about then, and a hard-eyed young face appeared in the entrance. "What is it? I am expecting . . . ," then his eyes lit on Arlaine, fell, and softened. "Mademoiselle Arlaine, pardonnez-moi." So the kid had a crush on Arlaine; well, hell, even though I felt a stab of jealousy, I couldn't blame him. Look at me. And if his crush got us a chance to question him, God bless young love.

"These gentlemen would like to ask you some questions, Paul. Is that all right?" Arlaine smiled at him gently, and I could tell she understood how he felt.

"The police have already been here," he said, turning his head away and retreating back into the flat.

I followed on his heels, not chancing rejection. "That may be true, but we need to ask you some more questions. We are working for Mademoiselle Sylvia."

At the mention of Sylvia's name, Dounat's expression turned to confusion, and he sank onto a threadbare couch. It was one of only a couple of items of furniture in the room—a table, two chairs, and a small writing desk. A little charcoal heater sat in the middle of the floor.

The kid was dressed in a simple shirt and pants. Nothing fancy. Cleaner than the overalls I'd seen him in the day before, more fitting for a student, but still not expensive. His hair was as dark or darker than I remembered it, and his eyebrows were heavy, thick; they joined as one above his nose. I'd never seen anyone with one, solid, eyebrow.

Arlaine sat down next to him. Hemingway and I centered ourselves on him. Dounat kept glancing sideways at Arlaine, his face a mix of pleading and confusion.

"We want to know about that night, two nights ago. Did you see Monsieur Joyce that night?"

He stared at the floor. "Oui. Around 11:30." The words came out in a mumble.

"What was he doing?"

"He locked the door to the shop and walked very quickly away."

"Did anyone walk up to him?"

"Non. There was no one."

"Was there anyone else on the street?"

"Non. Only Monsieur Joyce. He stopped only to lock the door, and then he went away very fast."

"What were you doing on rue de l'Odeon at that hour?"

Dounat just continued to stare at the floor. "Nothing. I was doing nothing. Merely walking home. Walking here."

"Did you think it was strange that Joyce was at the shop so late?"

"I think Monsieur Joyce is a very strange man. So, non, I did not."

"And then what did you do?" coaxed Arlaine.

"And then, nothing," he replied in that same, halting voice, still refusing to meet us eye for eye. "I had stopped to light a cigarette. I saw someone walking inside the shop, open the door, and then come out. I waited to see who it was. It was Monsieur Joyce. I lit my cigarette. I went home. That is all." From the way he was fumbling with his hands, I'd say he needed a cigarette about then.

"And you saw nothing else out of the ordinary?"

He chuckled nervously. "What is 'out of the ordinary' in a city like Paris, Monsieur? But, non, I saw nothing else. It is this that I have told to the police. This and nothing more."

"Hem?" Something bothered me. I wasn't ready to leave.

"I can't think of anything else to ask, Jack." Hemingway turned around and studied the apartment. He walked over to the table and picked up a couple of pamphlets, glanced at the covers, and held one up. "These yours?"

Dounat blushed. I swear he blushed. "Yes. I have been reading them."

"And making notes it looks like," Hem added.

"Sometimes it is necessary to write what I am thinking as I read them to better understand what they say," the boy replied with a shrug.

Hem tossed it back down. "What else do you do besides work for Mademoiselle Beach?"

"I take classes at the Sorbonne."

"What are you studying to be?"

"A medecin, a physician."

"Are you a Communist?" Hem waved one of the pamphlets again.

Dounat blushed again and quickly shook his head. "Non, I read many things."

I scanned the apartment myself while Hem continued the questioning. It looked pretty dull. A lot like mine. Something still itched at me, but when I turned back, it looked like Arlaine had scooted closer to the boy or that he had scooted closer to her. It didn't really matter; I didn't like it.

"Thank you, Paul." I cut Hem's question off, whatever it had been. "I'd like to say you've been helpful, but I'm afraid things don't look very good for Mademoiselle Sylvia, or Monsieur Joyce."

He looked at me then, finally, and his eyes were dull and worried. "I am very sorry, Monsieur Barnett. I wish I could have told you a different story."

Just like a kid. Tell the truth no matter how bad it hurts you or your friends. Just wait till he grows up, I thought; he'll learn. "C'mon guys," I said. "Let's get out of here."

Hem headed for the door, and I was on his heels, but not before I saw Arlaine give him a motherly pat on the shoulder. He couldn't have been any younger than her, but they say that girls grow up quicker than boys. Whatever, a motherly pat was better than the two of them trying to sit in the same spot as far as I was concerned.

After lumbering down the stairs again, past the smelly pissoir on the landing, I looked at my companions. "What the hell do you make of that?"

"Awwh, Jack, he's lying through his teeth."

"How so?"

"He was nervous, shifty. Hell, he couldn't even look you in the eye."

"Sure he was nervous. Two big oafs like us bust in on him and start asking questions."

"I'd stake my name on it, Jack. The boy's hiding something."

Hem was right. The kid was nervous, restless. And he wouldn't, didn't, look me in the eye. Maybe Hem had something. Maybe I'd been too preoccupied with Arlaine to pay close attention. That was bad. I waited for her analysis before I spoke.

She looked away from us, towards rue de l'Odeon, the wind tugging at her scarf, and she looked thoughtful. "He may be lying," she began. "He was certainly nervous. It's hard to tell." She smiled at me then; it was a look I'd been waiting for and when it came, I felt years younger.

"But, does just being nervous qualify you as a liar?" I didn't want to ignore any possibility. "If he really did see Joyce here at 11:30, then I'm afraid Jimmy-boy's in a world of trouble. As long as Duvall has that, plus the torn shirt, plus Karper's claim that he hired this Karl Pfeiffer to burn the books, to hold against Joyce, it's not gonna be easy to keep him from arresting our hero."

I pointed us towards Shakespeare and Company, figuring Sylvia would be there and we could talk to her some more, maybe find out something else about Dounat, and tell her about the Nazis and all. We hadn't gotten much chance to talk to her at Gertrude's the night before. I liked Sylvia; it was hard not to like her, even considering everything.

"Hem, what do you know about this conference thing in Genoa?" A change of subject was needed. We'd gotten too deathly quiet.

"Genoa?" Arlaine interrupted with a sharp look. "You're not going to Genoa, are you?" She faltered, searching for words it seemed. "I mean . . . , well, that means you'd be leaving Paris."

Hemingway grinned at me and I wanted to belt him one, but I kept on talking instead. "I haven't made up my mind yet. An editor I've done some stuff for in Cincinnati wants me to go, said he'd pay me the standard plus expenses."

"That'd be great, Jack. We could travel together. I'm covering it for the *Toronto Star*. The Rooshians and the Germans and the Brits are all supposed to be there. I could show you some places in Italy. It'd be a hell of a fine time. And we could earn a few seeds." That was Hemingwayese for dollars.

It was hard not to like Hemingway. He could take the idea of going to an international economic conference and make it sound like a day at the races. I looked at him then, and again, like earlier that morning, he almost bounced beside me as we walked. Hem was excited. Arlaine was just trudging along, quiet now that I'd said something about leaving Paris for a while.

"I'll cable him back and let him know I'll do it," I decided.

"We're gonna need some entertainment after this is all over. Besides, watching politicians lie to each other is more fun than chasing murderers." And getting drunk with Hemingway in Genoa sounded like a pleasant vacation. A thought struck me. "Say, Hem. What were those pamphlets on the kid's table? You know, the ones you picked up."

"Oh," he laughed. "Typical French student garbage. Communist crap. The kind of thing you'd hear at one of those cafes over by the Sorbonne. You know, 'Down with the Capitalists!' The kid had scribbled all over them. Things like 'Exactly! But of course!' He may have just been reading them for enlightenment, but he sure as hell agreed with a lot they said."

French students were notorious for arguing politics and every other current topic at their hangouts. You've got to give American students one thing—drinking is far more important to them than politics.

"So what do we do now, Jack?" Hem went on. "This morning never got us anywhere."

"We need to spread out and ask some questions. If Dounat is lying, there's a way to shake his story. If he's telling the truth, we've hit a dead end. Either way, we've got to find out. We need to catch up with Kopfmann, too. With the prospect of a bunch of Nazis involved in all this, I don't want to ignore any possibilities. And we've got to spend a little time with the Reverend Karper."

"Jack, I've got to tell you. I don't like the idea of wasting another night drinking with that arrogant Kraut. Besides, I think Hash would dump me."

"Who's 'Hash'?" Arlaine asked as we rounded the corner onto rue de l'Odeon and headed for the shop.

"Hadley, his wife," I answered for Hem. He was still shaking his head, probably remembering the night before with Kopfmann. I looked back up towards Boulevard St. Germain, and they'd gotten the honey wagon out of the way, but its unmistakable odor still flavored the air. An old Frenchwoman, bent-over and ancient, trundled past, a hard look in her eye.

She paused and sniffed in the air. "Merde!" she grunted, louder than she intended to. She glanced at me and stiffled a giggle with her hand. I smiled at her and nodded; she hurried on.

"Look," Arlaine said. "There's Sylvia."

I glanced up from the old woman, intent again on her morning chores, and saw across the bricked street that Sylvia was opening the door to the darkened bookshop. A sign graced the front window—"Fermé." The place was usually crawling with activity—people bustling in and out— but now it looked like a tomb. You couldn't see past the books in the windows, not even through the door, so complete was the darkness. And Sylvia wore the same kind of dark look.

And then I sucked in a breath of fouled air, because rounding the corner and headed straight towards Sylvia was the most Reverend Quintin Karper.

Nine

e hustled across the street in between a Citroen and an imported Oldsmobile and caught up with Sylvia before she got the door unlocked and before her pursuer caught her. She had a particularly harried look on her face, and she fought with the key in the lock, trying to get it to turn.

I stepped in swiftly and pushed her hand away. Sliding the key completely in the lock, I turned it easily and the door fell open. Sylvia wore a white blouse, the collar lapping over her tweed jacket, and a woman's bow at her throat. She pushed that perpetually errant lock of hair from her forehead and smiled.

"Good morning, Jack. Thanks."

"No problem. How're you doing?"

"Good." She nodded as if to convince herself. "Yes, good. How about you?"

"Reasonably well, but the day's about to change." I nodded up the street at the huffing, puffing figure of Quintin Karper bearing down on us like a freight train.

"Oh, my," Sylvia said softly.

"Miss Beach! Miss Beach! I *will* speak with you!"

"Reverend Karper, I really don't know what we have to discuss. You're not going to change my mind, and I'm certainly not going to change yours." Sylvia went on the offensive.

Karper stopped and wiped a handkerchief across his glistening forehead. "The Lord works in mysterious ways, Miss Beach. And I am a persistent man; now—"

"Very persistent," I interrupted. "Inspector Duvall told me about your little trip to his confessional yesterday."

Sylvia threw me a confused look, and Karper turned.

"I need no confessional, young man. I am zealous in the service of the Lord, and my actions are guided by His hand. It was only proper and Christian to tell the Inspector of my connection with Phillipe Jourdan."

"Jack," Sylvia began. "Do you want to fill me in?"

"No problem, Sylvia," Hemingway answered for me, and I let him. "The Reverend Karper here told Duvall that he had hired the dead guy to burn Joyce's books. That, of course, provides Joyce with a motive for murdering the guy."

Sylvia's thin lips grew thinner still until they compressed into a razor line stretching across her face. "Now, my dear Reverend, I *know* that I have nothing further to say to you."

"But I do," I interjected, moving between them and letting Sylvia slip into the shop.

Karper started to move past me, but Hem cut off his advance. Arlaine squeezed behind me, and I thought she was going to follow Sylvia, but she paused in the doorway and listened.

"Who are you, sir? And why do you involve yourself in this?" A strong bluster had reentered Karper's voice.

"I'm Lucifer, but you can call me Lou."

"Your humor is lacking." Karper wiped his forehead again, and his right eye began its rhythmic twitching. "Stand aside."

"In just a minute," Hem said.

"Where did you meet Phillipe Jourdan?" I began.

"I sought a certain kind of man and I went to places where I knew that men of that nature could be found."

"Didn't that go against your creed?"

"I have no creed but the Bible."

"Cut the baloney, Reverend. Where did you meet him?"

"I am under no compulsion to tell you anything. You have no official standing." The twitching in Karper's eye doubled in speed and intensity. He put the handkerchief to use again. "Inspector Duvall has my statement." He stopped wiping and glared at me. "Do not get in the Lord's way, young man. You may find yourself a victim of God's vengeance."

"How do you know I'm not already?"

Hem chuckled.

Karper stopped, started to speak, stopped again, and finally frowned. "You can always become more of a victim. God's vengeance knows no bounds."

"Is that what happened to Phillipe Jourdan? Was he a victim of God's vengeance?" Hem asked.

A look approaching fear stole into Karper's eyes. "What happened to Phillipe Jourdan is the province of the police." He paused, and something like calm returned to his face as if the tremor of fear had passed as quickly as it came. "Though," he continued, "evidence would indicate that he died at the hands of the heathen James Joyce."

Interesting, I thought, that Karper's thunderous accusations had trickled down from definites to possibilities. He sounded remarkably like a man hedging his bets. Maybe a man who knew that his lies would eventually catch up with him, and contingency plans had to be made. Or maybe a man who was playing a game unlike any he had played before, and the rules frightened him.

"Why did you come to Paris?"

"As I told you yesterday, I am a member of the executive board of the Society Against Immoral Literature. After we succeeded in preventing the continued publication of this perverted book in the United States, a rumor reached us that Sylvia Beach of Shakespeare and Company Bookstore here in Paris had undertaken to publish the book in its entirety. Since I was here during the Great War and understand something of this foreign land, I was asked by the remainder of the executive board to undertake a mission to persuade Miss Beach of the sinful folly in which she was engaged." He paused and took a breath.

"And?" Hem prompted.

"And," he continued, casting a menacing frown at my partner. "And, I came. Miss Beach refused to see me. Her refusal had the ring of finality to it. I explored other options."

God, it amused me how people like the right Reverend Quintin Karper could talk of sin in such non-sinful terms.

"When you sent Jourdan to burn the books, didn't you realize that they might just reprint them?" I reentered the fray.

"But precious time would have been bought, time that would have allowed me to pursue more," and he harumphed, "legal remedies."

"Didn't you worry about being charged with attempted arson?"

Karper's pudgy-faced smile returned. "Inspector Duvall seems more interested in an actual murder than in attempted arson."

"Obviously, he lacks a well-developed sense of priorities," I muttered. "Where did Jourdan get the faked typewriter salesman credentials?"

"How should I know?" Karper wrinkled his forehead. "We were not close."

"No, I don't suppose so."

"If you gentlemen will excuse me, I'd like to see Miss Beach." Karper tried to push through us, but Hem stood his ground.

"The bookshop is closed, Reverend. You ain't getting in." The look in Hem's eyes left nothing to the imagination. And when he shadow-boxed a punch or two for emphasis, I thought Karper was going to pass out.

The roly-poly preacher fell back, stumbling, and wiping at his forehead with renewed intensity. "I shall report you to Inspector Duvall." He turned, walked a couple of steps down the street, and then pivoted, the distance breeding a new look of confidence on his face. "I'm not finished with any of you. I *will* stop the publication of this sinful book."

"Take my advice, Reverend," I began. "Go back to the states. Paris is the wrong place for you. You're like a duck in a dry pond. But ducks like you can drown in this pond."

"The Lord is my shepherd, young man. I shall fear no evil." He spun and headed off down the street. "And David smote Goliath. . . ."

"He's mixing his verses," Hem pointed out.

I nodded and watched with satisfaction as a thin, scarecrow figure slipped from an alcove and fell into step behind Karper who noticed nothing at all.

"I've never seen someone more difficult to figure out," Arlaine said, breaking her long silence. "It's hard to tell if there's any truth to what he says."

"I'm taking nothing for granted."

"Me either," Hem agreed.

The three of us tromped into the shop, our steps sounding deep and dull on the wooden floor. Sylvia had flipped the switch at the back of the shop, brightening the darkness a little.

We found her shuffling some papers on top of her desk, ensconced in a wooden desk chair. "Did he leave?"

"For the time being. He's the kind that'll hang around and hound you to death, Sylvia."

She shivered. "I know. But I don't see any profit by giving him the chance to rant and rave at me. Do you believe that he hired that man?"

"I don't know what to believe." And I didn't.

"It's possible," Hem said.

"If he did," Arlaine added, "it certainly doesn't help Mr. Joyce any."

Sylvia frowned and shuffled her papers again nervously. "I received a message from Inspector Duvall this morning, Jack."

I grabbed a chair next to her, those weird posters about *Ulysses* peering over my shoulder, and leaned back. "So, what did the great inspector say?"

"He said I could reopen tomorrow. He also said that they would probably be confiscating all copies of *Ulysses*. I was not pleased."

"James Joyce won't be either; I'd bet you on that."

"Is Duvall about to do what I think he's going to do?" One thing I had to give Sylvia. Her world was collapsing, but she still managed to keep her back straight and her eyes dry.

"I'd say that within thirty-six hours, James Joyce will be securely locked away for murder."

"It's getting that serious?"

"Between the positioning of the corpse, the Molotov cocktail, the mysterious note from 'J.J.', Karper's accusations, and the bit of cloth, Duvall is building a hell of a case. So, yeah, it's that serious. Unless we do something."

"What are we gonna do, Jack?" Hem stepped forward and leaned on the desk. "I'm not seeing it. Sure maybe this Dounat kid is lying, but we have to prove it."

"Paul Dounat?" Concern flashed over Sylvia's face.

"Yeah, your handyman here. I must be losing my mind. I left that little tidbit out." I briefed her on what we'd learned from Dounat. Each piece of the story caused Sylvia a new wrinkle.

"But that proves nothing," she began.

"It proves that Joyce was here during the hours when this guy was murdered," I pointed out. "At least it proves it to Duvall's satisfaction. Somebody above him wants this thing settled quickly, and whoever that someone is doesn't care if James Joyce takes the fall for a crime he didn't commit. And either Karper or the real murderer (if they're not one in the same) has connections at the U.S. Embassy." I filled Sylvia in on that cheery news.

"What can you tell us about Dounat?" I prodded.

Sylvia thought for a moment. "I've really never talked to him very much. He stopped at Adrienne's some time ago, looking for work. She already had someone for odd jobs, but she knew I needed some help. He told me he was a student and needed a part-time job. He seemed nice, clean. I hired him."

"Anything odd?"

"No. He did what he was asked. Hardly spoke more than a greeting. Polite, respectful."

"In other words, squeaky clean," I said. "If he is lying, it's gonna take some fast footwork to break his story."

"Then it's over," she said dully, her voice holding all the life of a mute choir.

"I'm not convinced of that." I shook my head. "I didn't say it *couldn't* be done. I said it would take some fast footwork. I've still got a couple of aces up my sleeve. A couple of things argue against Joyce being the murderer."

"Like what?" Arlaine asked. She'd been quiet up till then, standing at a corner of the desk and playing with this twirly thing that held a bunch of rubber stamps.

"Like the swastika. Like the U.S. Embassy."

"But you don't know what any of that means yet. How can you say it argues against Joyce as the murderer?" Arlaine questioned.

"I'm not ready to say yet." I wasn't ready to say because I didn't have a whole hell of a lot left to say.

"Hey, Jack, we're on the same side," Hem reminded me.

"I know, I know." I waved him off. "The most important thing right now is to find out what's going on with this embassy business, and we've got to find a way to punch holes in the Dounat kid's story and in Quintin Karper's revelations, no pun intended. Knocking down those stories will help keep Joyce out of jail. Tracking down the embassy line should lead us in the direction of the real killer. I hope."

"That's the bastard I want to get my hands on," Hem agreed, flexing his muscles and rolling his shoulders for effect.

"Why should you even care about the real killer if you keep Mr. Joyce out of jail?" Arlaine asked, still twirling the rubber stamp thingamajig.

"Because somebody took a shot at me." My eyes narrowed involuntarily. "And I get pissed off when that happens."

"'Tis better to be pissed off than to be urinated on, my son," a deep, bass voice intoned as the rumble of heavy steps echoed across the shop.

"Frank O'Connor! I can't believe it. You actually moved your lard ass out of your store." A chuckle gurgled in my throat, but I didn't like seeing Frank. He only left the shop when he sensed a profit, or if he was trying to pull my fat out of the fire. Frank was there after my last patrol; Frank and two bottles of whiskey finally made me stop screaming.

He paused in the middle of the bookshop and scanned the walls, decorated with photographs. "So this is the infamous Shakespeare and Company, home of the expatriate writer, great, small, and flatulent. I've put off a visit to this modest hovel for too long."

Frank was no writer. And he had no time for writers, unless they were singing the glories of his antique shop and bringing in more wealthy customers. He leaned on his cane and surveyed the surroundings, his eyes finally coming to light on Sylvia Beach.

Only Sylvia could smile in the face of pompous insult. "Mr. O'Connor." She rushed forward, hand outstretched. "You must be the man Jack has told me so much about."

Frank's eyes widened as she shook his big hand. "Jack has told you of me?" he asked increduously.

"Why, of course?" She was puzzled and the answer really did come out like a question.

"Then, Madam, you are most certainly a lady of the highest order." He bowed, but while most people bow from the waist, Frank has to do it from the knees—his waist disappeared long ago beneath too many cases of pate de fois gras.

"And why is that, Mr. O'Connor?" Sylvia's eyes twinkled.

"Because you have heard Jack's scurrilous lies and will still shake my hand without requiring that it be disinfected first."

And everybody laughed at that, except me. "Don't laugh so soon, Sylvia," I warned her. "Wait a few days for the incubation period to pass."

Frank's bald head gleamed and reflected the ceiling light. He turned to Hem. "Mr. Hemingway, how perfectly ordinary to see you again." Hem's smile fell a half inch or so. But then, Frank saw Arlaine, and a glow rose in his cheeks. "Ah, Mademoiselle, you must be one of the great authors harbored in this bastion of free speech. But, your youth and beauty shout innocence from the rooftops, and so you couldn't possibly write of life's iniquities. I have it. You write love poetry. You must. Your carriage, your beauty bespeaks love. Your—"

"—full of crap, Frank," I cut him off at the pass, so to speak. "This is Arlaine Watson."

"An American student, filling in as a clerk for me," Sylvia added.

All of us smiled at Arlaine's expense. Frank, on the other hand, was completely unmoved by his exposure.

"Jack," he began, eyeing me severely. "You and I need to have a long talk about polite behavior. Your conduct is regrettably lacking in the conventions of propriety."

"Don't think I'm not touched by your visit, Frank, but why are you here?"

"I am wounded, devastated. I came here out of my deep and abiding devotion for you, Jack Barnett, and you dash me upon the rocks of insult and disdain. Move!" he commanded Hemingway, who jumped aside. Slowly, almost painfully, he lowered himself into a chair behind the desk. "I may never rise again, so deeply am I hurt." He tucked his three chins against his chest and closed his eyes for dramatic effect.

"Frank, get to the point."

The head flew up and a mischevious grin lit his face. "You, sir, are in deep shit."

"Mr. O'Connor!" Sylvia's mouth flew open.

God, he loved shocking people. "It wouldn't be the first time," I reminded him.

"Mr. Barnett, Jack!"

"Please, Sylvia, the man has information to communicate. Reactions only bring on more shocks," I warned her. Hemingway was grinning from ear to ear. Arlaine's face was expressionless. I was pretty sure she'd seen her share of Frank O'Connors before.

The light from the ceiling glared off Frank's bald head again as he shifted in his seat. "I had a visitor this morning, Jack. Two visitors actually. Both were dressed rather stylishly. I anticipated unloading some of my junk, uh . . . I mean my treasures . . . on them. But, it seems they didn't come to shop."

"And what did they come for?" I played his silly game.

Frank shifted into his most sickeningly smug look. "Why, for you, Mr. Jack Barnett of Liberty, Missouri."

Ten

ell, ain't this a hell of a fine time," Hemingway said, leaning on the edge of the desk. "Who were they?"

"They claimed to be from the U.S. Embassy staff."

"Claimed to be?"

"I seldom spend time with the embassy staff and so, therefore, I'm not acquainted with everyone there, nor am I acquainted with official embassy identification papers. Never take anything for granted, Jack."

I felt like somebody had shoved their size fourteen shoes in my stomach. First, my own embassy sends somebody out to take a shot at me; then they follow it up with a couple of bozos on a fact-finding mission. And, ostensibly, all because I was trying to prove that James Joyce didn't kill anybody. I don't know why I was surprised. Absurdities marked my life.

"What did they want to know about me?"

"And did they give a reason for their inquiries?" Sylvia added.

Frank nodded, folding his three chins into four. "Yes, they gave an excellent reason. They said they were investigating allegations that Jack was involving himself, illegally, in French affairs."

"Well, that covers a lot of territory," Hem said.

"And what did you tell them?" Sometimes you had to drag information out of Frank.

"I told them it was ludicrous, absolutely without foundation. I knew for a fact you had never had a French affair. And I told them so in no uncertain terms."

"Please, Mr. O'Connor, this is all very important." Sylvia's aggravation showed.

"No, Sylvia," I said. "That's exactly what he told them. How did they react?" I turned back to Frank who let a big smile spread across his face.

"With the appropriate disgust, reminding me that theirs was an official inquiry. I reminded them that I was under no compulsion to cooperate. They were, after all, representatives of a foreign power. . . ."

"But you're still an American!" Hem interrupted.

"No," I answered. "He's not. Frank renounced his American citizenship at the end of the war."

Frank nodded. "A fact which I was forced to flaunt in their faces. They grumbled and I told them that, unless they were buying something of course, they should take their questions, and their derrières, elsewhere."

"You're an interesting man." Arlaine finally had something to say. Her tone was soft, but her eyes studied him with more than just minor interest.

"You're a perceptive woman." Frank smiled.

"I think I'm gonna be sick," I said. I lost women to people like Hemingway, not to the Frank O'Connors of the world. Of course, at that particular moment in my history, losing a woman had already lost some of its meaning. "What else happened?"

Frank turned his attention away from Arlaine and back to me. "Nothing, actually. They grunted something about my not knowing 'who I was messing with;' I think that's how they phrased it. I considered breaking wind as a symbol of my disdain for them—and to punctuate my desire for them to leave—but they seemed hardly worth the effort. At any rate, they climbed back into their *black* Model T and went on their way. I grabbed my hat and cane and immediately came to find you, waiting, of course, for them to get out of sight."

"Thanks, Frank. Glad you did."

"This doesn't make a damn bit of sense," Hemingway fumed. He paced around the desk and frowned.

"It makes a little anyway," I said. "Somebody at the embassy doesn't want me messing around in this murder."

"Or," Frank interrupted. "Somebody in the French government doesn't want you to, and that somebody has pull at the embassy. Never underestimate the power of political string-pulling."

"Well, certainly, that must be it," Arlaine echoed.

"Of course," Sylvia chimed in.

"I'm not sure the French could coerce the American embassy into making an attempt on an American national's life," I reminded them. "That doesn't jibe. Sure, sending some guys around to bully me, yeah, I can see them doing that. But not taking potshots. They must have some other stake in this, more than just a complaint from a French official. Unless, of course, the Reverend Quintin Karper is at the bottom of their efforts."

Frank's chins almost disappeared, so quickly did his head pop up and his neck stretch out. "Whom did you say?"

I had never seen Frank so intent on what someone else was saying. "I said, 'the Reverend Quintin Karper.' Do you know him?"

He leaned forward on his cane. "Would this minister of God be about my height and half my circumference?"

"Yeah," Hem answered.

"Does he, perhaps, perspire profusely?"

I was leaning forward now. "Like a race horse at the finish line."

Frank reclined in his seat and those bright, lively eyes sparkled nostalgically. "Awwh, the right Reverend Quintin Karper. A face, a voice, a pain in the ass out of my past."

"You know this guy?" Somehow, I couldn't figure Frank for having spent much time with Brother Karper.

"Of course, Jack. I'm surprised that you're surprised. I've always assumed that you're as fatalistic as I am. Not to mention just as cynical. It's one of your most appealing qualities. We will always be confronted by our own, personal goblins. They attach themselves to our posteriors and we drag them along like extra baggage all our lives. But because they are of a perverse nature, they delight in swinging around in front of us occasionally, just to trip us up, you see. Yes, Jack," Frank continued, the sparkle never dimming for an instant. "I know the Reverend Quintin Karper. He was the Baptist chaplain that, shall we say, discovered me inflagrante delicto with the baroness."

"I'll be a son of a bitch." There was nothing else, after all, to say.

"What baroness?" Arlaine asked, her confusion obvious.

"Yes, what baroness?" Sylvia echoed, just as perplexed.

Frank started to answer, and I held a hand up. "Save it for another day, Frank. Stick with the present topic."

"So," Frank continued, lancing me with his most disapproving look. "If you count Karper among your enemies, I say only to never underestimate him. He is quite the conniver. He may be the most morally immoral man I've ever known."

"Your warnings are hardly comforting."

"But heed them, my dear Jack. What part does Karper play in this drama?"

So, I ran it down for him, up to and including our latest run-in.

Frank nodded. "Typical Karpathian interference. Never take him at his word, and never doubt the depths of his hypocrisy. As to whether he did what he claims, only he knows for sure. But if he does carry any weight at the embassy, you can be sure he's used it."

"Even to the point of sending someone to kill Jack?" Arlaine asked.

"Yeah, why would they want to mort Jack here?" Hemingway hovered around my shoulder.

"Man is a wicked creature by nature and Karper is no different," Frank conceded. "But I know nothing, really, of any of this. Jack has not felt comfortable in confiding in me." The wounded look came back, and I rolled my eyes.

After a nod from me, Hem detailed everything that we knew. Frank, his chins tucked against his chest, nodded, frowned, smiled, and occasionally grunted as Hemingway hit the high points. Sylvia, who had missed much of the action, listened in rapt fascination. Arlaine, who had missed little of the action, browsed among the books. I watched Arlaine.

Finally Hem finished, and Frank put both hands on top of his cane and leaned forward. "Intriguing, absolutely intriguing. However, it requires more physical activity than I care to engage in. Despite," he struggled to his feet, supporting his bulk on the cane, "the role being played by my former nemesis. I would tell you, Jack, that the boy, Dounat—if Ernest's story has any credence— probably knows a great deal of the truth in this matter. The description Ernest gave paints a picture of a young man on the edge of cracking. Discover a chink in his armor and drive your sword home. He will break. I've seen hundreds like him in the confessional. They begin with a lie. Then, after a couple of deftly placed inquiries, they confess to every act of perversion they've ever committed. Find the flaw in his story and hammer him with it. He'll talk. Karper, on the other hand, will talk only if you nail him to the proverbial wall (or a cross if one's available).

"This Kopfmann," Frank continued. "I've heard of him from

some of my more literary clients. Just this morning, I overheard a young, lean-looking man talk about meeting a Herr Kopfmann at Nathalie Barney's tonight. You should be there, Jack."

"Why?"

"I recognized the lean-looking man. You will, too."

"Why the mystery, Frank?"

He smiled. "Consider it my perverse sense of humor."

I shrugged. I'd put a lot of things down to Frank's sense of humor. One more wouldn't matter. I thought. Arlaine had rejoined us, and she stood next to me, her arms crossed.

"Thanks for coming over, Frank. I owe you, like always."

Frank grinned his evil grin and raised his eyebrows. "Just come by and see me some time. After Nathalie's party tonight. We'll pretend it's the old days and you can confess more of your lurid perversions. And, Jack?"

"Yeah."

"Avoid black Model Ts and embassy officials. I suspect they're hazardous to your health." On that note, he spun around, quickly for a man of his bulk, and lumbered out of the shop.

"Lurid perversions?" Arlaine threw me a sharply pointed look.

"Frank exaggerates," I countered weakly. "Besides, I knew Frank in another time, another place. And," my voice grew stronger, "I never confessed to him in the traditional sense."

A laugh crinkled up around her eyes. "Well, where does that leave us?"

"Yeah, Jack." Hem circled the desk. He blocked out the posters of Arnold Bennett proclaiming the virtues of Ulysses. "Where does that leave us? I'd say we've got a hell of a fine mess on our hands, and some legwork to do."

"It's a hell of a mess all right," I agreed. Sylvia dragged a couple of chairs over, and we sat around the desk. Arlaine went back to twirling the rubber stamp thing. She seemed lost in thought. I found myself hoping I was the thought she was lost in. "Let's divide up chores. I've got to get a cable or two off on this Genoa Conference thing and some other things to get done. Hem, get back on Kopfmann. He'll be rolling out pretty soon probably."

"Jack!"

"Hem, you've already established a relationship. I've got a feeling he's connected to all this. Frank must feel that way too. And I trust his hunches." It was plain to see that Hem didn't like not being in charge, but he liked me—I knew that—and so he frowned and said okay. I turned to Sylvia. "Can we borrow Arlaine today?"

She nodded. "We're not officially reopening until tomorrow. And, anything to get Mr. Joyce out of this situation." Wrinkles were deepening around her eyes. "I tell all of you, under the strictest of confidences, I've committed a great deal of money to publishing *Ulysses*. If this isn't resolved and we're not allowed to complete what we started, Shakespeare and Company will close."

"Don't worry, Sylvia," Hem assured her. "We'll get it straight. Right, Jack?"

"Sure, Hem." But I wasn't convinced. Lurking around in the back of my head was the awful thought that maybe Joyce did kill this guy. How? Why? I didn't have any answers. But Joyce was in deep, scalding water.

"What do you want me to do?" Arlaine asked.

I stared into her eyes for a minute. God, she was lovely. "Check with some of Sylvia's neighbors and see what you come up with. Maybe somebody saw or heard something. I know." I put my hand up to stop her protest. "The police have already done that. But sometimes people don't tell the police everything. Some people, especially lecherous old men, would prefer talking to a pretty, young American girl."

She closed her mouth and pursed her lips. "Okay. What do you want to know?"

"Anything that will blow a hole in Paul Dounat's story or Quintin Karper's, and anything that will confirm Joyce's version of the events."

"What if I find something else? What if I find someone who not only corroborates Dounat's story, but adds to it? Or someone who saw Karper and Phillipe Jourdan together?" The look in her eyes was hard, almost brittle, daring me to answer.

Sylvia and Hem both scooted forward expectantly in their seats.

"Then we don't tell Duvall. Let him find his own information. And then we go to James Joyce and ask him just exactly what the hell he thought he was doing and how he expected to get away with it. And Sylvia cries into her empty bankbook. And Hem and I get drunk."

I'd never seen anyone more depressed than Sylvia Beach at that moment. From what she'd said, her whole ball of wax was riding on this crazy Irishman. If he went down, she'd be taking the fall too. And all of that was reflected in the sharpening angles of her face. She was one of the kindest people I'd ever known. I couldn't conceive of disappointing her. At least I didn't want to face that possibility.

"Hem, do you think Joyce did it?"

"No way, Jack, not after everything we've seen. He never morted anybody." Hem crossed his arms for emphasis.

"Arlaine, do you think Joyce killed that guy?"

She looked away for a second and then turned back, the hardness slowly smoothing. "No, Jack. Not really." The admission came softly.

"Well, I don't believe it either. Too much is going on here. We've just got to get it figured out before Duvall arrests Joyce and before the American Embassy shoots my ass off. I'll meet you two at Nathalie Barney's later." That was the good thing about Paris. You could always meet at a party or a bar later.

Arlaine and Hem headed for the front door, and I started after them, but Sylvia's hand closed on mine.

"Be careful, Jack. I don't like seeing friends of mine get shot." The smile in her eyes was genuine.

I slipped my hand out from under hers. "I don't want to get shot any more than you want me to. We'll get it worked out, Sylvia. I promise. Sylvia?"

"Yes, Jack."

"Is that the only light switch in the room?" I pointed to a back wall.

"Certainly."

"Okay."

"Thanks, Jack." She smiled again, and I slipped out the door.

• • • •

But being careful wasn't in my cards that day. I realized that when I felt the gun barrel poke into my back.

It didn't seem complicated at first. I left the shop and headed to a cable office to finalize the business about the economic conference. It'd been my unhappy experience that if you didn't let editors know your willingness to take on a job, you lost the job. And there were plenty of alternative reporters in Europe.

Winding my way through the street traffic on the Boulevard St. Germain, I stopped in front of a bakery to tie my shoe. Well, actually, I liked to smell the pastries and bread baking. Paris was a city of smells, some pungent, some delicate, all enticing, seductive.

But as I bent over, I sensed somebody walk up behind me, and then I felt the unmistakable thrust of a gun barrel stab me in the kidney.

"Stand up very slowly," a harsh, eastern European voice demanded.

"Is there a problem?" I straightened, but didn't turn around. The barrel was blunted, and I figured he had it concealed in his coat pocket, especially since nobody else on the street seemed very concerned.

"You are the problem, Mr. Barnett. Walk to the automobile at the curb." He used the American tag, but the voice was heavy Russian.

Without turning my head, I swung my eyes over to a brown car, a Citroën. My heart had skipped two of its last three beats and was now pumping double time to cover lost ground. Running for it seemed like the best idea. At least, it seemed that way until I caught a glimpse of the guy's eyes as I turned to check the sidewalk traffic.

Penetrating brown eyes, unmoving, unyielding. Brown is supposed to be a warm color, but I've never seen colder brown eyes before.

Nope. Running was out of the question. I knew from that one glance that this guy would shoot a dozen other people just for a clear shot at me.

He jabbed my kidney again, and I stumbled forward towards the car. Without turning around I crouched and climbed into the backseat. My companion, dark brown hair to match his brown eyes, slipped in beside me. The front seat had a blond-haired occupant, and the driver pulled the auto away from the curb without any instructions.

"Want to tell me where we're going?" I figured even a condemned man had a right to a last request, and I wondered how long they would wait before they shot me.

I got a sneer for my trouble. This guy knew how to sneer. One whole side of his upper lip rose past his nose. He was clean-shaven, young, twenty-two or so, I figured. His clothes weren't very fashionable, workmanlike, rough and sturdy, but he didn't hide the pistol in a pocket after we got in the auto, and it looked clean, shiny, and efficient.

"Someone wishes to speak with you," he finally snarled.

"Great," I said with a smile, my heart bouncing between my stomach and throat. "Who?"

This time I was left with just the sneer for an answer.

Since they didn't seem intent on killing me, I leaned back in the seat and tried to enjoy the ride. It didn't take long to figure out they were headed south of the city, one of the suburbs probably, but my companion wasn't inclined to talk a lot, and the driver never turned his head, so I spent the time staring out the window and wondering why in the hell I'd gotten myself mixed up in this mess.

After at least a half hour, we pulled into the courtyard of a small farmhouse. I didn't know enough about Parisian suburbs to know exactly where we were, and the house was fairly nondescript. Stone walls, a brown roof, a cow and chicken loitering around the house. Another Citroën was parked in the circular driveway. Change the stone to clapboard and it could be Missouri. For some reason, the resemblance didn't give me any comfort.

"Out!" my companion commanded.

I climbed down out of the auto and looked around. No way to escape. I was an expert at escape. Twice during the war I was captured and sent to Germany. Twice I got away. Hell, the second time I made it back just in time to go on my last patrol. I should have stayed in Germany.

Right then, though, clear escape avenues weren't plentiful. Nonexistent was a better word. I had one guy poking me in the ribs again with his pistol. The driver was walking up to the front door. A third man lounged at the corner of the house, making no effort to conceal his rifle.

"You mind telling me who you are?" If my heart kept pounding like it was, I wouldn't need to escape. It would explode.

Sneer (my new name for him) just grunted and shoved me toward the house. I regained my footing and crunched across the gravel, onto the cobblestone walk, and up to the door. The driver held the door, and I felt a jolt of blunt pain as Sneer's gun tried to dig a hole in my back again.

It was dark in the house. The shutters were closed and a single coal oil lamp, centered on the one table, provided the only illumination. The lamp sent spiked fingers of light around the room, leaving patches of darkness just beyond its fingertips. The room held only the table and two chairs.

The lack of furniture wasn't the strangest thing about the scene, though. A man sat in one of the chairs, facing the table, but his features were shrouded in darkness, and only his linen shirt caught the light. It was eery.

Sneer pushed me into the empty chair and faded into the background. The lamp's glare blocked the man's face even more effectively than the darkness, and I squinted against the light.

"Who are you?" I took the offensive. What the hell, I was either dead or I wasn't.

The figure shifted slightly in his seat. "Why do you investigate the murder at the bookshop? Do you work for the Germans?" His voice was a guttural, deep Russian like my other new friend's.

"No." No harm in telling him that. "My friend owns the shop. Sylvia Beach. James Joyce is her friend."

"But why?" His tone was harshly insistent, and his body leaned forward slightly, light hitting his square chin and thin mouth.

"I told you. She's a friend. She doesn't think Joyce did it and neither do I."

"What do you know of April 7th?"

"It's the seventh day of the fourth month."

"Answer me!"

This guy was crazy. "I don't know *anything* about April 7th!"

"Tell me what you know!"

"Are you deaf, you moron? I don't know anything about April 7th!"

He nodded, and I felt the rush of air before the fist collided with my temple. Jesus! This pink haze floated over everything, but I stayed in my seat and shook my head to clear it.

My interrogator straightened, receding again into the darkness. "You will stop your investigation immediately. The Irishman killed the pig rapist. Do not pursue it."

"Sorry. Can't do it. The pig may have been a pig, and he may have deserved killing, but James Joyce didn't do the honors," I said, keeping the trembling in my voice to a minimum.

He must have nodded again; I saw the bottom of his chin sink from the shadows and dip into the light, revealing a dark, block cut mustache.

"Oh, Shit!" The words slipped out as the fist made a repeat visit to my head. I jerked back, the stinging shudder rippling across my face.

"You will stop your investigation." The voice showed no emotion.

"You've already said that." My head was still spinning. From the corner of my eye, I saw the head bob again.

I rode out the next slap as best I could. Knowing it was coming helped, but the ringing in my ears got louder and the spinning got faster, and the force of the blow sent me to the hardwood floor. A fingernail must have scraped my cheek. I felt a thin trickle of something warm start down my face.

I struggled upright and climbed back into the chair. You've heard of "stubborn as a Missouri mule?" Well, I was the jackass they were talking about. "Hey!" I shouted to still the spinning in my head. "The hell with you! I'll do whatever I damn well please!"

My hand hurt; I'd picked up a splinter from the floor, and the warm, slow trickle at my cheek reached my chin. I looked around and saw Sneer and the driver standing by the front door. Another door was centered in the wall behind my table companion. I measured the distance and decided against it. Sneer would tackle me in a heartbeat.

The guy across the table hadn't spoken for several seconds. Finally, he leaned forward. "Leave . . . Paul Dounat . . . alone!" The words came out in a shouted whisper.

"Leave what alone? Shit!" I went tumbling again. No way around it. I was gonna look like hell. Lying on the floor, I wiped the blood from my cheek and gently touched the lump growing on my temple.

In the shadows I saw a figure move next to the man at the table. Something wet touched the corner of my eye, and I guessed he must have split the skin somewhere up there too. My head throbbed and my heart raced. I stayed on the floor and tried to regain my senses. But, I heard a voice, a French voice, whisper to my interrogator, and my head started clearing real fast.

"Comrade. Someone may have seen him leave with us."

So they were Communists. I kept acting like I was mortally wounded, which was more real than act, and the guy at the table nodded towards the voice.

Suddenly, I was jerked up by my arms and dangled between Sneer and the driver. The man at the table sat impassively, never moving.

"Do not interfere!"

I didn't answer, just let myself be suspended between the two. As long as they were holding me, I figured I couldn't get hit. After a second, they spun me around and marched back through the front door, across the courtyard, and tossed me into the auto.

Curled up in a corner, I licked my wounds, so to speak, while Sneer and the driver took up their places again, and the vehicle started moving back towards Paris.

"You know," I said finally. "It's not polite to invite somebody over and beat the hell out of them." If they hadn't killed me already, they wouldn't do it then.

Sneer sneered and looked out the window. He crossed his hands in his lap, and I noticed that his trimmed fingernails were streaked in blood. So, he was the one who had administered my beating. I studied his features for a long second; I'd remember him. And I hoped a chance came around to repay the favor.

Another thirty minutes of silence passed, and we were back on the Boulevard St. Germain. The auto pulled to the curb, and Sneer gave me one of those looks. Our time together was over. I can't say I was sad.

I slipped open the door, and as I half-climbed, half-tumbled out onto the sidewalk, I turned back in time to see the Citroën slide back into the traffic.

Straightening my clothes, I touched my wounds softly. One cut on my temple, one on my cheek, and the left side of my lower lip was swelling. If I looked bad naturally, I looked even worse after Sneer's beauty treatment. But a new piece had been added to the puzzle. The Communists absolutely wanted nothing done about the murder. James Joyce could fry as far as they were concerned. And Paul Dounat knew something. That was obvious. Our little visit to Dounat's flat must have scared the hell out of them. All of a sudden the thing seemed to start boiling down into some kind of grudge match, and James Joyce was a convenient scapegoat.

"Herr Barnett?"

I shuddered at the accent and turned slowly, right into the business end of a German Luger. It was definitely *not* my best day.

Eleven

'D o not be concerned." He was about five feet ten inches, wearing a nice suit with one of those leather cape-looking things over his shoulders. The pistol barrel protruded from within, but just beyond the edge, of the cape. "Someone wishes to speak with you."

My head hurt, my temple throbbed, and I could feel the crusty blood cracking on my cheek as I spoke. "So what else is new?"

He motioned toward a waiting Hispano-Suiza—a fine, sleek, touring car—parked at the corner. I looked around for some help, but I didn't see anybody I knew. The sidewalk was pretty full, but nobody noticed the gun; they all had somewhere else to be. Lucky them.

I climbed into the car and tried to ease back into the seat, but my shoulder was getting sore, from slamming against the floor of that farmhouse probably, and I couldn't get comfortable. My new escort slid in beside me, but this time there were two goons in the front seat. At least, I sighed to myself, nobody's sneering.

"Your friends were not gentle with you," my gun-toting companion said. He let his hand stray up towards my temple, and I caught it in my paw.

"Are you a doctor?"

"No." His eyes locked with mine.

"Then, don't mess with it." I'd seen his kind before. "Where are we going?"

He tucked his hand back into a coat pocket, keeping the gun in the other trained on me. "I told you. Someone wishes to speak with you." He spoke precisely, with little accent.

"I must be a popular person. Who is this 'someone'?" I thought it was a fair question, but my host didn't answer, just smiled a subtle kind of smile.

Didn't take long to figure out that we weren't headed outside the city. The two guys in the front didn't speak at all as we winded our way through narrow streets, headed deeper and deeper into one of Paris' more seedy districts. These three weren't as surly as the Communists, not that I cared for any of them. But, despite the gun pointed at my belly, these guys were less hostile, and I considered that a good sign.

The automobile finally stopped in front of a small pension—a boarding house—on the outskirts of the city, in the 13th Arrondissement I figured it. It was a plain, brown, dull-looking building. My buddy in the backseat motioned for the door, and I slid out, the pain in my shoulder becoming more than just a little unbearable.

The cobblestone was uneven and jarred me as I walked across. The guy behind didn't prod me along with the gun, and I was thankful for that. My kidney couldn't take another jolt.

"Upstairs," one of them directed. "Deuxieme etage." His French was weak and came out with a rough, Germanic accent.

We climbed the stairs to the second floor landing, and the guy with the pistol stepped in front of me and opened the door without knocking. I walked in.

A musty odor lingered in the air, like the place had been shut up for a long time. My kidnappers had something about rooms without furniture. This one, too, just had a single table with two chairs. They must all have the same manual, I thought. But then, I couldn't see the Communists and the Nazis playing out of the same book. And, if the ones before had been Communists, these Germans had to be members of the NSDAP.

The guy sitting behind the table had a vaguely familiar look to him. Thin-faced, his skin looked a little windburned, and he held himself erect in his dark business suit. He smiled at me with a tight little smile.

"Herr Barnett, sit, sit." He waved a hand at the chair opposite him. His voice was friendly and relaxed. "Cigarette?"

My companion from the auto appeared beside me with a pack. I shook my head. "Do I know you?" Something about my host was damn familiar, too familiar.

He smiled again. "We have never really met, but we have seen each other before."

"You hang out at the race tracks?"

"Nein." He shook his head and kept that tight little smile.

"I know, you spend time at the Brasserie Lipp?" That had to be it.

"Nein," he said, waving his hand. "It is not important. You will remember some day and we will have a drink to our common history. At this time, I would like to ask you a few questions."

I leaned back in the chair, adjusting my shoulder for comfort. These guys were being reasonably polite. "Shoot."

He smiled again at that. "You are investigating the death of Karl Pfeiffer?"

"Yeah."

"You do not believe it was the Irish writer, James Joyce?"

"No, I don't." That was pretty safe to admit.

"This reporter, Ernest Hemingway, he does not believe that Joyce is the murderer?"

"The last time I checked he didn't." These guys were being too polite to be killers. "Look," I began. "Who are you people and where is this headed?"

He held up that hand again to silence me. "Please, just a few moments more."

I shrugged.

The guy turned his profile to me, and another vague memory poked me in the ribs. I *had* seen him before, but I just couldn't remember where. He stared off across the room and out a window for a long minute. "Karl Pfeiffer," he said finally, "was a good friend of mine. We shared many beliefs, and it was very unfortunate when he was killed. We must learn the details of his death. It is important that we know everything surrounding his murder. I take his death as a personal insult."

God, these Junkers, and that's the way he held himself, took everything as a personal insult. But, I was intrigued by something else he said. "By 'we' I assume you're referring to the NSDAP."

Shakespeare could have been describing this guy when he said "a lean and hungry look." His head whipped around, and a wolf-like expression streamlined his face. "What do you know of the NSDAP?"

I checked my watch. It was getting on up into the afternoon. I didn't have time for this bull. "Let's get to the point here. You—

whoever you are—are a German nationalist. I just came back from a little discussion with the Communists. You guys nab me and—though I admit you have more manners—you're playing the same cat and mouse game the Reds did. Just get to the point. What do you want with me?"

That same tight smile tempered the sharp angles in his face. He puffed on a cigarette lazily. "You are an interesting man, Herr Barnett. I knew that. I knew that should we meet on a more personal level the challenge would be just as great as our more professional meetings. We would like to hire you to investigate the death of Karl Pfeiffer. Since you are already involved, we simply require that you pass along the identity of the murderer when you acquire that information. Money is not one of our greatest resources, but on this occasion we can afford to be generous. We will pay you five hundred U.S. dollars for your assistance."

I gulped. Five hundred bucks was a lot of money. I tried to keep the idiotic grin off my face and replace it with something approaching boredom. "Look, pal. I've already had a collision with a pack of blood-thirsty Bolsheviks; the fact that you're part of the Workers' Party is hardly a secret at this point. What I can't figure out is why one of your boys ended up with a knife in his back in Sylvia Beach's bookstore, and why the Reds want me to keep my nose out of it?"

He smiled again. "Precisely our problem as well. Will you accept our offer?"

I waited a good long time. My buddy from the Hispano slipped a cup of coffee on the table in front of me, and I sipped it. It tasted warm and good. "Under one condition," I said finally.

"And what is that?"

"That you keep your goons away from me and give me some breathing room. I've got too many people interested in what I'm doing. It makes it difficult to work. How can I contact you when I need you?"

He pulled a pen and piece of paper from a breast pocket and scribbled something. Almost in slow motion, he slid the scrap across the table towards me. "Send me a telegram at that address when you have information."

"I've got a couple of questions." The guy raised his eyebrows like he was interested, so I plunged in. "What was Karl Pfeiffer doing in Paris?"

"He was here on business."

"Political business?"

"Perhaps, in a manner of speaking. You might say it was a collaborative effort."

"With who? The Commies?"

A laugh rose from him, loud and scoffing. "Never the Communists. They are a disease. I am not at liberty to reveal our, 'partners' shall we say. Besides, what I know of this murder, it may have nothing to do with his business."

"Was Pfeiffer connected with the American preacher, Quintin Karper?"

If he could have looked more puzzled, I couldn't imagine it.

"I do not know this Quintin Karper. He had some relationship with Karl?" The innocence seemed genuine.

"Forget it. Just a question. I've got to ask you. Why all the interest?" Five hundred dollars was a lot of interest.

"It is important that we know the truth of it." He nodded, almost unnoticeably, and my traveling companions appeared on my flanks. "They will take you anywhere you wish to go."

I stood and started towards the door, escorted by my new friends.

"Herr Barnett?"

I turned back around.

"You really don't remember me, do you?"

"Somewhere in the back of my mind," I admitted, "I know I've seen you before. But for the life of me, I can't figure out where."

He laughed. "Perhaps, when we meet again, I'll be able to refresh your memory." And he laughed again.

I turned back and kept moving towards the door. Behind me, he laughed over and over and over again.

• • • •

The shoulder still hurt like hell as I paid the girl for the cable to Cincinnati. I rolled it around, trying to loosen the muscles while I pushed the door open. A little bell jingled, and I stepped back out onto the sidewalk. My new employers had dropped me off at a cable office on the Boulevard St. Germain and sped away in their auto.

My watch said four in the afternoon, and I wondered where the day had gone. Not much had gotten accomplished, that was for damn sure. My nose twitched a time or two, and my stomach rumbled. It occurred to me that I hadn't eaten anything all day, except that cup of Nazi coffee. Which wasn't bad coffee, mind you, but it wasn't a good strong cup of Missouri joe.

"Hey! Jack!"

I looked around and saw Hemingway headed down the sidewalk. As cocksure of himself as he was, I couldn't help but like him. His grin was, well, infectious. "I thought you were following that German."

"He got out of bed about an hour ago. Now, he's encamped at Michaud's for a late breakfast." Hem was out of breath by the time he caught up with me.

I checked my watch again. Yep, four o'clock. "No wonder the Heinies lost the war. Hell, they don't know what time of day to eat breakfast."

"What in the hell happened to you, Jack. Somebody try to mort you? Jesus H. Christ! You've got enough bruises on your face to have gone ten rounds with Sullivan."

"No, just some Communist bum."

"You've got to learn to lead with your left, Jack. Maybe you better join Ezra and me for a few rounds." Hem's eyebrows knitted together in concern.

"No thanks. I've already had a few rounds." The last thing I wanted was Ezra or Hemingway taking pokes at my face. "Let's go grab a bite and I'll fill you in."

"Sure, Jack, sure."

We headed to the Cafe aux deux Magots since it was closer, and my stomach was sending out shock waves that could rattle Notre Dame Cathedral. Hem told me about his short and singularly uneventful day with Kopfmann. He'd come up with a big goose egg, zilch, zero. I almost wished I could have said the same. The only wounds Hem had to show were from boredom. My shoulder punctuated the thought with knife-like pains as we sat down at a back corner table. This time, I sat with my back to the wall. I figured there was no use tempting fate.

"So where'd you get the bruises, Jack?"

"Well, let's see. First, I was kidnapped by the Communists. They banged me up."

"Geez. But that means. . . ."

I held up my hand to stop him. "I'm not finished. Then, I was kidnapped by a bunch of German Nationalists and they served coffee."

Hem's eyebrows made one thick, dark line across his forehead.

I'd never seen him in such deep concentration. "This thing's a mess, huh? Coffee. Geez, pal. Maybe this Nazi crowd ain't so bad after all."

"They're just as slimy as the Communists; the only difference is they're more polite about it. Besides, they hired me to investigate the murder at Shakespeare and Company."

"Gawd, Jack! You're working for them?"

"Why not? Hell, they offered me five hundred dollars for the name of the murderer. Why not take their money for doing something I was gonna do anyway?"

"But what if you don't find the murderer?"

"Then I don't get paid, I guess. But, I think I'm getting pretty close." I told him about the conversations with both groups. "None of them would be showing any interest if they didn't think I was zeroing in. And this German guy's reaction to Quintin Karper told me everything I needed to know. Unless Pfeiffer was doing some kind of independent job for Karper, then the Reverend is lying."

"Don't rule out that Pfeiffer had two bosses. Look at you. But ain't none of this pulling the noose from around James Joyce's neck either," Hem pointed out.

"There's still time. I've just got to nail down all the loose ends. That's all." I noticed a shadow fall across the table. Thinking it was the waiter, I said, "I'll have some sausages and eggs" in French.

"Sorry, I don't take orders from you." But the voice and the words were as American as apple pie.

I looked up, and two guys in brown, double-breasted suits hovered over the table. One had grayish hair and bags under his bespectacled eyes; the other was as redheaded as Ezra Pound.

"You Jack Barnett?" the redhead asked.

"What's it to you?" Hem jumped in.

The redhead didn't like it, and I saw his fist tighten. The older guy put a hand on his shoulder, and he relaxed, reluctantly.

"Mind if we sit down?" the gray-haired guy asked.

"Go ahead," I answered.

He reached inside his suit pocket as he and his partner dropped into chairs. A card of some kind, official-looking and embossed with the U.S. seal, appeared in his hand. It identified him as one H. Winston Miller, special attaché at the U.S. Embassy.

"So, Mr. H. Winston Miller, what can I do for you?" I figured that if they were willing to identify themselves, they weren't gonna

138

kill me in the middle of a crowded cafe. They had something else on their minds.

He smiled in a fake, political kind of way. "We understand you have some interest in a murder committed at Shakespeare and Company Bookstore two nights ago."

I smiled back. "That's right. I do."

"It would be in everyone's best interest, Mr. Barnett," the red-head began in a rough voice, "if you found yourself other things to occupy your time."

"A little late for that, I think," I replied with a tight, smug look. Out of the corner of my eye, I saw Hem grin.

"And how is that?"

"I'm currently employed by two interested parties—Miss Beach, owner of the bookstore, and certain German gentlemen." Okay, I was stretching the truth a bit, but what the hell.

"You seem to be misunderstanding us, Mr. Barnett." The old guy got back into it. "This is really more of a," and he coughed politely, "directive as opposed to a request."

"You seem to be misunderstanding me, Mr. H. Winston Miller. This has been one bitch of a day. I've been interrogated and beaten by Reds, served coffee by German Nationalists, and now I'm being threatened by my own government. Rubbing elbows with lunatic fringe groups—and right now the U.S. Government fits that bill— has never been my idea of a good time. Make no mistake, pal, I don't take kindly to 'directives,' especially from people who shoot at me from black Model Ts." H. Winston Miller flinched, and I didn't care. My shoulder hurt like hell; I was in a bad mood, and H. Winston had planted himself on my wrong side. "As a member of the press, I think the American people would find it odd that their embassy personnel have time to drive around and shoot at one of their own citizens."

"And," Hem added, a hard, nasty look in his eyes, "as another member of the press, I'm sure that my editors would truly love to get some copy on this."

"You see, H. Winston, too many people know about the pot-shot that you folks took at Mr. Hemingway and myself. Were you to get that dramatic again, I'm sure that certain people in the States would have questions for you. I've been around long enough to know that the Secretary of State isn't always pleased with actions his ambassadors take. Don't forget, Miss Beach's family is very well-connected in Washington." That much was true. Her father had been Woodrow Wilson's preacher.

The redhead started to say something, but Miller touched his sleeve. "Perhaps we got off on the wrong foot." Miller's tone oozed diplomatic slime. "Perhaps some early decisions were in error. Let's start over. Your government would greatly appreciate it if you could arrange to move more slowly in this affair."

"Sorry, I'm working on a deadline as it is. But tell me something, H. Winston. Why are you people so interested in the death of a member of a small German political party? You're not, by chance, working on something with them? Or maybe you're involving yourself at the request of the right Reverend Quintin Karper?"

I received an utterly blank look for my efforts and a noncomittal, "Sorry, Mr. Barnett. That's something we can't discuss."

"Then, I'm afraid Mr. Hemingway and I can't be cooperative."

The redhead stabbed across the table and jerked my arm. "Look, you moron, this is none of your affair! Somebody's already worked your face over. You're out of your league. Get out before you get hurt."

I didn't see Hem move. But the next thing I knew, the redhead was laid out on the floor, and Hem was rubbing his knuckles. H. Winston Miller sat silently shaking his head. "This won't sit well," he said finally, while his partner lay on the floor and the other patrons stared at him. He stood and helped the redhead to his feet. "I'm sure we'll meet again, Mr. Barnett." And they were gone.

"Did you hurt your hand?" I asked him as our guests disappeared from view.

He grinned, spreading his mustache into a thin line. "Naw. The guy's got pitiful reaction time. Ezra could take him in three rounds."

The real waiter showed up then, and I ordered sausages and a beer. "Well, the day's almost complete, Hem. All three parties have been heard from."

"Yeah," Hem laughed. "And you look like you've been to three parties." He stopped chuckling and turned half serious. "What I can't figure, Jack, is why these guys from the embassy are up to their necks in it. I mean, these German nationalist grunts and Communists, sure. They chase each other all over the place anyway. And this thing at Sylvia's is beginning to look like a blood feud between them. But, why are our guys into it? Why could we possibly care about these idiots killing each other off?"

The waiter showed up and delivered my sausage and beer and gave Hem his rum St. James. I dove in and chewed for a while without answering Hem's mostly rhetorical question. We fell silent, and Hem pulled out a pad and pencil and started scribbling.

"What are you working on?"

"A story." He didn't look up. When Hem got into what he was doing, he wrote with an almost fierce concentration.

I got the feeling he didn't want to be disturbed, but I couldn't help myself. "What's it about?"

"It's about the war," he grunted, pausing for a second and considering his words. "But," and he crossed something out, "I don't want to mention the war in it."

"Neat trick if you can pull it off," I said, shoving another sausage into my mouth.

A few more minutes and the meal was rumbling around in my stomach. I wiped my mouth, and Hem stowed his pad and pencil away. "I don't know, Hem," I began. "I don't like the looks of any of this either. Obviously, something about the murder is of pretty strong interest to Uncle Sam. I think it's clear now that the shot they took at us was just to scare us off. H. Winston and his buddy wouldn't have been here today if they wanted to kill us. If they wanted us dead, we'd be dead. It's as simple as that. Karper is one possible explanation. If he's got any connections at all, he might get the embassy to give him a hand."

"But something about the Nazis hiring you bothers me. It don't seem right."

I shrugged. "Hey, you and I both know that they'd slit their mothers' throats if the need arose. Their man got axed. It makes them look more respectable if they hire me to look into it. Plus, I obviously have some limited connections with the Paris police. That doesn't bug me as much as the Communists slugging me across the jaw and telling me to leave Paul Dounat alone. Which tells me–"

"Which tells me," Hem interrupted, "that we need to go have another little gab fest with him."

"Right. But let's not rush into anything. He's not going anywhere and I want to see what Arlaine came up with. If he's lying the way we think he is, we're going to have to break his story some way. She stands the best chance of doing that." I checked my watch. "It's four-thirty. What time does Nathalie Barney start her little soirées?"

"Five usually. The earlier you get there the better. Sometimes there'll be a couple of hundred wandering around the Temple de l'Amitie," Hem let the phrase roll off his tongue, and his face held a silly grin.

"Yeah, right. Let's go by my place first and get me cleaned up." I touched the scrape on my cheek tenderly, flinching at the sting. "Later, all three of us can pay a visit to Paul Dounat again."

•   •   •   •

Nathalie Barney was an institution on the Paris social scene. She lived in an old, old house over on rue Jacob. I didn't know her very well, but once I went to one of her parties because somebody told me lots of women were always there. But, as my luck ran, my informant neglected to tell me that the women went there for exactly the same reason. Needless to say, I was somewhat disappointed.

To be fair, though, Nathalie wasn't exclusive in her preferences. She was partial to a girl named Romaine Brooks who I knew vaguely. But Nathalie did have a few male friends. And, except for certain personal problems, I wouldn't have minded being one of those friends; Nathalie was a damn good-looking woman. Some weird things went on at Nathalie's "salons," as she called them. In the garden behind the house, she had this big Greek temple built. Engraved over the entrance were the words "Temple A l'Amitie"— Temple of Friendship. I'd heard about some of the dances and concerts Nathalie had sponsored. Anyway, she was a character.

Hemingway and I paused for a minute outside her house and just stared up at the big stone building. "Hell of a house," I grunted.

"Yeah, ain't it though," Hem agreed. "I try to stay away from these things. Miss Stein doesn't care a lot for Nathalie, but Ezra hangs out here some. I think Joyce even comes over occasionally. He's not exactly welcome at Miss Stein's."

"I've heard, and if I hadn't, last night was a pretty good tip-off."

"Yeah, you'd have to be deaf and blind to have missed it." Hem nodded.

A quartet of young Parisian girls, early twenties I guessed, giggled past us and into the house. From the courtyard, I could hear the strains of violin music. Things were heating up early. Several autos already lined the street.

"Well, Jack. Might as well dive in." Hem ushered me ahead of him.

"Chicken," I accused, stepping through the front door and into the foyer.

A dozen people milled around in the ornate entranceway. Since it was still early, I didn't see any of the activities I'd heard about. Even more people came in behind us and sort of pushed us through the house. Some little Chinese fellow stuck cups of tea in our hands, and I sipped mine while I scanned the growing crowd for Arlaine, with more than just a little anticipation rumbling in my stomach.

"Hell of a crowd," I mumbled. A pair of women were in a corner holding hands, and they weren't just being best friends. It's not so much that I had a problem with that—hell, a lot of my friends lived in that world—but something in my Liberty, Missouri upbringing kicked me in the ribs when I saw it in public.

"It ain't real pretty, is it, Jack?" Hem nodded at the couple.

"Where are you from, Hem?"

"Illinois, more or less."

"Things in Paris are a little more cosmopolitan than Illinois or Missouri, I figure. Most of the time I like the way things are here. You know, nobody holding me up to some stylized measuring stick of behavior. But, other times, the Missouri in me comes out."

"Yeah," Hem agreed, a distant look occupying his eyes. "It makes me think of other times, times when it," and he looked back at the couple in the corner, "didn't seem so cultured. Times," he went on, lightly fingering the cup of tea, "when a man had to use a knife to avoid . . . some things."

I looked at him then. "You're a funny guy, Hem."

"How so, Jack?" His eyes began to laugh again.

"One minute I've got you pegged one way, and then you come out with something like that."

"I'm not that complicated, Jack. I just want to write."

"A noble ambition, young man. One I aspire to myself some day." The voice boomed from behind us. I didn't even bother to turn around.

"I thought you wanted me to come over *after* this thing, Frank," I said as Frank O'Connor's hand draped itself over my shoulder. "And besides, don't you find the atmosphere here a little stifling for a man of your heterosexual inclinations?"

He winked at me. "Ahhh, Jack. You misjudge some of these fine young women. Many of them are very liberal in thought and not so narrowminded as you. I've often found some pleasant diversion as a result of one of Nathalie's salons. Besides, my desire to see you with my visitor from this afternoon got the best of me."

"That's right, Frank. This is some kind of world's record. You left your shop twice in one day."

Frank chuckled and Hem had the gall to laugh at us.

"You two ought to start a vaudeville routine. I knew the minute I lamped him that he was a hell of a good guy," Hem pronounced. Something beyond the door in one of the other rooms caught his attention, and he discreetly motioned someone towards us.

"Jack?" I heard her voice and turned towards her. She looked good. Okay, what the hell, she looked great. Arlaine was wearing one of those pretty new dresses that came just below the knee. It was ivory, and I was warming up already. And that was something that hadn't happened to me in a while, a long while.

"Yeah." I couldn't say much else. She was looking only at me, and I saw from the corner of my eye that Hem and Frank weren't real pleased. As Hem would say, we were a hell of a crew—nothing but a bunch of centers of attention.

"What happened to your face?" A hand went up and brushed the scrape at my temple. It felt better than good.

"I ran into some new friends." I pulled my little troop over into a corner and quickly explained the day's events to Arlaine and Frank.

"Then it's settled. Paul Dounat was lying." She quit looking at me and stared blankly at a wall.

"He may be," Hem began, "but we've got no way in hell of proving it."

"Right now we don't. Unless," and I turned back to Arlaine, "you came up with something to dynamite his case."

She quickly shook her head. "No. Nobody saw anything, or if they did, they aren't saying. Did you find anything out about the German, Ernest?" she asked Hem.

"He likes to drink, but then so do I. How long are we going to stay here, Jack? I'd sort of like to get back to Hash."

"Just hang on to your pants. I want to see who this German, Kopfmann, is going to meet here."

"Yes, yes, by no means can we forego that little pleasure," Frank interjected. "That's the sole reason I came."

"Let's make a move towards the courtyard," Hem suggested. He was looking sideways at two women in the opposite corner. One was sliding her hand up the dress of the other.

"Yeah." I grimaced. "Looks like they need to make a move upstairs."

We weaved through the crowd and into the courtyard where Nathalie's impeccably Grecian temple stood. Four Doric columns fronted the building, and a set of concrete steps led up to the porch and two tall, wooden doors. A string quartet played soft music on one side of the courtyard. The slight hum of spring insects blended with the music and made it seem almost like an evening concert in the park back in Liberty, Missouri. But, sure enough, there, in front of the temple, stood Kopfmann, tea in hand, right next to the lean Nazi who had been so accommodating that afternoon. The man turned towards me.

"Herr Barnett, so good to see you again. Herr Hemingway told me much about you last night. I hoped we would have the chance to speak again." Kopfmann was all smiles. He paused long enough to turn to his companion, "Allow me to introduce a countryman of mine, indeed one of our heroes from the recent war, Hermann Goering."

Twelve

I t all came rushing back, and my brain was in a nosedive. I numbly stuck out my hand and shook his. The smile on his face was priceless. He knew he had me.

Hermann Goering had commanded Manfred Von Richthofen's squadron after the old Red Baron was downed in April of 1918. He was right, back in that room in the 13th Arrondissement; we had met before—at 8,000 feet and flying one hundred miles an hour. Twice I crossed swords with Goering. And twice we called it a draw. Once, in fact, we both ran out of ammunition almost simultaneously. The other time we nicked each other's fuel lines and had to call it quits. Neither instance lasted more than a few minutes, but we knew each other in ways that others could only imagine.

Hemingway was quiet. That was the first thing I noticed. I'd been staring into Goering's eyes for a long minute, the wind of memory whipping against my face, and the conversations around us had died to fragmented whispers.

"Herr Goering," I croaked finally. "It's good to see you again, under more . . . comfortable circumstances."

His wolf's smile never wavered, and no hint showed in his face or voice that we had met earlier that day. "Herr Barnett, I remember your exploits very well. You were a remarkable adversary."

"So were you. So were you. What brings you to Paris?" I changed the subject.

"The springtime, Herr Barnett. Everyone talks of Paris in the springtime. I came to see if what they said was true."

"And?"

The smile never faltered. "Paris is a beautiful city. And I get the chance to see old friends. A most worthwhile visit. But, it's so seldom that I'm able to see one of my old enemies."

"That must have been a hell of a fine time," Hem said, a look of wonder in his eyes.

Goering glanced at him casually. "It was; it was. Herr Barnett was a skillful pilot, difficult to manuever in front of one's sights. We often wondered what happened to you, Herr Barnett." He turned back to me. "We heard that you landed suddenly after flaming one of our planes. An observation balloon spotted you scoring the victory, but then saw you make what seemed to be an emergency landing. And then, nothing. Your plane never appeared in the sky again."

Everyone focused on me then—Frank, Hem, Arlaine, and a bunch of others I didn't know. Sweat beaded on my forehead. I only faced that flight in my dreams, never in the open, in daylight. "The war ended soon after, Herr Goering," I stammered. "And we were all anxious for that."

"True, true," Goering agreed, his eyes boring into me even deeper. "But not so soon as that." He paused and my stomach fluttered. "The past should be left in the past, Herr Barnett." The smile broke across his face again. "Why, look at us; we are no longer enemies. We can talk here like old comrades."

I almost slumped in relief. "Of course."

"You flew against Jack in the war?" Arlaine asked, sending my stomach sweeping into Immelmans again.

Leave it alone, I thought. Leave it the hell alone.

But Goering didn't hear my silent pleadings and turned his charm on. "Oh, of course, my dear Fraulein—"

"Watson," she answered, extending her hand which Goering leaned down and kissed gently.

He straightened and sipped his tea. "Herr Barnett was a pilot to be feared. He was a patient and cunning hunter. I consider it an honor to have flown against him."

"Things weren't so lovely down in the trenches," Hem interrupted. I could have kissed him. "Got pretty dirty there."

Goering turned to Hemingway. "You were in the war?"

"Ambulance driver," Hem said proudly, squaring his shoulders. "I was wounded in Italy."

"You are right," Goering agreed. "Our war was more orderly, more civilized. I pitied those who fought in the trenches."

"What have you been doing since the war?" I asked, still eager to

147

steer the conversation into safer waters.

"Restoring some order to my life, raising my family," he said, his blue eyes smiling. "And you?"

"Enjoying Paris." I noticed out of the corner of my eye that Arlaine was still watching us closely. "And how is the German political scene?" I couldn't help the jibe.

But Goering didn't flinch. He sipped his tea again before answering, that smile still perpetually hanging on his lips. "Interesting. Now is a tremendously interesting time to be a German."

"What do you think about Rathenau?" Hemingway asked. Rathenau was the new German Foreign Minister. From stuff I'd picked up in the papers, the Nazis weren't overly fond of him. Good old Hem. Always the writer. Always looking for news.

Goering turned his gaze on Hem, the smile never fading. "He is a dangerous man, but Germany has survived dangerous men before, and it will again."

Across the way, I saw Djuna Barnes, a female writer I'd met. She smiled and raised her teacup towards me in recognition.

"Isn't that right, Herr Barnett? Herr Barnett?"

"Huh?" I'd been watching two women dancing quietly and closely to the music of the string quartet. The Temple de l'Amitie stood behind them with its door open. It was pitch black in the interior, and Nathalie Barney suddenly materialized in the door. Something about her mesmerized me, held me. I shook it off after a second and turned back to see Kopfmann looking my way.

"I asked you, Herr Barnett," the German said patiently, "if you agreed that the admission of the Russian Communists to the Economic Conference in Genoa was a mistake?"

"I try not to get involved in politics," I said.

Kopfmann looked flustered. "But Herr Hemingway says you are being credentialed as a journalist to attend the conference."

"That's different. That's work. And I'm not involved. I'm an observer."

"But certainly you have an opinion."

Everybody was looking at me again—Frank, Hem, Arlaine, Goering. I really *didn't* have an opinion, but what the hell. "I think the Communists are here to stay for a while, and so you might as well scoot down and set another plate for them at the table. They've just about eliminated all their major competition inside Russia, and Lenin strikes me as the kind of guy that's gonna be real thorough about shoring up his position. In fact, from what I've read and seen, Lenin is the one you want to deal with. Some of the younger crowd, this Stalin guy for example, won't be as benevolent in their dealings with us capitalist heathens."

Goering didn't like it worth a damn and said so. Frank nodded. Hem launched into a speech about what he thought, and I never really got a grip on what that was. Arlaine smiled at me, and I started over to her, but about that time Kopfmann grabbed her elbow and wheeled her away into a corner with a "Miss Watson, you must tell me where you bought your perfume. It's magnificent, sehr gut."

I looked around and saw a few other people I knew. Ezra was sipping tea and eating cake. Bob McAlmon was talking to James Joyce in a corner. Paul Valery and André Gide were into a deep conversation with Nathalie. I started to go over and talk to Joyce, but, to my surprise, he broke away from McAlmon about then and headed my way.

"Mr. Barnett," he said, his eyepatch wiggling a little as he talked. "Have you any news?"

"Nothing of any substance." I didn't see any reason to tell him about the Nazis and the Communists. He wouldn't care.

"Oh." His one, visible, blue eye watered almost constantly. "But you will let me know of anything you discover?"

"No problem. What brings James Joyce to Nathalie Barney's?" I tried to change the subject. Arlaine was looking too happy glued to Kopfmann's arm, and I tried to focus back on Joyce.

He adjusted his patch. "Many of my friends are here. I first came to Nathalie's looking for beds when we moved to Paris. I needed four beds, a not inconsiderable number."

"Yeah, I guess." Despite my best efforts, I was watching Arlaine more than listening to Joyce. "I figured you'd be writing or something," I said just to keep the conversation going as I watched Kopfmann kiss Arlaine's hand for about the fifth time, and they whispered familiarly to each other.

"I am working on something new, but it takes me so long to write." He touched his eyepatch. "I must use the big pieces of paper as it's so difficult for me to see."

His words seeped into my ears as they reddened at watching Arlaine smile as Kopfmann kissed her hand again. "What did you say?"

The one good eye blinked at me. "I said I must use big pieces of paper because it is difficult for me to see."

That's all it took. That and the vision of Nathalie Barney appearing in the door of her Greek temple. I got this incredibly warm feeling all over as more than a couple of things clicked. "Please excuse me, Mr. Joyce. I need to see Hemingway."

"Of course," he stammered.

"Hem!"

I saw his big head poke around Goering's shoulder. "What?"

"We've got a trip to make."

You could see the lights flash on in his eyes. God, he could make the worst things seem like fun. "Let's go."

I turned around looking for Frank, and he appeared at my elbow. "Want to come?"

"No," Frank decided. His eyes lingered on two women headed up the stairs. "I think I'll find a more interesting, and certainly more challenging, hunt here. But, good luck to you, boy."

"Your choice," I shrugged. Something touched my shoulder, and I looked over my shoulder to see Arlaine. "I thought you were busy."

"I got unbusy," she said. "What happened? Where are we going?"

"Hem and I have a stop to make." I was feeling too good to let her bring me down much. "You can stay here if you want."

"No way, buster. I signed on for the full trip."

Half of me wanted to give her a hard time about Kopfmann, but her lips were moist and just slightly parted, and I couldn't bring myself to rib her. "Come on."

We started threading through the crowd. Hem threw a "sorry, Nathalie, thanks for the invite" over his shoulder, and we hit the front door where Herman Goering stood with that damnable wolf's smile still painted on his face.

I didn't know how Goering beat us to the door, but Hem buzzed by him and outside with Arlaine close on his heels. I nodded as I went by, but he snagged my arm and stopped me. "Does this have anything to do with that discussion we had this afternoon?" he asked.

"Everything," I admitted. I felt too good to lie. "Be at Shakespeare and Company on rue de l'Odeon at noon tomorrow. I may have something for you."

He released me and maintained his smile. "I had great faith that you would work this out. You were always a formidable adversary. You knew how to dive out of the sun and hit a pilot in his blind spot. You knew how to manuever your machine to get the most from it. You were good, Jack Barnett."

"You were okay yourself," I answered. "But we can trade stories another day. I've got business right now, boss."

"Certainly."

I headed out the door, but his voice reached me as I hit the street.

"And will you tell me of that last patrol, Jack Barnett?"

I didn't answer and I didn't stop, but I heard him and some of the warmth left my bones. Hem and Arlaine waited for me on the sidewalk, and I joined them without saying a word and headed off towards the rue de l'Odeon.

• • • •

A few people still walked down the sidewalk in front of Shakespeare and Company. The shopfront was black and dark, like a cavern that could swallow you up in its depths if you strayed too near the edge. It was nine o'clock by the time we walked over there, and the sun was long gone.

"Well," Arlaine finally said. "We're here. What's so important?"

"Oh, Jack. You're a helluva fine detective." Hem was looking straight at the door to Shakespeare and Company.

"Pretty simple, isn't it." I knew he was seeing it. Arlaine still had this confused look on her face.

"What's going on inside the bookshop?" I asked her.

She squinted at the shopfront. "Nothing."

"You mean there's nothing going on, or you can't see anything?"

Arlaine shrugged. "I guess I mean I can't see anything."

And she was right. The streetlamps reflected off the glass, and all that could be seen were the books Sylvia displayed in the window. The door, the interior of the shop, was an impenetrable, pitch black.

"There you have it," I said.

"Right," Hem agreed.

"I don't get it," Arlaine answered. We looked at her like she was crazy. "I'm sorry. I just don't see the point. You can't see inside the shop. So what? It's night time."

"That's right. Come on, Arlaine." I was obviously gonna have to spell it out for her. "Paul Dounat claimed that he saw somebody walking around inside the bookshop, that he stopped to see who it was, and when he recognized James Joyce, he moved on."

"This is swell, Jack," Hem began. "If the kid was lying about this, then God knows what else he's been lying about."

Arlaine didn't speak; she stared at the darkened shop. "Could there have been a light on inside? That would have made a difference."

"Yeah," I agreed. "That would be different. But I asked Sylvia yesterday morning if there had been a light left on when she came in that day. She said no. That everything was as it had been. And the only light switch in the bookshop proper is at the back of the room."

"See." Hem picked up where I left off. "Dounat couldn't have seen someone moving around inside the shop. The glass reflects the streetlamps and throws off a hell of a glare. So the son of a bitch was lying."

"Okay, okay," she said, throwing her hands up in submission. "You've convinced me. I just needed to play devil's advocate a little. But this doesn't do anything to kill that Karper man's story."

Arlaine's warning didn't matter. I felt good. And the longer I looked at Arlaine under that streetlamp, the more I felt like trying what I had avoided the night before. God, she was lovely—blond, blond, hair and icy blue eyes.

"Let's go get him," Hem said.

"No," I answered, still looking at Arlaine. "He'll hold till tomorrow. He doesn't know his story's been poked full of holes. He's not going anywhere. I want Duvall and his boys there when we confront him. Maybe in the process, we can bring Karper's story down, too."

Hem shrugged. "Okay, but I think we ought to strike now."

"No," Arlaine said, suddenly looking very tired and worn. Her eyes had lost something of their gleam, and I felt sorry for her. "Jack's right. He'll hold. I'm beat down to my socks, guys. I've got to call it a night. All this running around is tough on a girl from Iowa." Her voice wavered just a little bit, and I thought I knew why.

I felt really good, the best I'd felt in days. And I wanted her to stay and go home with me. I wanted that so bad the urge just swirled around me and wrapped me up in its warmth, but she wasn't used to lies and murder, and that's what stole the luster from her blue eyes. So, I didn't argue with her. I just said, "Okay. Get some rest." And she was gone, leaving me and Hem alone on the sidewalk. The breeze turned cold, cold and repellent. I turned and looked at Hem.

He shrugged. "Can't win 'em all, Jack."

"I can't win any of 'em. You up for a drink or two?"

"Sure, Jack," he said without a hint of doubt or regret in his voice, and I loved him right then for that. "What the hell are pals for? You and I ain't got drunk together for a brace of diurnals." That was Hem's inimitable way of saying "the last two weeks."

"The Dingo?"

"The Dingo," Hem agreed. He clapped me on the back, and we headed off toward Montparnasse and the Dingo Bar. "You know," Hem began, "Arlaine would look a lot better if she'd cut her hair. Short hair would look great on her."

I just grunted in reply.

• • • •

The long, battered wooden bar at the Dingo couldn't be seen for the crush of customers. For every person on a stool, three hung over their backs yelling orders at Jimmy Charters, the bartender. Everybody loved Jimmy. He was a great guy to tell your troubles to. Leaning on one of the big wooden posts stationed a few feet in front of the bar, I spotted a table, one of only six in the whole place, just then emptying and directed Hem towards it.

The crowd at the bar turned out to be some Brits singing loud, obnoxious, British drinking songs. Poor Jimmy. The literary crowd hadn't left Nathalie's yet, but later the Bob McAlmons, the Ezra Pounds, the James Joyces would all find their way here. We'd been quiet on the way over, too quiet. I knew that Hem's mind was working a thousand miles an hour when he got that quiet.

"Look, Jack, tell me if I'm off base here, but I've got to ask you. What was that Kraut's thing about your last patrol?"

He'd fetched two drinks from Jimmy, a rum St. James for himself and a scotch for me. I dipped my finger in the glass and swirled it around, sucking, finally, the dregs from my finger. The peculiar taste of scotch touched only my tongue, and I savored the sensation.

"Not much of a story, Hem," I lied.

He shrugged. "Forget it then, Jack. You don't want to talk about it. I guess we've all got stories like that." But he didn't like being turned down. The half-pout gave him away.

153

I downed my drink in two gulps and let the stuff work its healing magic for a minute. "It was a long time ago, Hem," I began. "Somewhere over the eastern border of France."

"Late in the war?"

"Late, later, latest." I caught Jimmy's eye and signaled for another drink. He could tell by looking that I needed it. Bartenders like Jimmy Charters are one in a million. "I'd just escaped from a German prison camp. The squadron commander gave me a week off, here in Paris actually, and then, after I got back, sent me up one day. Simple patrol. Just fly up to the front lines, make a sweep across, and then return."

"Were there many like that?"

"Oh, yeah. Sure. Lots of them. We spent part of our time flying escort to reconnaissance patrols, another part busting balloons, and finally, the bulk, flying simple patrols. And we didn't always find something. Rickenbacker and his crowd have romanticized it, made it seem like Sir Goddamn Walter Scott and his knights and damsels fair. It wasn't that daring. I flew probably a dozen patrols where I never saw a German machine. Especially in those last days. The Krauts didn't have many planes left. And they had fewer veteran pilots."

"What happened on that last one?"

I sipped the scotch and let it warm my throat again. Hem sat across from me, that eager look lighting his face. I knew I couldn't tell him all of it. Only Frank O'Connor knew it all. But I would tell him a little, enough to satisfy his curiosity.

"I spotted a lone scout heading over Allied territory. I claimed him as mine and sent my patrol on ahead."

"Yeah?"

"There was a dogfight. I shot him down, but he wounded me. I landed to help him, but his plane had gone down in flames. There was nothing left to help. He burned up in front of me." It all sounded so simple, even the little white lie.

Hem's mouth was fixed in a comforting, satisfied, expression. "That's hell, Jack. I was wounded, too, you know."

"Yeah, I know." He'd told me a hundred times.

"Where'd he get you?"

I considered his question. God, I liked this kid. He was young and brash, opinionated and accepting, playful and earnest, all at the same time. He made you want to be open with him. "Somewhere awkward, Hem," I admitted finally. "Somewhere vital to certain functions. Somewhere a man shouldn't be wounded."

Ernest Hemingway didn't have to be kicked in the stomach. "Gawwd, Jack! That's awful. Are you still . . . ?"

I sipped my drink and nodded, a little flush filling out my cheeks, a little anger drifting in because I had revealed so much, too much.

"So you and Arlaine haven't. . . ."

"No," I said curtly.

We fell silent then, and Hem pulled out a little pad and wrote something down. "Grocery list?" I was glad to change the subject.

Hem grinned a little uncertainly. "Naw. Just making a note to myself for later."

"Why do you want to be a writer so bad, Hem?" The change of subjects stole the heat from my cheeks and calmed me.

"I don't know, Jack. But I do. It's the one thing that calls to me, the one thing that catches my attention and holds it."

"You work a hell of a lot harder on it than most of your pals."

"I just try to write down one true sentence and then go from there. I just want it to be right, to say something. I figure I'll do things my way and they can do things theirs."

"I envy you your focus."

"Where's your focus, Jack? Why are you here? Why Paris? I mean, you don't really enjoy writing. You've told me that before. You don't seem crazy about Paris."

"Paris is Paris, Hem. It's everywhere and nowhere all at the same time. It doesn't matter where I came from; it doesn't matter what I've been, done, or seen. Paris isn't yesterday or tomorrow. Paris is, and always will be, today. This minute. And nothing else matters."

"You almost sound like you don't like Paris."

"Maybe I don't," I shrugged. "But maybe I like the other places I could be, like Liberty, Missouri, even less."

"Gawd, I love Paris. I can write here, and be with other writers. It doesn't cost much to live. And this is where things are happening. I wouldn't want to be anywhere else."

"Then, my friend," I said with a little slur in my words. "Here's to Paris." I raised my glass and touched Hem's. "For it seems we're here for the same reason. We couldn't stand to be anywhere else."

"Monsieur Barnett?"

The voice jolted me a little, and I looked up bleary-eyed at the man from Madame Mariette's.

Concern crinkled the corners of Hem's eyes, and I saw his right hand ball up into a fist.

"It's okay, Hem. He's a friend."

The hat bobbed and weaved in his hands again, but at the word "friend" something like a smile broke on his face.

"What do you have?"

The smile grew wider and revealed blackened, abandoned teeth. "If you can come with me, please. I have something to show you, something I think will be of interest."

I was just drunk enough to be glib. "Lead the way," I instructed, but deep down I wondered what he had done, if maybe he had taken it on himself to dispose of the right Reverend Quintin Karper. I worried enough that I wanted to know before we got there.

"Arrêtez-vous."

He stopped and turned back to me, a question in his soured eyes.

"Did you . . . ?"

"Non, Monsieur. Nothing like that." The smile returned, and he continued leading us out the door.

• • • •

Our companion led us back through the streets of Paris to the rue Zacharie, just beyond the Place St. Michel. The picture was getting clearer and clearer the further we went. And when he stopped in front of a laundry across the street from Madame Mariette's, I knew exactly where he was taking us.

"Upstairs?"

The man nodded.

"What in the hell is going on, Jack?" Hem was scratching his head.

"Just hold on a little bit longer. Do you know Madame Nathalie Barney?" I asked the man.

"Oui."

"Go there and ask for Monsieur Frank O'Connor. Tell him Monsieur Barnett needs him here immediately. Hurry. We'll wait for your return."

And he was gone.

"Come on, Jack, give! Why are we wasting a good drunk out here in front of a laundry?" Hem weaved a little as he spoke. "Hell, isn't that a Bureau de Police?" He pointed across rue de la Huchette which crossed rue Zacharie to the east. He was right. A little station house sat catty-cornered to the laundry. I knew the station. It didn't even have a squad car.

While we waited, and I filled Hem in on the laundry and the "real" business it did upstairs, a young girl emerged from La Panier Fleuri and slinked across the street. She was a haggard kind of pretty, and her teeth were crooked. "Monsieur Jacque," she said with a smile. "You've come to see me again?"

Her arm slipped around my waist, and I hugged her tightly. "No, Marie. Not tonight. My friend and I are working."

She gauged Hemingway with one long look. "Perhaps your friend needs some time off." Marie started towards him, but I held her against my side.

"Not tonight, my dear." And I could have sworn that Hem blushed, but, in the dark like that, it was impossible to tell. A thought struck me. "Marie, I need a favor."

She caressed my cheek. "Anything for you, Jacque."

I whispered in her ear and she grinned.

"De rien. Consider it done." She disappeared into the laundry.

Hem cocked an uneasy eye at me. "What was that all about?"

"Just wait and watch."

And minutes passed.

Finally, from down towards the lights of the Place St. Michel, I saw a giant shadow moving in our direction.

"You, Jack Barnett, are in deep trouble." The voice rolled down the darkened street.

"You, Frank O'Connor, are in for some fun."

Frank narrowed his eyes at the laundry and at La Panier Fleuri. "I was having plenty of fun when your hired help here summonsed me. Why are we at a brothel?"

"To take care of some unfinished business."

"And you want an audience?"

"Not that kind of business, Frank. Just pay attention. You'll enjoy yourself."

"I've never been much of a voyeur, Jack," Frank grumbled.

Hem laughed at us and I led them, swaying just a little from the scotches, into the laundry. The air smelled of a detergent-scented cleanliness, and two girls worked behind the counter. A third stool was conspicuously absent. An older woman appeared from behind a curtained door. She had once been very pretty, and in her sixties she still retained a sensual charm. Grey streaked her once brunette hair in wide swaths. And when she smiled, it was all in her eyes.

"Monsieur Jack." She held out her hand, and I kissed it lightly. "You have been away too long. Has my man served you well?"

"Absolutely, Madame Mariette. He's been most helpful. Did Marie speak with you?"

"Oui."

"May I borrow your . . . ?"

"Certainment." She slipped a hand beneath the counter and emerged with a camera.

"Room?"

"Room Three." She smiled with her eyes. "You are certain that word of this will not slip out? I have my reputation to think of."

"Trust me."

Frank had remained uncharacteristically quiet during this exchange, but I could see the excitement growing in his cheeks. Hem wasn't saying anything, but I think he was getting the picture too.

We mounted the stairs and headed down the hall to the door marked with the number 3. Strange squeakings and rumblings emanated from behind the closed door. Then, a woman's soft moaning turned into a spiralling, ascending, catlike screech that pivoted on its apex and padded off into a murmur so low only a sensitive ear could catch it. The time had arrived.

I grasped the camera in my sweaty palm, checked the flash attachment, and nodded to Hemingway.

He grinned, lowered his head, and plowed his shoulder into the door just as an unmistakable "God Preserve Us!" reverberated inside the room.

Thirteen

Rushing in on the heels of a stumbling Hemingway, the sound of splintering wood still crackling in my ears, I stepped to the side of the bed, focused as quickly as I could, and caught a look of stun on the flushed cheeks of the right Reverend Quintin Karper as I pushed the button and the exploding flash brightened a truly horrific scene.

"No need to hurry, Jack," Frank said, stepping over the fallen door and positioning himself at the foot of the bed. "Reverend Karper is, shall we say, indisposed."

And he was all of that. Martinique, God love her, was sitting bare-assed naked, astride Karper's considerable, and equally naked, bulk. Maybe it was the blinding effect of the flash; maybe it wasn't. Whatever it was, something held Karper motionless, staring at us as if we had caught him with his pants down. Well, I guess we had. Literally.

"You!" Karper finally showed some signs of life. He struggled underneath Martinique, but she was young and strong and merely turned towards me with a question on her face.

"Monsieur Jacque," she said. "Is there something wrong?"

"Nothing at all. Stay where you are, dear."

She flashed a smile at me and wriggled her finely shaped bottom back down on him, giving every sign of staying there in perpetuity.

"You!" Karper gasped again.

"Which of us do you suppose he's speaking to, Jack?" Frank asked.

"Could be either one, I guess."

"Maybe we should ask," Hem suggested, a smile the size of the Arc de Triomphe covering his face.

"This is outrageous!" Karper carped.

"Yes," Frank agreed, nodding his bald head enthusiastically. "What would your congregation think? Did you get his good side, Jack?"

"Does he have one?" queried Hem.

"I'll have you arrested!"

"No," I said, grabbing a chair, turning it backwards, and lowering myself. "No, you won't. While there's nothing illegal about prostitution in Paris, there's also nothing illegal about taking photographs of men engaged in sex with prostitutes. However, as your old friend, the former Father Frank O'Connor, just pointed out, your congregation would find this scene somewhat enlightening."

"Be more understanding, Jack," Frank pleaded. "Man does not live by bread alone."

"True, true, Frank," I said before Karper had a chance to interrupt. "But where does that leave Martinique?" Actually, Martinique was still astride Karper, her wonderful breasts quivering as she restrained a giggle. She'd been in the business long enough to enjoy a little exhibitionism.

Frank cocked his head to one side, considered Martinique's curves, and leaned heavily on his cane. "As manna from heaven, I suppose."

"I'll second the motion. I haven't seen manna like that in a brace of diurnals," Hem added.

Karper tried to roll Martinique off, but she righted him and tweeked his nipples with a laugh. Beads of sweat were doing more than popping out on his forehead; they were shooting off rapid fire. Finally, he collapsed back on the bed.

"What do you want with me?"

"I'm enjoying the opportunity to repay the favor you paid me some years ago, Pastor Karper. Although, I must in all honesty admit that this dear girl's treasures seem far superior to the baroness'. If one is going to be defrocked, then it would seem only appropriate that the pleasures of the sin equal the pain of the punishment. Frankly, and how could I be anything else, being stripped of my priestly vestments caused me less pain than the loss of yours will cost you. But that is *my* purpose, not his." And he nodded towards me.

"Phillipe Jourdan, or Karl Pfeiffer if you prefer."

"I've told the police everything," Karper said, struggling under Martinique again.

"Not good enough, Reverend."

"Jacque, do you need . . . la vérité, the truth?" Martinique asked. I nodded.

She grinned with evil eyes. Reaching around behind her, she squeezed something, rather ungently I thought, between his legs. When he spoke again, the pitch of his voice had changed noticeably.

"Okay!"

"Goddamn, she has a way with him!" Hem noted.

"Unquestionably," Frank concurred.

"The truth, Karper," I said. "Karl Pfeiffer."

Karper's eyes were bulging by then, and his face was as red as I thought it could get. "I didn't know him," he choked out. "I saw an opportunity and I took it. I lied to Duvall. Oh, goddamn! Get her to stop!"

"Do you have any contacts at the U.S. Embassy?"

"No, no, Jesus Christ, no! I thought about going to talk to them, but, oh shit, Jesus, the dead guy showed up in the backroom at the bookstore before I had a chance. I figured—Jesus, man, make her stop—I figured that I'd save that for a last resort."

"What do you think, Frank?"

"I think that the Reverend should promise to tell Duvall the truth," Frank decided.

"Oh, shit! Yes! Yes!" And Karper's voice went up another octave.

"Ernest," Frank continued. "Does he sound sincere to you?"

"I don't know. . . . Seems like a man that would lie once would lie again."

"Martinique," I instructed, and she caressed him again in her inimitable way.

He shrieked.

"That ought to work," I said. "And, besides, we've got the photo to hold over his head."

"You will see that I get a copy," Frank requested.

"Absolutely. We'll leave you to your evening's entertainment, Reverend," I continued. "Merci beaucoup, Martinique."

"De rien," she said, releasing her grip on Karper who shuddered once or twice and immediately passed out. Jiggling in all the right places, she crawled off her client.

"You're absolutely right," Frank said to her, studying the now fully exposed Karper. "It was nothing."

• • • •

"That settles that," Hem said once we had made our way back to the street.

"Another loose end tied up," I agreed.

"That was a treasure, Jack," Frank said, twirling his cane. "Hypocrisy is never better than when fully exhibited. And Quintin Karper exhibited just about everything he had."

I laughed. And they laughed.

"You know, guys," I said when the chuckling had calmed down. "I can tell you exactly who didn't kill Karl Pfeiffer, but I haven't the slightest damn idea who did."

"I'm not sure that's our problem, pal," Hem said.

Frank gave Hemingway a look of growing respect and then turned to me. "At the risk of experiencing a flashback to earlier days, accept the blessings God bestows on you, Jack. Greed is more a curse than a virtue. And some things are destined to be mysteries forever."

"I guess," I answered. But down deep, I was greedy for that last bit of knowledge, that need to know the whole truth. And I had already learned one truth; Quintin Karper was no copy of my father. He was a cruel caricature at best, a cartoonist's rendering of hypocrisy. My father's religion—my father—was made of sterner stuff, inflexible, unbreakable. More to be admired, I decided, than ridiculed.

• • • •

Flames ring the barn, the orange fingers spewing their black and grey smoky vomit into the sky. I circle lower and lower, my body soaking in the scent of burning flesh. The plane bumps to a violent stop in the field as the doors of the barn burst open flinging bloody, pink hunks of flesh across the landscape and destroying my father's image. Through the door, through the flames, I see all three of them—the child pilot, and the man and woman wrapped in a lover's embrace. But the man's genitals have burned off and he enjoys the pleasures of penetration no longer. Their heads, devoid of flesh or hair, blackened and charred, turn together and join the child pilot in pointing long, accusatory fingers at me.

I cover my eyes and cry.

I sat straight up, bathed in a sticky, unpleasant sweat.

Something new, something cleaner, dropped on my face, and I looked up to see a leak forming in the ceiling. Goddamn it to hell, I thought, using my sheet to dry my skin. A headache banged between my temples, and I clutched my head.

Last night. The night before. The Dingo. Ernest Hemingway. Quintin Karper. Frank O'Connor. Martinique. Some of it came storming back in between drum-banging pains. I remembered talking to Hem. I remembered the scotches and Madame Mariette's man coming for us. And I remembered our encounter with Quintin Karper. And, through the pounding in my head, I smiled. One more loose end tied up.

Awkwardly, I stumbled to my feet and looked out the window. The rain was back. All the warmth and confidence of the night before was shot to hell. Arlaine's departure and my drunken revelations to Hem—slanted though they had been—played hell with my assuredness. No matter how easily I'd been able to puncture Karper's story, I felt exposed, shiveringly, embarrassingly exposed. If the rest of the day went like this, they'd hang James Joyce by his testicles on the Champs Elysees by sundown, and me with him.

I put some water on to boil for coffee and struggled into a pair of pants. My stomach was losing some of its tone and lapped over my beltline just a little. Got to cut down on the beer, I thought. A boyhood of Missouri farming didn't lend itself to putting on a lot of weight. But, it had been a long time since I worked a field, and two years of gambling with the other pilots—not to mention the booze I drank to melt the perpetual knot in my stomach—had worked their peculiar magic on me.

Every morning before a patrol, I got out of my bunk, ignored the officer's mess, and drank two or three good jolts of brandy. After a couple of minutes, the warmth would blossom in my stomach, and I forgot about the knot, forgot about it long enough to climb into my Spad 13 and make my ascent to the sky. Then, another nip up there in the clouds, and I was ready to do my job—to hunt down and kill other people, for God and Country, for Missouri and the Baptist Church. For my mother and father and the Quintin Karpers of the world. But especially for my father.

I was feeling that same knot again. Never mind that I was confident of the outcome. It was the uncertainty, the fact that we didn't have *all* the loose ends tied up.

The coffee was good and hot and ready to drink by the time the knock sounded at the door. "Come in!" I yelled.

163

Hem's big head poked through the opening door. "Ready?"

I frowned at him through bloodshot eyes. "What the hell do you think?"

"Let's get this thing over with, Jack. I need to spend some more time earning seeds. And Hash's started to get jealous of you. It took a hell of a long time explaining last night away. Especially when I let slip where we ended up."

"My, my," I chided. "If she could see us now. Me half undressed. And, as a married man, you're supposed to know that slips are not allowed. Did you send a message to Duvall?"

"Yep. Now, knock off the malarkey and let's go."

So I gurgled down a cup of coffee, threw socks, shoes, and shirt on, and followed Hem to Shakespeare and Company.

• • • •

They were all there: Sylvia, Joyce, Arlaine, Duvall, Goering, and a couple of gendarmes hovering behind Duvall. Hem and I walked into the shop, and they turned to look at us. I wondered if Arlaine had already told them about our discovery of the night before. But Duvall answered that question quick.

"You're late, Jack. What do you want?" Duvall was short-tempered. He smoked his cigarette in jerky puffs.

"Get up on the wrong side of the bed, Inspector?"

His dark eyes shot around the room. "I have cabinet ministers calling me demanding that I arrest Monsieur Joyce. My position has been threatened more times than I care to recall. I warn you, Jack, if this is another attempt to stall, I will not be gracious. And," he said in a whisper, passing close to me, "who is this man?" He could only mean Goering.

"My employer and one of Karl Pfeiffer's colleagues," I whispered back as Duvall frowned. "Don't worry, pal," I said aloud. "Hem and I have it wrapped up. At least the Joyce end of it. Did Karper come to see you this morning?"

Duvall flicked his ashes on the floor, and they fell slowly, like orphaned snowflakes. Sylvia frowned at this assault on her property. Arlaine stared at Joyce. Joyce's one visible eye watered; the other rested mysteriously behind the patch. Goering looked more than mildly interested.

"Oui, but his confession sounded more like the result of blackmail than the truth."

"But?" I sensed the rest of his answer.

"But I never truly believed his story anyway. Talk," Duvall ordered.

"Hem," I prompted.

Ernest Hemingway loved to be in charge. He ran a hand through his hair, adjusted his pants, and began. "Inspector, when you questioned Paul Dounat, didn't he say that he was walking home when he saw movement here inside Shakespeare and Company?"

"Oui, he made such a statement." Duvall's eyes narrowed.

"Have you ever tried to look through the front windows of this place at night?"

"From across the street?" I added.

"Non," Duvall admitted. "But what of it?" The question was stubbornness; he knew where we were headed.

"You can't see anything inside this shop. It's like the windows were painted black." Hem loved it. "We checked it last night."

"Perhaps Monsieur Joyce left the lights on?" Duvall continued.

"Sylvia," I said, spinning to face her. "Did you find any lights on when you came in the next morning?"

"No, Jack, like I told you that morning, everything was as it should be." A smile was finally lighting in Sylvia's face, and I liked seeing it there.

"Then he turned them off as he went out the door." God, Duvall was stubborn.

"There's only one light switch in here, Inspector," Hem picked up the argument, moving towards the wall next to the storeroom door. "And it's here in this wall, at the opposite end from the front."

"You could all be lying. Perhaps, I should take Monsieur Joyce into custody until this evening when we can test your 'theory'?" He motioned for the gendarmes, one of who moved forward with handcuffs.

"But I have done nothing!" Joyce exclaimed, speaking for the first time. His eyepatch wiggled up and down as frustration moved his face.

"Then you would be freed. I can't take your word on this, Jack. Too much pressure is coming from above. The revelations of Karper's lies aside, you and your friends are prejudiced in this matter. Please, Jack. There is the note, the bit of cloth from the jacket in Monsieur Joyce's apartment. The fact that the victim was apparently trying to burn up his book—"

"The fact," I interrupted, "that the victim was a Nazi, unknown and unconnected to Joyce. And that's not all we have, Duvall."

Duvall's eyes flickered over towards Goering who responded in kind.

You've got to give Hem credit; he was a quick study even at that age. His eyes said, "It's not?", but his mouth said, "That's right, Inspector. Go ahead, Jack."

I walked over to Joyce. "Mr. Joyce, would you write me a brief note?"

Joyce's one eye blinked wetly. "What would you like me to say?"

"Anything. Just jot a note."

"Miss Beach, do you have—"

"Yes," Sylvia said, jumping up, "right here." She reached into her desk and produced a large pad, placing it in front of Joyce.

He slowly extracted a pen from his breast pocket, paused for a second as if in thought, and then scrawled something on the pad. Finishing, he passed it to me.

I held it against my chest. "Inspector, you mentioned the infamous note arranging the meeting here behind rue de l'Odeon?"

"Mais oui, of course."

"How was it written?"

"By pen."

"No kidding, but what did the handwriting look like?"

"A very tight, controlled writing."

I ripped the sheet off the pad and flashed it for everybody to see. "Like this?" Joyce's scrawl covered half the pad; it was a tortured hand, written large and sprawling, practically indecipherable.

Duvall snorted. "It is a trick, Jack, unworthy of you."

"No, Inspector," Sylvia Beach said. "Mr. Joyce's eyes are quite bad. He must write in such a manner to be able to read what he has written. I'm not sure why I never realized it at the beginning."

"A hell of a touch, Jack." Hem smiled at me.

Duvall blinked two or three times really fast and puffed quickly on his cigarette. He turned to Joyce. "Your doctors can confirm your condition?"

Joyce nodded.

"Then, obviously Monsieur Dounat has more to tell us than we thought at first." When Duvall saw the handwriting on the wall (no pun intended), he didn't waste any time. "I apologize, Monsieur Joyce." Duvall was sincere. I could hear it in his voice.

Joyce didn't smile, but the concern wrinkling his forehead faded.

"It was only a small bother," he said in his thick, Irish brogue.

And I believed that.

Duvall turned towards Sylvia. "Mademoiselle, we will not be confiscating Monsieur Joyce's books. At least, not at this time. You may resume your usual business." He bowed and spun towards his companions.

Goering stopped me as I moved to follow Duvall. "This is what you called me here for? I expected to hear you name the real murderer, not clear someone."

"Just tag along. You'll get what you came for." I wasn't half as certain as I sounded.

"Gentlemen, we have business at Monsieur Dounat's flat," Duvall said.

"Mind if I come?" I asked.

"Me, too," Hem said.

"And me," Arlaine added. She hadn't had much to say, and I was surprised to hear her jump in.

Goering didn't bother to ask permission.

"Pourquoi? Why?" Duvall didn't understand.

"Let's say I still have a business interest in this affair."

Duvall shrugged and motioned for us to follow.

"Thanks, Jack," I heard Sylvia say behind me.

I waved over my shoulder. "Just call me 'Jack, the Literary Giant Savior'."

"Isn't that 'Jack the Giant *Killer*'?" Arlaine asked.

"Sometimes, my dear, there's a thin line between killing somebody and saving them."

• • • •

"Knock again," Hem suggested. We were standing in the hall outside Dounat's apartment, the smell of urine strong in the passageway. Duvall had banged his fist on the door twice already. He threw a jaundiced look at Hem, but went ahead and hammered the door again.

Arlaine huddled against me in the drafty hall. I liked feeling her warmth on my arm, and she buried her head into my shoulder. The two gendarmes stood up the hall and waited patiently for their boss' instructions. The concierge, a woolen-sweatered old lady, watched anxiously as Duvall pounded the door.

No answer.

"Madam, avez-vous la clef pour la porte?" the Inspector asked the concierge.

A quick shake of the head. No key for the door.

Duvall motioned for the gendarmes, but Hem stepped in and waved them off.

"Let me," he offered. Duvall shrugged.

"One, two, three—" and Hem battered his shoulder against the door. It creaked and groaned, but didn't open.

Again, Hem rammed the door. It splintered, but didn't surrender.

A third time, and the door sprung back, splitting the wood at the jamb and sending Hem tumbling into the room.

"Uh-oh." I heard Hem say.

I followed Duvall and his boys in and said, "Uh-oh," too. Goering looked unmoved. Arlaine took one look and buried her face in my chest with a whimper.

Fourteen

P aul Dounat wouldn't be answering our questions that day or any other. The young student was sprawled back on his sofa, a pistol lying next to one of his outstretched hands, and the side of his head (not to mention half his brain) splattered pink and red against the wall.

"Holy shit!" Hem swore.

Duvall and the gendarmes swung into action. The two uniforms checked the rest of the flat while Duvall knelt on the sofa next to the body and looked it over.

I shook Arlaine gently off, and she went to sit in a chair at the table. As I got closer, I saw that the kid's eyes were still open, but they didn't tell me anything; a glaze had settled in. His face was pale, and his lips were slightly parted. The blood had congealed to a dark, almost black red, matting his hair in long streaks, and little bits of drying flesh clung to the fabric of the sofa. Suddenly, I was pretty damn glad I only had coffee that morning. No, he wouldn't be telling anybody anything anymore.

"What's that?" I asked Duvall who was reading a soiled, crumpled piece of paper.

The inspector looked up and frowned. "A suicide note, I believe you call it."

Hem stepped over. "What does it say?"

Duvall looked for a long second at the kid's body and then went back to translating the note. "I cannot . . . keep my secret any longer. The guilt . . . washes over me like a fire. I killed the German in the alley behind Mademoiselle Beach's bookshop. I was ordered to infiltrate the NSDAP circle in Paris. When I met with Karl Pfeiffer that night, he . . . exposed me as a Communist and tried to kill me. We struggled and I stabbed him. He had told me that others were coming. I panicked. The light . . . was extinguished . . . in the storeroom of the bookstore. I waited a few minutes and then . . . broke . . . the door, putting the scum fascist on the floor, concocting the note blaming Monsieur Joyce, and fabricating a Molotov cocktail."

Duvall's translation got smoother as he went. "I hurried around the building and stole Monsieur Joyce's key, hoping his failure to produce it would make him look even more suspicious. Later I planted the jacket I wore in his apartment while he and his family were eating at a restaurant. But I cannot live with my lie. I have done what I had to do for the cause and now, I end this miserable existence."

"Jeeesus!" Hem exclaimed as he surveyed the scene. "He sure made a hell of a fine mess doing it."

I grabbed the note from Duvall, who, surprisingly, let it go without a fight. The handwriting was the same, tight hand as the note at Shakespeare and Company. My stomach was beating a Latin rhythm, and I felt like I was spinning out of control. I stepped back from the couch and tried to breathe deep. The gendarmes came back and shook their heads. They hadn't found anything else.

Arlaine stood abruptly, turned away from the grisly sight, and walked to the window. She didn't cry, but tense ridges of muscles showed in her back. I started to go to her, but Duvall held me back.

"Give her some time to herself. She is unaccustomed to such sights."

"And I am?" I started to say, but shut up instead and nodded.

"Well, that pretty well tells us everything we needed to know," Hem began. "Mr. Joyce is completely off the hook."

"Yes, it would seem so," Duvall said, producing his match out of nowhere and lighting another cigarette. His beady little eyes were narrowing, and his forehead wrinkled up like the Grand Canyon.

I grabbed the suicide note from his hand and studied it. "This sounds like a bunch of romantic claptrap, almost too sentimental for the Communist propaganda I've read, too self-indulgent." The image of the kid lying there with half his head gone started to recede into the background, and I focused on the argument.

"I don't get it either," Hem began. "Something doesn't ring true about this. It's too convenient."

Duvall smoked his cigarette for a long time without saying a word. His eyes were locked with those of Paul Dounat. Finally, he sighed, expelling a cloud of smoke, and stood. "I have my murderer now."

"You're gonna buy this?" I asked.

"Your Mr. Joyce is off the hook, as you say. I have a murderer and a confession. Karper's allegations have been revealed—by whatever methods you used—as lies. My superiors will be more than happy. I can move on to other things." A flatness marked his eyes.

"You can't be serious," I said. "What about the U.S. Embassy and the potshot somebody took at us? Don't you think that it's awfully convenient, just when we know that Dounat was lying, that he has an attack of guilt and suddenly commits suicide. Too many questions are dangling in the wind, buckoo."

"It's over, Jack. C'est fini," he said with just the slightest of edges in his voice.

Hem wandered over to the kitchen table, looking at some papers lying haphazardly across it. I saw his eyes narrow, and he picked up one of the pamphlets and shoved it in his pocket. Just as I started to ask him what he was doing, I felt someone snag the suicide note out of my hand.

"Paul Dounat killed Karl Pfeiffer." Duvall's voice was flat, dulcet.

Goering edged up to me. "I am satisfied. I will be in touch." He slipped out of the flat without another word.

I didn't argue anymore, but it wasn't over, and standing there with Ernest Hemingway, staring at what was left of Paul Dounat, I had a gut feeling that the last word was a long way from being written.

• • • •

Hem knew it was wrong too—his silence told me that much—but we had Genoa to get ready for, and I wanted to spend some time with Arlaine, away from murders and policemen, and Heinrich Kopfmann. Hem wanted to get back to Hadley and his writing. It didn't matter that there were a thousand unanswered questions. Hell, if I'd said it once, I'd said it a thousand times; this was Paris, and in Paris you didn't have to make sense. It was a natural law.

Joyce dropped by one day to tell me he was glad that the whole affair was finished. That's right. No, "thank you." No, "I'm really grateful." Just, "I'm glad it's over." But, by then I realized that that was James Joyce, and he didn't act like ordinary men. I kept the writing he scrawled on the big pad at Shakespeare and Company that day. It took me a little while, but I finally figured out that it was a signature—somebody named Leopold Bloom.

And Arlaine. The sight of her arm in arm with Kopfmann had hurt me more than I wanted to admit. Maybe what I experienced was just lust, but I got the feeling that there was something deeper rumbling around inside my stomach. I really, honestly, liked her. I enjoyed having her around. Hell, I even enjoyed those probing questions, the ones that took me to the edge of my sanity, to the point where I almost broke. But, I would never break again, and, it didn't matter then anyway. Arlaine was gone.

I dropped by the bookshop the next day, and Sylvia told me that Arlaine had left, to travel, Sylvia said, and see some of the countryside. I sort of figured that the innocence—the Midwestern farm girl—buried inside her couldn't take the reality of Paul Dounat's shattered skull. Well, to be just perfectly damned honest, I wasn't dealing with it very well either, and so, I could hardly blame her. But I hoped for so much more. Obviously, she hadn't. I bandaged my ego with a couple of nights hitting the hot spots in Montparnasse. I wound up with a Brit named Duff Twysden one night. She was long-legged and good looking, but no matter how hard she tried, she couldn't repair my machinery. It was broken; I was broken.

Duvall threatened to arrest Karper, but in the end, the pudgy little preacher went back to his congregation. Frank suggested that he might want to leave Paris before a certain photograph was posted to the states. Karper condemned us all to eternal damnation and went home. If the truth be known, Frank mailed a package of photographs the day after I got them developed.

And Herman Goering proved to be just as slippery a bastard on the ground as he was in the air. I tried to reach him to collect my five hundred, but the jerk had flown the coop, maybe even literally. For lack of anything better to do, I even went down in the 13th Arrondissement and checked the place they'd taken me to that day and the address Goering had given me that day. But there weren't any Germans either place. Both flats were empty. I sucked up the loss and headed home.

· · · ·

And the three grinning skulls beckon to me from their red and orange inferno. And as always their fingers of bone point accusingly at me, blaming me for the flames that extinguish their lives, blaming me for the loss of their flesh, the loss of their humanity. For they are all just alike now; I can't discern the woman from the men. And I weep bitter, hot, acid tears that scar my cheeks and burn at my pride, the pride that sent them to their flaming hell. But, as I begin to turn away, to hide myself from their hatred, a new vision floats above my victims. And no longer is it my father's face. No longer do his familiar features silently chastise me, burden me with my guilt. It is the unwrinkled, youth-smooth, face of Paul Dounat, untouched by the flames. He locks into my eyes and shouts, "Why!" but no sound is heard.

And his head explodes, covering me with the sticky wetness, the metallic taste of his blood.

And my body shudders and won't stop.

Sweat stung my eyes as the lids flew back, and I lurched straight up. My heart raced, and my hair was sopping wet. It was the worst yet, the worst in four years of hellish dreams. I think at that moment a gun and a bullet would have been my best friends, anything to help the burning in my head and gut.

According to my father, the sin of pride ranked right up there with murder and adultery. And I had committed that crime on my last patrol. I let pride in the guise of compassion dictate my actions, and three people died. As long as those three people haunted my dreams, I could never go home. For my father could look into my eyes and see their faces, and there would be no rest in his house. In Paris, no one saw their faces in my eyes, since all their eyes carried the faces of their sins as well. And so we existed together, saying what we pleased, doing what we pleased, and drinking to dull our memories and obscure those horrible faces.

But another face had entered my dreams, accusing me of a crime I didn't think I'd committed, and that gnawed at my heart. The worst part was that I was fully awake by then, and still I couldn't get Paul Dounat's face out of my head. I had two days before I left for Genoa. I needed Hemingway and I needed Duvall. Nothing could be done about three of the faces, but I'd be damned if I'd let Paul Dounat join them without a fight. James Joyce might be off the hook, but I wasn't.

• • • •

Hem was at his favorite table at the Cafe des Flores over on the Place St. Michel, the joint I met him at that first day. It was a bright, sunny day, so I first tried the hotel room, but he wasn't there. No accounting for the movements of artists, I figured, and I trudged over to the cafe.

Head bent, wrinkles in his forehead, he was scribbling like crazy on a pad. I watched him for a minute. I'd never seen anybody work with the intensity that he did. I think it was then that I realized that being a writer was not just an affectation for Ernest Hemingway; he really meant what he said; it *really was* what he wanted out of life.

"How's it going?" I walked up and grabbed a chair.

"Just a second, Jack," he said, not lifting his head. The pen scratched across the paper a couple more seconds, and then he stopped, a grin spreading on his face, and looked up. "It's going great. Really good." He paused. "But, Jack, you look like hell."

"Bad night."

"If that's what happens after a bad night, Jesus, try not to have a bad day."

"Your concern is overwhelming. Look, Hem, I didn't track you down so you could feel sorry for me. I've been thinking about this thing with Paul Dounat and Sylvia and Joyce and all. You and I both know something was screwy in all that. I can't sleep nights thinking about it. We've got a day or so before Genoa. How about helping me poke my nose back into it a little?"

Hem didn't say anything for a long thirty seconds. He stared at the pad on the table. For a second, I was afraid he'd gotten lost back in his story.

"Why can't we just leave it alone, Jack? I mean, Dounat's dead. Joyce is free. Sylvia's happy. Why mess with it?"

"I can't get that kid's face out of my mind, Hem. Think about the U.S. Embassy, the Commies, Goering and his buddies. Do you really think they would have been involved if it was just some young, idealistic kid trying to strike a blow for Bolshevism? All we did was flirt around the surface. This thing runs deeper. For some reason, I see this Dounat kid as the real victim."

"I don't know, Jack. I see what you're saying, but, well. . . ."

I laughed at a sudden thought. "This is funny."

Hem looked at me quizzically. "What?"

"We had this same conversation last week, only *you* were trying

174

to talk me into it and *I* was looking for a way out."

He shook his head back and forth and an amused grin lit his face. "Okay, you're right. What do we do first?"

"I figured we've got two or three places to hit. First, we can look into Dounat's background. Second, there's this U.S. Embassy question. Finally, we need to see Duvall. We need to get our hands on all the information he collected."

"What if he doesn't want to give it to us?"

"Then, we'll twist his arms. You said you wanted to write one true thing. Well, maybe this is the story I need to write, the one true thing I can leave behind, and I'm not gonna let him stand in my way."

"Uh-oh," Hem said softly as I finished.

"What?"

"Number Two on the list just came to us."

I looked up and sure enough, H. Winston Miller and his red-headed protégé were advancing on our table with serious frowns on their faces. "Jesus, they work fast. We just decided to stick our noses back in their business and here they are."

But as they drew closer, I got the distinct impression that the frowns were general in nature and not really intended for us. In fact, H. Winston let his frown slowly slide into something approaching a smile. The red-head, sporting the vestiges of a black eye, kept his frown intact.

"Mr. Barnett, Mr. Hemingway. May we join you?" The question almost had a pleading quality to it.

I jumped for the offensive. "Sure, sure. Sit. We were just gonna come see you."

The pair exchanged glances and eased into chairs. "You were?" Miller said.

"Absolutely," I answered, nodding my head vigorously. "We wanted to talk to you about Paul Dounat."

If my earlier statement made them exchange glances, this one had them exchanging thunderbolts. But the shock was quickly replaced with something approaching sheepishness, even by the red-head.

H. Winston Miller held himself erect and squared his shoulders. "That's why we came here, Mr. Barnett. We," and he paused for a second as if he begrudged the admission, "need your help."

"With what?" Hem asked.

"We'd rather discuss that at a more appropriate location."

"Like where?" Hem continued.

"The embassy." H. Winston looked around cautiously. "Gentlemen, this is a rather delicate affair and we would prefer to discuss it in a more secure place. A great deal rides on our ability to handle the problem before us."

I realized then that I was in the presence of a master of doubletalk. And I wasn't sure I wanted to help him out. "You know, H. Winston, you put me through a lot of horsecrap, and I'm just not positive I want to get mixed up helping you."

The red-head leaned across the table with a heavy pink growing in his cheeks and temples. "Look, funny man, there's something goddamn serious at stake here. It's time to quit playing games." His straight talk had something that H. Winston's diplomatese didn't have—a ring of honesty. "I don't like you or this clown either one, Barnett," he continued, with a flip of his head towards Hemingway. "But you've got something we need. And if you don't help us, some other people are gonna die. I watched enough people die at Verdun. I'd like to avoid another war if we can."

Hem and I looked at each other for a long second while the red-head's statement sank in. "Okay," I said finally, with a certain blink of Hem's eyes giving me his assent. "Let's go."

• • • •

The U.S. Chancellery was at 5 rue de Chaillot in those days. Miller and his buddy—who we knew by this time was named Howard Brown— pushed us past the secretaries and clerks and into an office up on the second floor. Panelled with a deep, rich, dark wood, the room was both expensive and depressing at the same time. Miller glided around behind the big oak desk and sat down like it was his own. A window, with curtains closed, graced one wall. Behind the desk, a door opened into another room.

We were planted in a pair of chairs and the red-head, Howard, paced almost frenetically from the desk to the window. He looked at H. Winston every once in a while with this "get on with it" expression, as H. Winston settled in and pulled a file from his desk drawer.

"Does the government always do things this slowly?" Hem complained, and I smiled.

H. Winston frowned his disapproval. He had his own pace, and, by God, come hell or high water, he was gonna stick to it. Flipping open the file, he studied the top sheet for a second before he began. "A circle of intensely anti-Western Communists has arisen in the Kremlin. At least one of their number—a young man named Stalin—moves at powerful levels. They are highly isolationist and quite opposed to any contact whatsoever with Western powers." He sounded like a schoolteacher, and he must have thought so too, because he stopped for a second. "Gentlemen, to save time, I'll be brief; according to our information, this splinter group of radical Communists intends to assassinate British Prime Minister David Lloyd George tomorrow as his train stops in Paris on the way to the European Economic Conference in Genoa."

I contemplated the implications of that for a second and almost messed in my britches. Hem's mouth was hanging half-open, and his eyes were sort of glazed over. "Jesus! That would mean—" he began, but Howard stepped back into the picture.

"That would mean a whole hell of a lot of things," the red-head interrupted. "David Lloyd George is a key figure right now in European stability. Stalin hates the West with a passion that almost equals the suspicions we have of the Communists. Just recently, this Stalin wrote an article for *Pravda* denouncing the Soviets' participation in the Genoa Conference. He's unalterably opposed to any kind of connection with the West. So, Stalin stands to gain a great deal if Lloyd George is permanently removed from the scene. First, the Genoa conference goes down the tubes. Second, if they try to blame it on French Communists, as we suspect they will, and are successful, peace in Europe becomes a shambles. Finally, hysteria against the Communists will reach new proportions, fueling Stalin's claims that isolationism is in the Soviet Union's best interests. The United States is not so much concerned with the Genoa conference, but the rest of it causes us great concern. A second world war this quickly on the heels of the first could be catastrophic, and that's what we're facing if the French and English face off."

I was lost. Something was missing in this picture. "What in the hell does any of this have to do with Ernest Hemingway and Jack Barnett? I hardly see how we can be of any benefit to you."

H. Winston harrumphed meaningfully. "Well, you see—"

"The murder at Shakespeare and Company," Hem finished for him, and then it all clicked for me.

"Paul Dounat had something to do with this." I was beginning to see things quite clearly.

"So did Karl Pfeiffer," Howard added. He glanced at Miller with more than a little disgust in his eyes. "Some weeks ago, a military attaché named Truman Smith, at our embassy in Berlin, was assigned to investigate an emerging political group in Germany, the NSDAP, known more familiarly as the Nazis. They've been growing in popularity, and though they're still small, taking a closer look at them seemed a prudent thing to do. It was pretty routine at first. But, during his investigation the Nazis gave him some interesting information." Howard paused. "Okay, more of a hint than any really hard evidence involving this attempt on Lloyd George. The trail led here, to Paris."

"Where did their information come from?"

"One of their members, some guy named Hitler, was assigned by the German Army to investigate left-wing political groups. It was while he was checking out the Commies that he got wind of this plot. The Nazis told us, figuring it couldn't hurt their standing to be pals with the U.S. We followed up and sent an operative to attempt an infiltration of the group.

"The Nazis had some people already here and since our abilities in these matters are somewhat limited, they were eager to help provide some contacts for us—"

"Why?" It seemed odd to me, that the NSDAP, who were about as radical as the Bolsheviks, would cooperate with the United States.

"The Nazis are striving for serious respect as a political party. Like I said, they sensed, I'm sure, that cooperation with us on this would only create sympathy for their efforts. They hate the Communists with a passion, and any chance to strike a blow against them is a chance the Nazis won't pass up," he explained. "We've also had hints that the German foreign minister, Rathenau, is courting the Bolsheviks for some kind of secret deal. Pfeiffer had been in Paris trying to raise funds, as well as keeping an eye on the French Communist movement. We used him as a contact for our operative, again because of our limited personnel and to keep the embassy removed from the situation. He knew the area and wasn't a new face. It was during a meeting between our operative and Pfeiffer that the murder occurred."

"Wait a minute," I began. "You're not telling me that Paul Dounat was your operative?"

H. Winston Miller and Howard Brown cleared their throats simultaneously and avoided looking at me.

"No, Jack." The voice floated from the open door behind the desk. "I was."

My heart pounded like a teenager's.

I looked to make sure, and I was right.

Arlaine Watson.

Fifteen

She stepped through the door and into the room. But this wasn't the young, innocent Arlaine Watson I first met two weeks before. This Arlaine had deep, dark circles under her eyes, and new wrinkles had hardened into crow's feet. Even her blonde hair hung limply, as if it were tired. This was an Arlaine in anguish.

"You." That's all I could say; I was locked into a spin and couldn't pull out. A dozen thoughts hit me all at once, but I pushed them to the back. Some were too much for me to handle. Through the fogbank rolling across my mind, I remember thinking that I sounded just like Quintin Karper when we caught him inflagrante delicto, to use Frank O'Connor's favorite phrase. Hemingway couldn't say anything. "You killed Karl Pfeiffer?" I finally blurted out.

She slumped into a chair beside the desk and stared at the carpeted floor. "No. Paul Dounat killed Pfeiffer."

"Well?" I wanted an explanation, and I wasn't waiting.

Howard slipped up beside me. "Go easy. The last couple of weeks haven't been a picnic in the park for her."

But I wasn't interested in going easy. I wanted an answer. "Well?"

"Paul Dounat," she began without looking at me, "was my contact with the conspirators. He was a young, idealistic French Communist. We became . . . close." She winced at the admission. "My instructions were to find out the specifics of the plot and the names of the Soviets involved. Then, Howard and his people would shut it down. I'd made some headway. They were trying to convince Paul to kill Lloyd George, trying to convince him that it was the best thing for the cause. But, he was young and frightened; he would never fully commit. And he told me more than he should have, but not enough to close their operation down.

"I arranged a meeting with Karl Pfeiffer that night to pass along some new information. It was safer to meet with him in secret than for me to come here. Someone might have seen me, and I was getting closer by the minute."

"Wait a second," Hem said, finally finding his tongue. "Why were you working at Shakespeare and Company?" He had an edge to his voice that I'd never heard before.

"There was an opening. It was easier to connect with the Communists as a clerk at a bookshop, just arrived from the states, than as a recently transferred embassy employee. The Communist movement is stronger here among the students than anywhere else. Sylvia's seemed a natural location. She wasn't told because, to be blunt, she didn't need to know. Anyway, I got lucky. The first student I met was Paul Dounat. He was perfect for their purposes—young, idealistic, just arrived from a small town in Normandy, eager to be involved.""

"I want to know about the alley."

Her eyes flickered up and met mine for an embarrassing second. "Paul was young, and jealous. We had been together and we parted in front of the bookshop that night. I told him I had agreed to help Mr. Joyce with his work. He didn't like it, but he finally started off for home. As soon as I thought he was out of sight, I headed around behind the shop to meet Pfeiffer.

"It didn't feel right. I had a hunch that Paul hadn't gone home. He had become so jealous that he avoided taking me to any of the cafes where the students hang out." She pounded a fist against her thigh as a hint of moisture gleamed in the corner of her eye. "I should have listened to my instincts." It took her a second, but she straightened herself. "Well, anyway, we had just begun our meeting when I heard something. Just a noise. A faint footfall. But enough to tell me that somebody was out there. I whispered to Pfeiffer to grab me, that I would push him away and run. He could chase me out of the alley, and we would arrange another meeting later. We couldn't take any chances on being discovered. We were just too close to paydirt. Paul was telling me more and more.

"So he grabbed me by the arm and pulled me to him. I slapped him, broke away, and ran to the mouth of the alley. Pfeiffer roared like a bull and came after me. But as he reached the street, he stopped." Arlaine shivered, crossed her arms and hugged herself.

"He looked at me like he wanted to ask a question and, then, he fell."

"Yeah?" I prompted.

"Yeah, well, it was Paul Dounat. My hunch was on target. He hadn't been out of sight like I thought. He saw me go around the building and became curious. He followed. He thought I was being raped. I told him I had heard a noise and went to see what it was. I told him that I found the man at the back door of the bookshop trying to break in. I told Paul that the man attacked me. I told Paul what he wanted, expected, to hear."

"And so you framed James Joyce," Hem said with a hint of anger in his voice.

She wouldn't look at us even then. "I didn't know what to do," Arlaine continued. "While we talked in the alley, the light disappeared under the bookshop door. The idea of making it look like Mr. Joyce did it just came to me in a spurt. I sent Paul around to get the key from Joyce. When he returned, I had him bash in the door. We carried Pfeiffer in and laid him on the floor. The Molotov was Paul's idea. We planted the note and the piece of cloth, and then left out the backdoor."

I didn't ask where they'd gone; I didn't want to know. "Did you think that hanging it on Joyce would last forever?" I finally said.

She shook her head quickly. "No. It was just to stall for time. I knew that eventually the police would look in other directions, but I just needed a little time. That's why Howard took that shot at you. We didn't bank on you or anybody else getting involved. By then, I'd met a few others from Dounat's circle. They were beginning to trust me. And the conference was getting closer and closer. I needed more time. We only meant to scare you off, but, obviously, it didn't work."

"What about Kopfmann and Goering?"

"They were two of our contacts with the Nazis. Kopfmann was working with Pfeiffer. Goering came in to bring some new information from the Nazi leader who gave us our first hint of this thing, this Hitler guy." Brown answered that one.

"So when you talked to Kopfmann at Nathalie Barney's . . . ," I began, looking at Arlaine.

She smiled softly. "I was touching base with my new contact."

"But why did Goering come to me and hire me to find out who killed Pfeiffer?" It didn't make sense to me.

Brown cleared his throat. "We . . . uh, we didn't tell them the truth. It didn't seem prudent to let that cat out of the bag so to speak. We let them think that we were as in the dark about Pfeiffer's death as they were."

"What happened to Dounat?" Hem asked.

"I guess the pressure from the Russians to kill Lloyd George and then the business with Karl Pfeiffer were too much for him to handle," Arlaine answered with a shrug. "And, maybe, at the end, he thought he was protecting me. Paul was a boy who cared too much. I found out that he'd killed himself at the same time you did."

I felt sorry for her. I really did. Nobody wanted to look at her. Not Miller, not Brown, not even Hemingway who sat and silently stared at his hands, a look of curious concentration on his face.

"Which," H. Winston interrupted finally, "leaves us in something of a sticky wicket. Dounat never told Arlaine who the Russians were nor where they are hiding. As far as we know, the plan is still on. We've spent the last week trying to ferret out their location, but they've simply vanished. None of the students they contacted early on has seen them in the last few days. It's like they never existed."

"At this point," continued Howard, "we assume they've gone into hiding and will try to carry out the plan themselves. But that still leaves us with the problem that none of us, including Arlaine, knows where these bums are or what they look like."

"Which makes me an important man," I realized aloud.

Arlaine looked straight at me then. "You've seen them, Jack. They picked you up and carried you to their hideout. It wasn't important then—they thought they had Dounat primed for the kill and you were just a fly in their ointment—but you're the only one now who can identify them."

"I didn't see much." For some reason, I didn't like being compared to a fly in anybody's ointment, and I got the distinct impression that I had just been a fly in her web as well.

"What did you see?" Howard Brown circled and came to roost on the edge of the desk. The question was edged; Brown was the most intense person I'd ever met.

I shrugged. "Two guys picked me up in an automobile, a Citroën I think, and drove me out in the country."

"What *did* it look like?"

"The auto or the country?" Something in his tone put me off. A red to match his hair creeped up his cheeks and his hands gripped the edge of the desk until the knuckles turned a sickly white. "This is no game, Mr. Barnett. Two people have already died over this. We've got to stop them."

"Jesus," Hem exhaled. "Why don't you just flood the station with police?"

Howard looked at the curtained window, letting the red drain from his face while H. Winston answered with a polite cough. "The, uh, French are not being highly cooperative with our investigation. And, we have not deemed it wise to provide them with all the information at our disposal."

"Jesus," I exclaimed. "In other words, you didn't want to have to explain to them why you had kept them in the dark?"

"It did pose certain problems in that area. However, there will be a significant number of French security present anyway," H. Winston hurriedly answered. "Our best understanding at this point is that Premier Poincarè will meet with Lloyd George as the train travels between stations in Paris, which means the French police will be out in full force. But that's really of only minor comfort; if they make any appearances at all outside the train, a good rifleman can take Lloyd George out regardless of the number of policemen."

"Then don't let them outside the rail car," Hem suggested.

Miller looked distinctly uncomfortable. "While that might be preferable, we can't completely control the movements of politicians."

"There's something I don't get here," I began. "Why aren't the Brits involved in this?"

Miller, Brown, and Arlaine all exchanged embarrassed looks and a long pause ensued.

"Well," Miller started. "It was decided at higher levels that a lid should be placed on this in order to avoid exposing our investigation."

"And," Hem nodded with a cynical smile growing across his face, "if you're successful, that would be a feather in your cap for dealing with the Brits."

"Or," I countered. "You didn't have enough hard evidence to convince the British that a conspiracy really exists, or some ambassador somewhere—Berlin it looks like—wants all the glory for himself."

I could have sworn that H. Winston Miller began sweating. "A little of all three," he said. "But, in our defense, a massive investigation would tend to spook the conspirators."

"It's a wonder you haven't spooked them already. I mean, I start investigating; their patsy, Paul Dounat, commits suicide after killing a Nazi in an alleyway. Seems like a lot of activity."

"And we've gone too far now to turn back," Howard added. "But, gentlemen," and I could tell he used the term loosely, "if the conspirators intend to play it out, and if you don't help us, then Lloyd George may die two days from now. And Europe may end up in another world war."

"And if they've already packed it in?" Hem asked.

"And if they have," Miller conceded, "then you will have merely wasted a couple of days in your country's service."

Arlaine hadn't said anything in several minutes. She sat in her chair and stared at the floor, never lifting her eyes, never meeting my gaze. H. Winston Miller and Howard Brown had finally shut up. I thought about Arlaine. I thought about how she had made me feel. But as my eyes touched her blond hair, the face of Paul Dounat floated through my mind. And another face replaced his— Sneer, my Communist friend. I flinched again, reflexively, as I remembered the hand colliding with my cheek. Out of the corner of my eye, I saw Hem give me a look. The message was simple.

"Look, guys," I began, "Hem and I are no heroes—hell, I'm not even sure I rank as high as coward—but we'll do what we can.

• • • •

"What the hell do you mean we're no heroes?" Hemingway was aggravated with me.

"You know, Hem, in some ways you're a hopeless romantic." We sat in an embassy car outside what I thought was the country farmhouse where the Communists had brought me. Howard Brown and Hemingway were in the front seat. Arlaine and I were in the back. H. Winston Miller had, of course, other duties to perform. As much as I disliked Brown, he was preferable to Miller's kind of animal. The Miller's of the world are only one step removed from the Quintin Karpers. Their hypocrisy is marked more by sublety than bombast.

The pit of my stomach was raw, torn and stung by the last two weeks. It was like being back in the cockpit. That morning, after our little conference at the embassy, I'd found some milk and brandy. The mixture eased the pain, but set my stomach on a different edge, like a see-saw that was perfectly balanced. If I shifted the wrong way, I'd fall.

"Why didn't you call Duvall like I told you?" I complained. Nobody had come or gone from the house since our arrival. We were parked in the edge of some woods, just up the road from the entrance to the courtyard.

Brown shrugged. "This isn't his jurisdiction. Besides, we can handle this ourselves."

"Yeah, right. You've been doing awfully damn well the last few weeks, haven't you?" I was less than impressed by his squad of makeshift spies.

"Come on, Jack. It's just a few Russkies." Hem was spoiling for a fight. He hadn't sparred with Ezra in days, and his energy level was near the bursting point. He continually cracked his knuckles and flexed his shoulders. He even shadowboxed in the auto.

Arlaine didn't say much. I wanted to know what was going on behind her eyes, but she seldom gave me a chance to penetrate their depths. Once though, while I was staring out the window at the farmhouse, I felt her fingers stroke the top of my hand. That one touch did more to ease the burn in my stomach than milk and brandy ever could.

We'd been there an hour. I studied the facade of the house for long stretches. This *was* the house. No mistaking that. But something was wrong. Something was missing. I tried to remember the day I'd been dragged out there. I tried to remember the setup, the scene.

"What's wrong, Jack?" Arlaine spoke for the first time in a long while.

I shook my head to clear it. "I'm not sure. Something isn't right."

"Like what?" Hem asked.

I turned to Brown. "Are you sure they don't know we're on to them?"

The red-head nodded. "I don't see how they could. Except for Dounat's suicide and your intervention, they've not been touched by our investigation. In fact, if nothing else, your little brush with them should have convinced them you were just amateurs playing around the edges."

"Better to be an arrogant amateur than a professional asshole," I grumbled and stared at the house for another moment or two. "They're gone. They're not here anymore." I said it with assurance. I knew it. I could feel it.

"What do you mean?"

"The day when they brought me out here, there was a guard at the corner of the house and another car in the courtyard. The guard wasn't hiding his rifle. Activity—more activity." I was right. The place was dead. In the hour we'd waited, there'd been no sign of life. Nothing. Zilch.

The three of them started really paying attention then. And when they all turned back to look at me, I could tell that they knew I was right. Almost right, that is. Never class anything as a certainty.

Because just then, the glass shattered in the front window, a crack echoed in the French forest, and Howard Brown's shirt turned a scarlet red.

The blood frothed and bubbled at his chest, and his eyes telegraphed their surprise before they glazed. I'd seen it before.

He was gone.

Hem had splatters of blood on his shirt and cheek. Arlaine stared, almost paralyzed it seemed, as Brown slumped in the seat.

"Kick him out the door, Hem! Now!"

Ernest Hemingway didn't have to be told twice. He leaned back against his door and rammed his feet into Brown's limp body.

The door wouldn't give.

Another shot shattered the glass, passing through the front and exiting the rear between me and Arlaine.

Hem thrust his legs forward again, with a vengeance. Brown went out, and the driver's door, the twisting metal screeching like a wounded animal, flew out with him.

I tried to get a bearing on the gunman as Hem slid into the driver's seat. Somebody had to go crank this jalopy, and I guessed I was elected. Having no luck targeting the gunman, I cracked open my door and started to make the dash.

"Don't, Jack!" Arlaine shouted.

"And sit here and get killed? No thanks. I've been a sitting duck before. It's not fun."

Slipping out the door, I hugged the car, figuring that I presented less of a target.

No shots.

My heart was doing the mamba, lodged somewhere between my stomach and my adam's apple. The brandy and milk I'd had that morning were about to make a nasty reappearance.

I gulped the rising flood back down and made my move.

God bless that auto. Two revolutions did it. And no gunshots.

Something had to work right. And just as I made a beeline for the door, a bullet dug a hole in the ground where I'd been standing.

"Go!"

Hem threw it in gear, and with a jolting lurch, the auto hopped out of its hiding place and onto the road. Arlaine pulled me down in the seat, and Hem slid lower in his as another pair of gunshots sounded, but we were moving too fast and too erratically for an accurate shot.

As we careened off down the lane, I chanced a look back and saw a figure carrying a rifle run from the woods opposite where we'd hidden. But he didn't try another shot, and I turned around and slouched down, my breathing coming in hard painful bursts and my fingers, surprising me just a little, entwined with Arlaine's, but gripping her like I used to grip the joystick of my Spad 13.

• • • •

"Going back to the embassy makes no sense," I argued. "Miller will wring his hands, pull his hair, and act like a typical diplomat, a species remarkably incapable of doing more than making promises it can't keep. *We've* got to figure out what to do. And we've got to stay off the streets. They may think they've spooked us by killing Brown. Or they may be out there in droves trying to find us. But, I don't think they'll change their plans. They've come too far now." The Bolsheviks I'd met in 1919 hadn't seemed much like the kind that would change plans too readily. As a matter of fact, I'd always thought it was that irreversible singularity of purpose that gave them victory.

"Okay, okay," Arlaine finally agreed.

We were back at my flat. It seemed as good a place as any. Hem had commandeered a bottle of rum, and we were settling our nerves with a couple of shots around my kitchen table.

"Yeah, well, somebody's gonna have to tell H. Winston what happened to his auto," Hem joked grimly. We'd abandoned it, minus the door and front windshield on the rue de Chaillot near the American Chancellery. But the thought of the abandoned auto reminded me of something—someone—else we had abandoned, Howard Brown.

"You don't have time to get a message or any real instructions from your boss in Berlin. And I wouldn't trust anything H. Winston said to do." I ignored Hem and kept arguing with Arlaine.

"Nobody knows what these guys even look like except me, so flooding the station with cops—and it'll probably be flooded anyway—doesn't really help us out. In fact, going to Duvall might just increase the risks. They might try to change their plan. At least this way, we know what it is." I paused and thought a minute about my next statement. "No, the only thing to do is to be at the Gare de Lyon when Lloyd George's train stops. I'll find myself a place where I can get a good look at everybody. You two will be in the crowd. When, and if, I spot him, I'll signal you to move in, and I'll get there as soon as possible."

"Jack," Hem began, shaking his head. "The Gare de Lyon is a big place, and it's gonna be damned crowded tomorrow. I'm not sure three of us can get the job done. We might end up with one dead prime minister on our hands."

I looked at Arlaine, and her expression told me she agreed. Pondering the situation, I tossed another shot of rum back and set the glass on the table with a thunk. We only had one resource. We only had one answer to the problem.

"Okay, Hem, here's what I want you to do." And I explained in detail how we were gonna solve that little problem. "Don't show up tomorrow without them," I warned as I finished.

"No problem, Jocko. I'm gonna allez right now and get to work. Stay indoors. I'll stick to the back alleys. And watch out," he said without a smile.

A knock on the door stopped him.

All three of us froze like grotesque caricatures of Greek statues.

"Hem," I whispered and nodded towards the entrance.

He caught my meaning and stationed himself behind the door.

I directed Arlaine away from the door's line of sight. The knock sounded again as I approached. My very own collection of butterflies were whipping their wings around in my stomach.

My hand gripped the doorknob and turned.

I pulled the door to me an inch at a time.

And that unmistakable mop of brown hair bobbed down around my waist.

"Your mail, Monsieur Barnett," Julien announced, pushing the door back with stern confidence.

"Jesus!" My heart raced like an airplane engine.

Hem wiped the sweat off his forehead as a grin wrapped itself around his face. "Christ, kid, you could give a corpse a heart attack."

"What have you got for me?" I leaned against the doorframe and prayed for my stomach to settle. "I said, 'what have you got?'"

But Julien was staring at Arlaine with approving eyes. "Elle est la belle mademoiselle!"

A little of the tension fled from Arlaine's face, and she managed a smile. "Merci beaucoup."

"My mail, Julien?" I reminded him.

"Oh, oui, Monsieur Barnett." He handed the slim stack of letters over and then left his hand out.

"C'mon, Julien. Not every time." I was tired of having to pay extra.

"Fifteen francs, Monsieur," Julien said.

"Damn expensive mail," Hem noted.

"Forget it. Nothing's worth fifteen francs, kid."

"Some men came looking for you earlier this evening, Monsieur." A coy look covered Julien's face.

My stomach began twisting again, and I glanced quickly at Hem and Arlaine. "Who?"

"When?" Hem asked.

Julien rolled his eyes. "There is nothing to worry about. I told them you had gone away, in a hurry, this afternoon. That you said you would not be back for a week." He tucked his hands in his pocket and smiled smugly.

"What did they look like?"

"Just men, with foreign voices. One, he . . . ," Julien searched for the words, frowned, and continued in French, "il fut ricanment."

"He sneered, huh?" I repeated. No need for further explanations. Reaching into my pocket, I pulled fifteen francs out and slapped them in Julien's palm. "This time you did save my life, kid." I ruffled his hair, and he grinned. "Now get out of here."

The door closed, and he was gone. Fifteen francs richer.

"That explains some things."

"Yeah," Hem said. "Like why nobody's messing with us now. But stay inside anyway." He turned and headed towards the door.

"You watch out, too," I said to Hem's broad back as he slipped into the hallway. He was smart and reliable. I'd grown pretty fond of him. "And quit calling me 'Jocko'!"

Hemingway threw a forced grin over his shoulder and was gone.

I flipped the mail on my bed and turned back to Arlaine. She was fingering an empty glass, staring at the tabletop. "What's wrong?"

"Howard," she said softly. "He was a good guy. Real dedicated, honest. Had a bad temper though."

"Yeah," I agreed. "No doubt about that." And I remembered Hem decking the red-head at the cafe the week before. It seemed a long, long time ago.

Suddenly, she shoved the glass across the table, and it fell, rolling to the edge. "And we just left him lying in the woods, dead."

Tears washed across her cheeks, and her eyes reddened quickly and boldly. The rum gave me courage, and I went to her, taking her arms in my hands and moving her from the table to the sofa. I retrieved the bottle and our glasses and sat down next to her.

She let me hold her while she sobbed, and it felt good to have her warmth against me. Other women I saw around Paris, Hadley Hemingway for one, seemed to always keep their hair short, but Arlaine's reached down past her shoulders and gleamed in the room's yellowed light. I let my fingers roam in that golden forest until I could feel her head beneath my fingertips.

"Sorry," she said, pulling away a little. "Howard and I worked together in Berlin some and we were friends."

"Just that?"

She smiled almost sadly. "Just that." After a moment's pause, she looked back at me and took my hand in hers. "I wanted to tell you what was going on, but the whole thing was too sensitive. Too much was at risk. When it became obvious that you were going to investigate Pfeiffer's murder, Howard insisted that I stick with you and sidetrack you."

"You did a pretty good job of obscuring things," I admitted.

"My job. I always do my job." She squeezed my hand tighter, and we sat silently for a minute or two. "Howard told me to slow you down. I did as good as I could. My job."

"How *did* you get this job? A few nights ago you were telling me that Arlaine Watson was just what she seemed to be. Obviously, that was a little less than the truth."

"I finished Radcliffe a couple of years ago. My father has been a diplomat all his life. I wanted to go to Europe. He arranged a job for me in Berlin with the military attaché, Truman Smith, the guy that first got wind of this thing. I speak German and French, a little Russian. I wanted some excitement, some adventure. Truman let me do some little chores for him around Berlin, so I was used to the routine. When he needed somebody to go to Paris and infiltrate the French Communists, I begged for the assignment. Truman finally—reluctantly I might add—said yes. He told me to expect anything. He told me that it could get rough. I said I believed him, but I'm not sure I really did until it got that way."

"And when it did?"

"And when it did, does, you find yourself doing things you never thought you could or would."

"The Education of Arlaine Watson."

"At least I passed all the subjects," she said, looking not at me but at some far distant something beyond the walls, and I noticed again the lines that had deepened at her eyes.

"You seem to have a real knack for it."

"Is that a compliment or an insult?" A hint of concern marked her expression, and I was afraid that I'd touched a nerve.

"I'm not sure," I said, truthfully unsure of which answer was the safest.

She laughed and the sound—or the quick jolt of rum I downed—eased my stomach. "At least you're honest."

"Jack?" she said after a minute.

"Yeah."

"What was Goering talking about? Your last patrol?"

I didn't answer.

"Jack?"

I sipped from the glass again. The rum had my stomach feeling nice and warm, and that blocked my usual warning flags. The whole thing seemed less important through my alcoholic fog. It seemed natural to tell her. She had shared with me; maybe it was time for me to repay the favor. For the first time, I *really* wanted to tell somebody. I threw back another shot of the rum to bolster my courage.

"I'd been flying with the 94th Aero Squadron, Eddie Rickenbacker's old unit. But during the summer, I was offered a chance to transfer to No. 56 Squadron at Cachy. I did. By late October of 1918, the war was winding down. The Germans were running out of pilots. Hell, only Goering, commanding Richthofen's Flying Circus, had any real pilots left. They were sending up kids—I mean just plain children barely out of their teens.

"Anyway, on Halloween, October 31st, I was leading a patrol out of the aerodrome at Cachy up to the Somme and then east towards Cambrai. We were over farmland, just a few minutes from the airfield. Still over Allied territory. I was feeling pretty good. I'd just nailed my twenty-first victory, and I wasn't too far behind

Rickenbacker. And, the week before, I'd escaped from a German prison camp. I knew war was hell, and I was living off brandy, milk, and shattered nerves, but some of my old cockiness had come back. Yeah, I was feeling good. Maybe it was because I knew the end was pretty near. Hell, who knows."

I took another hit of the rum and sat silently for a second.

"Go on." Her voice was soft but insistent.

"I saw him before the others did. He was flying west in a Fokker D7, sort of erratically, like he didn't have a good idea of how to keep the crate in the air. I sent my patrol on, signalling that I'd take care of him. They waggled their wings, waved, and headed to the east.

"He was a mile away, so I pushed in the throttle, banked towards him and got ready to jockey behind him. Poor guy." I paused and shook my head. "He never saw me coming. He didn't try to manuever. It was all he could do to keep the plane flying relatively straight. He was young, a kid, with silky blond hair. I figured I'd plug a hole in his engine and force him to land. Then, he could spend the rest of the war safe, in one of our camps. I was feeling compassionate that day. And I just knew I could do it. I was pretty damned good, and I couldn't pass up a chance to show how good I was.

"Well, I lined up, gauged his engine, and let go with a burst. I missed." I wasn't on the couch anymore. I was back in the cockpit of my Spad 13. The wind was whipping around me and the drone of the rotary engine pounded my ears. And only the rum kept the knot in my stomach small enough to withstand. "He must have seen a tracer go by then because he looked over his shoulder and panic showed in his eyes. He banked left, hard and tight. I followed, turning my machine on its side. When he straightened out, I was still on his tail. I slowed just a little and anticipated his next move, banking right just slightly.

"I couldn't have planned it better. He banked right and I fired, hoping to catch the engine broadside. I didn't. I caught the fuel line instead. With a tracer." In my mind I could see the bullet heading for his machine. I could see it pierce the fuel line. I could see the fuel ignite.

"And then?" Arlaine was staring at me intently.

A shiver ran through me, and I realized that I had locked my glass in a white-knuckle grip. A sheen of sweat made my forehead damp and hot.

"Then," I said, trying to relax, refilling my glass and taking a sip. "Then, smoke started pouring out of his engine. And then the smoke turned to flames. And the crate started spinning.

"I followed the machine all the way down. The flames were fanning back in his face, and I could even see his shoulders jerk as he tried to unbuckle himself. But he panicked and before he could do anything, his Fokker became a ball of fire, and it slammed into a barn, sending that too into a burning shambles.

"The field out beside the barn was pretty flat and I landed to see if I could do anything. A lorry of French soldiers was passing by and they stopped to help put out the fire. They patted me on the back for the kill, but all I could see were the flames licking at that kid's face. And all I could smell was that sick, sweet scent of burning flesh."

"I'm sorry, Jack. That must have been . . . , well, I don't know what that was like." Her hand caressed mine.

I laughed, a hollow kind of laugh. "Oh, that was just part of it. See, when we finally got the fire out, it seems that a boy and a girl were making use of the hayloft just as the kid crashed into it. We found them, burned and shriveled, still entwined. The fire, the explosion, it all happened at once. They must have been right next to where the plane hit. The guy was melted in between her legs and the flesh was almost burned off their skulls." I could still see them; I'd always see them, and smell them.

"Oh, God, Jack." Arlaine shivered and I felt it.

I took another hit of the rum, and it went down smoothly. "The next thing I knew, I was screaming and Frank O'Connor was holding me, telling me I was gonna be all right. But, I wasn't. I'm not. Since then, I haven't been able to. . . ." I paused. "You see ever since then, any time I had the chance, I could only think of those bodies entwined, entangled, melted together."

"So that's why the other night—"

"I bolted and ran like a stuck pig," I finished for her. "See, I was beginning to feel, well, I was scared it wouldn't last." If it hadn't been for the rum, I would never have had the nerve to say it.

A hand pulled the glass from me then, and I looked into Arlaine's blue, blue eyes. They were big, almost luminiscent. Her other hand began massaging me.

"Why?"

"Because I like you," she answered. "Maybe I even love you. Because tomorrow is going to be one hell of a day. And, most of all, because I want to." And then her hand swept away the tear rolling across my cheek, and her lips met mine. I returned the pressure, tentatively at first, then more forcefully, more intently.

I pushed her back on the sofa and unbuttoned her blouse, removed her bra, and touched her breasts. Her hands were busy, too, and what I thought would never happen again became a possibility. And some minutes later, after I entered her and we moved together, it became real. Reality and fantasy merged into one exquisite moment. But what should have been over quickly lasted a long time, and Arlaine, murmuring in my ear, seemed to share my complete happiness. I wanted to howl at the moon.

I slept without dreams.

And as I lay next to her while the sun reached through my window, feeling the press of her bare breasts against me and her rhythmic breathing, I thought about what she said. Because tomorrow had arrived. And when I got up and passed the table, saw the packet of mail that Julien had dropped off the night before, saw the handwriting on the top envelope, I knew that the world was topsy-turvy. Because the handwriting was my father's, and, unquestionably, it *was* gonna be one hell of a day.

Sixteen

L loyd George's special was scheduled to arrive any minute. And the gnawing in my stomach was washing away the pleasures of the night before, and the shock of the morning after. I hadn't had the nerve to open the letter from my father. With a pang of guilt, I'd stowed it off to the side, out of sight, but not completely out of mind. I checked my watch. Almost noon. And that son-of-a-bitch Hemingway still hadn't shown up.

I kept circulating through the platform area, walking up and down, looking at faces. It was shaded; the huge roof, held up by an intricate arrangement of iron girders, defused the light enough to cast a light shadow over everything. The place was lousy with reporters, gendarmes, and railroad employees. The reporters were all jockeying to get close to the train. The gendarmes were trying to maintain some kind of control. And the employees—porters, janitors, and some mechanics—were just trying to do their jobs.

Arlaine was stationed at the entrance to the platform, holding a bag like she was going somewhere. I hoped she'd see one of Dounat's friends, anybody, that might be linked to all this.

"We're here!"

I almost jumped through the roof. "Jesus, Hem, couldn't you give me a little warning. I'm about to throw up as it is."

Hemingway stood behind me, grinning from ear to ear. "They're in position."

I looked around and saw that he was right. I prayed to God that the Bolsheviks weren't using a bomb. If they did, Paris' literary community was gonna take a heavy hit. Ezra Pound loped up and down the platform, eyeing every person that came within range.

Bob McAlmon, hair parted down the middle and combed back like always, lounged against a trashcan.

"Where's Gertrude?"

"C'mon, Jack, be serious."

"Okay, okay."

"Mr. Barnett, where would you like me?"

I turned around and there was James Joyce, eye patch, bow tie, and white tennis shoes in place, leaning on his cane. "What are you doing here?"

"I am here, Mr. Barnett. Now, where would you like me?"

"Up there," and I pointed towards Arlaine. Appropriate, I thought, that the framer and framed should be stationed together. He spun and made his way through the crowd.

"Why?" I asked Hem.

He shrugged. "Who knows? He does things for his own reasons. He and Ezra were boozing it up at the Dingo last night. I explained the situation, and he volunteered. Actually, I think he likes you."

"Too bad the feeling's not mutual. Listen," I continued. "When the train comes in, be as close to it as you can."

Hem nodded.

"Nothing to do now," I said, my stomach rumbling almost rhythmically, "but wait."

• • • •

The train was late. I spent the time circulating through the crowd and trying to figure out how it would happen. Lloyd George and Premier Poincaré were meeting onboard the train. The killer would wait until the French leader left. Poincaré opposed the Genoa Conference, so there'd be nothing to gain by killing him too. Lloyd George would come out to see him off. As soon as the two were separated, that's when our guy would strike.

I could give no guarantee that I'd recognize anybody. My total contact had lasted less than thirty minutes. And the room had been dark. I could really only remember Sneer's face clearly. Five of them. I remembered five. But only Sneer stood out. Only his insolence stirred my memory.

People began to rush past me. In the distance, over the babbling of the crowd, I could hear the rhythmic clattering of the train.

Goddamnit, I thought.

Still no Sneer or any of his buddies.

I glanced back over the crowd towards the door, and Arlaine shrugged and shook her head. Nothing. That area was clearing out. Only Arlaine, Joyce, and a couple of janitors sweeping. The train pulled into the station, slowing and hissing, slowing and hissing. The rush soon became a mob, and people were pushing and shoving to get closer.

A square-jawed man, sporting a big block mustache, elbowed me hard in the side. I yelled some unkind things in his ear as he went past. Reporters had their pads and pens out, ready to see whether Poincaré had changed his mind and would go to Genoa.

Still nothing. I jumped in the middle of the pile. A reporter. That had to be it. Reporters could be both obnoxious and invisible at the same time. I shoved my way through, signalling to Hemingway to meet me halfway.

I scanned the reporters.

Nothing.

I looked again. My attacker of a minute before was right in the middle of the mob. Something about his square jaw sparked a memory. Maybe it was the half light in the platform, maybe not. The man who questioned me, the Communist, had a square jaw and a block cut mustache. I could see his chin dipping into the light, the light just touching the heavy mustache.

Jesus, I thought.

It was him.

"Hemingway!" I pointed hard and fast at the man.

He nodded, and we started wading through the crowd.

Lloyd George, old and a little hunched-over, and Poincaré, haughty and arrogant, appeared at the train door together. Neither man smiled.

I felt like I was swimming. The knot in my stomach grew larger and more painful with each second. Blood rushed into my face. I felt hot, flushed. Shouts rang in my ears. Questions. But our target kept his mouth shut. Didn't shout questions of his own. Maybe he wasn't there to ask questions, I thought. Maybe he had something else on his mind.

I pushed on, fighting for each inch.

The two leaders were exchanging some words of farewell. They shook hands.

I reached the man first.

My fist closed around his shoulder just seconds before Hemingway grabbed him around the neck.

Surprise lit his eyes as we dragged him back out of the crowd to the jeers, shouts, and curses of everyone around.

"Watch for a gun, Hem!" I warned as we put him on the floor.

Hem planted a knee in his chest, and I breathed a heavy sigh, the relief in my stomach almost as satisfying as the night before had been. We'd done it.

Behind us, I heard Poincaré bid Lloyd George a farewell, and then the questions began in earnest.

"I say, chaps, is this quite necessary?"

The man on the floor looked up at me and blinked.

"What did you say?"

He blinked again, unruffled and unperturbed. "I said, 'is this quite necessary.'" The voice was unmistakably British, no hint of heavy Russian.

Hem pulled the knee out of his chest, and I backed off.

Crawling to his feet, the man extended a hand, "Lester Carrington, *Liverpool Daily News.*"

The knot exploded in my stomach again. Jesus! How wrong could I get? "Sorry," I mumbled, spinning and checking the train. Lloyd George and Poincaré were shaking hands again, and the French premier began to take a step away.

"Jack!"

I was back in flight then. I banked and turned on one wing. Arlaine stood across the station at the door and pointed back towards the train. Her mouth hung open in a shout. Everything was moving slowly.

He was halfway between the door and the crowd surrounding Lloyd George, maybe fifty feet away. A pistol appeared from within his coveralls as he let his broom fall to the side. Somehow, above the incredible din of shouts and questions, I heard the broom clatter against the concrete floor.

My old friend, Sneer, dressed as a janitor.

I bolted across the platform, glancing over my shoulder and shouting at Hemingway. But I caught a glimpse of the Brit holding his arm and asking him a question.

Sneer saw me.

He turned the pistol towards my stomach.

Arlaine seemed frozen in position, the shout still echoing from her mouth. Joyce took a step forward.

I was fifteen feet away.

Sneer sneered, and I could see the muscles tighten in his hand as his finger closed over the trigger.

I closed my eyes and dove towards the barrel.

Maybe he wasn't expecting a suicide dive. Who knows? He took my head butt full in the chest, and I heard no explosion, no gunshot.

We collapsed together on the floor. The pistol went skidding away, and I slugged him across the jaw, the feel of my fist crushing his cheek sending a chill of pleasure along my arm.

"Jack!" I heard Hem roar behind me.

Sneer's face had lost its surprise, regained its smirk, and I looked down.

A knife was heading for my belly.

Sneer's grin grew wider.

The knot in my stomach turned cold.

I could feel the knife point push the fabric of my shirt.

I sucked in my stomach, hoping in my panic that the extra fraction of an inch would make a difference.

But then the knife suddenly, magically, flew out of his hand, and a wooden stick lodged itself against his throat.

"I will gladly crush your windpipe," a voice, thick with an Irish brogue, said.

"And if he doesn't, I will," another, brash and brazen voice added.

The stick was James Joyce's cane, and he and fiery-haired Ezra Pound stood over us as only he and Joyce could do, with an air of complete superiority. Assholes.

Hem appeared at my side, and we turned Sneer over to the gendarmes who suddenly crawled out of every hole.

Lloyd George and his bunch didn't seem to notice what was going on. The reporters were focused on them, and so our little drama was played out with few observers.

Suddenly, Ezra, McAlmon, Arlaine, Hem, hell all of them were pounding me on the back. And there was Duvall, lighting a cigarette, and smiling on the platform. His boys had Sneer and were hauling him away.

"Is this what it was all about, Jack?"

I nodded. "Part of it anyway."

The little group broke up. Ezra, McAlmon, and Joyce went off to get drunk. Arlaine and Hem hung around with me and Duvall. The four of us watched Lloyd George safely reboard his train and listened with satisfaction as it squealed out of the station headed to Genoa.

"C'est fini, Jack?" Duvall asked, his eyebrows arching ever so slightly.

"C'est fini, pal," I answered as Arlaine slipped her arm in mine.

• • • •

And it would have been, except that Hem and I arranged for Hadley and Arlaine to meet us in Spain for a couple of days after Genoa.

We shot to our respective homes after the incident at the Gare de Lyon, threw some clothes together and took off for Genoa ourselves. Arlaine hustled off to the embassy to make her report. After that it was three boring weeks of listening to political crap. Nothing was accomplished except that Russia and Germany announced a new treaty which scared the hell out of everybody. And there was some talk of a secret military codicil that would allow Germany to rearm and to train their army in Russia, thus breaking the Treaty of Versailles. I could just see Goering and Kopfmann stomping and shouting already. They didn't like the Commies. They certainly wouldn't like being in the political bed with them. At least that's what I thought then. But, anyway, they'd scored some political points with the United States by helping with the Lloyd George conspiracy, and that's what they had been after anyway.

We wired the girls to bring us some extra clothes and meet us in a little village I knew of along the Ebro River. It was a quiet, peaceful place. Beautiful trees, in that first green flush of spring, lined the river banks. The long hills marking the valley of the Ebro were a peculiar chalk-like color that stood in distinct contrast to the heavy green of the foliage.

The girls were down in the cafe. Our hotel was across the narrow street from the train station, and a small cafe dominated the ground floor. A tattered awning protected the customers from any rain and from the hot Spanish sun.

Hem and I had gone up to the room to change clothes. It had been several days since we'd gotten any duds washed. And I'd told Arlaine to just bring what she could find. Searching through the bag she brought, I caught myself whistling senseless, happy tunes. Until I found the letter from my father, and I stopped whistling. Hefting the thin envelope, I realized that I didn't want to know what was in it. I stowed it in my pocket for later and went back to whistling.

Hem was quiet while I changed. He'd been sort of stand-offish ever since the Gare de Lyon and even before really. Buttoning the last button on his shirt, he wandered over to his bag and reached in, pulling something out and cloaking it in his hand.

"Jocko?"

"Yeah, Hem." I pulled my trousers on and buttoned them.

"Something I need to tell you." An edge marked his tone that I didn't like.

I stopped what I was doing and turned to face him. His shirt was rumpled, and he could have used a shave. But his face was tortured, almost wrinkled. He looked older than I did. "What is it, Hem?"

"I've thought long and hard about telling you this. It may not make any difference to you, but, Jeez, I don't know. You're my pal, Jocko. It's been great being around you these last weeks. I mean, you're a great pal. You, I don't know, I think you really understand me. And," this was tough for him, whatever it was, and the words were hanging up in his throat, "and, I just figured you ought to know."

"Know what?" My perpetual knot had reappeared in my stomach. I didn't know where he was driving, but his whole manner told me I wouldn't like it. In all our friendship, I'd never seen Ernest Hemingway search so completely and futilely for the right words.

He opened his big paw and revealed a crumpled pamphlet. "This is that Commie pamphlet I took off Paul Dounat's table the day we found him . . . well, you know."

I remembered seeing him pick it up then. The knot grew bigger.

"You need to look at this." He handed it over and looked away, a glistening in his eye that he wiped away quickly. "Don't hate me, Jocko. I just figured you needed to know, before things went too far. I'll be in the cafe." And he was gone.

I looked down at the crudely-printed leaflet, its margins covered with handwritten notes in a large, looping hand, and got sick as the realization, the significance washed over me. I didn't need Hem to explain it to me. That stupid, socialist pamphlet transformed into a sledge hammer, and it crushed a part of me, some something way deep down inside, with a single blow. I've never felt so cold and alone, and so completely like an idiot, in my life. And a thousand little nitpicking, nagging questions were finally answered for me. I'd never gone down in flames before, but I knew what it felt like then. The blaze burned cold in my stomach and consumed my insides. And, for just a second, I became that boy in the Fokker, watching the flames lick at my own goggles.

And then I did the only thing I could do. I packed another bag and went downstairs to try and salvage my soul.

Hem was sitting by himself at a back corner table against the building, head bent over his pad. Arlaine, a smile on her face, sat near the street, staring off across at the station.

"Where's Hadley?" I stopped by Hem's table.

"Went for a walk," Hem said.

His tone told me he was there if I needed him, but he hoped I didn't. I walked on by and towards Arlaine.

That incredible, beautiful face looked up at me and, for a second, the innocence was back, in full, intoxicating force. And I wanted to believe in it. I wanted to believe in it so much.

"Hey," she said, softly, the smile curling her lips even more.

"Hey," I said, sitting down across from her. Extracting the pamphlet from my pocket, I laid it gently on the table.

"What's that supposed to be?" She smiled a little tentatively.

"It's a pamphlet from Paul Dounat's apartment."

"Oh." Her voice was stripped bare of any recognition. I willed it to be the truth. "Where'd you get it?"

"Hem picked it up the day we found Dounat dead."

"Why?" She asked me the question, but her eyes cut around towards Hem. He wasn't looking our way.

"Look at the handwriting." I pointed to the large, irregular, looping notes scrawled in the margins.

She glanced down, but it was a brief, fleeting look that told me more than I wanted to know. She didn't need to see it. Moisture sprang up in her eyes, and her neck muscles went rigid as she tried to block the tears. For a long second, she stayed like that, unwilling, or unable, to speak.

I was begging inside. I wanted to hear her tell me it wasn't true. I wanted her to tell me that she had no choice but to kill Paul Dounat. I wanted the decision to be one of Providence, unambiguous necessity, not Arlaine Watson's.

She exhaled finally, a deep penetrating sigh. "How long have you known?"

"Just today, just a few minutes. I should have known a long

time ago. I should have seen it. But I didn't know before the embassy that day that you were in the alley with Dounat. I didn't know until then that you wrote the note framing James Joyce. And when I found out, when you threw all the Communist conspiracy stuff at me, I didn't take time to think it through. I must have let stopping the Commies become my uppermost thought. I put the connections off in some corner of my brain. Until Hemingway made me face facts."

"Maybe there was no connection to make. Maybe Hemingway wrote these notes himself. Maybe he wants me for himself." One, last valiant effort.

I looked into her eyes, those incredible, blue eyes, blinking now in evasion, the innocence washed out by her guilty tears. "You don't know how much I wish that were true. But, Arlaine, I saw him take this pamphlet off Paul Dounat's table. And the fact remains that whoever wrote the note framing James Joyce at Shakespeare and Company and the person that wrote Paul Dounat's suicide note were one and the same. And these little notes prove that it wasn't him. And . . . ," I paused for a second as the lump grew in my throat, "since I know you wrote the note at the bookstore, that can only mean you killed Paul Dounat."

Tell me something, I wanted to scream, something to make it right, something that makes you innocent again. I wanted her to be that impulsive diplomat's daughter, impetuous, but innocent. But I kept remembering that wonderful night in my apartment when she told me, "I always do my job." The lump in my throat threatened to choke me.

"I was doing my job," she said, as if she could read my mind. She wasn't looking at me then; she was looking at those long white hills across the valley of the Ebro.

"You had to of course." I wanted to help her.

She thanked me with a grateful smile and nodded. "He would have exposed me. Gone to the police. You kept getting closer and the lies and deceit were tearing at him. But we didn't just want to stop the conspiracy; we wanted to get the Russians. I couldn't let him take me out of the game, just as I was getting close. He would have ruined all the work I'd done. A suicide, I figured, the Russians would accept. But if he went to the police, my usefulness would be at an end. Too many people would be involved. We would just drive them underground." Her fist started to slam down on the table, but she held it just an inch short of the mark, flattened it and slapped the table, her fingers shaking with tension. "I thought I could use the contacts I'd made through him to get even closer to the Russians. He had just begun to trust me, to believe me. I was almost in a position to meet the Russians. I was inches away from success. I was in control."

I shook my head as disappointment washed over me. "It doesn't make sense, Arlaine. You would have been better off telling him the truth about yourself, pulling him to your side. He was your link. He was your connection. No, I don't suppose it would have helped your position if he'd spilled his guts to the police. But, goddamnit Arlaine, he loved you. You could have handled him. I'm trying awfully hard," and I was, "but I can't see any real justification for killing him." And I really *did* want to see.

"He threatened you," I suggested. "He discovered that you were working with the Germans and he attacked you. He wanted to tell his Communist buddies about you. Your *life* was in danger."

Her eyes cut back to me, but she said nothing.

"Goddamnit, Arlaine! Tell me something real. Tell me something true! Don't fidget and squirm to come up with something you think I want to hear. Just tell me what happened."

She didn't look at me then, either. She watched those long hills, watched the birds flit from housetop to housetop, and watched the people wander in and out of the train station. "I panicked," she began softly. "When I realized that you had found the flaw in his story, I panicked. I knew he'd cave in. It had taken all I could do to keep him in line that long. I was already scared, but I got even more scared. We had come so far, and I had kept my part a secret. I needed more time to regain control. I needed control. Keeping him from talking seemed . . . like the logical thing to do. The smart thing. He'd decided to tell the Russians he wouldn't do it, wouldn't kill Lloyd George. Truman told me I'd have to make some rough decisions. I thought that was one of them. I thought it just went with the job. I tried not to think about it. I just did it."

"And then?" I prompted her.

"And then I was going to set myself up as the patsy. Let the Russians think that I would kill Lloyd George. I thought I was good enough to fool them. I thought I could dig into the Communist movement even deeper without him. He seemed like a liability. I was proud of myself for getting as far as I had. I knew that Truman would be proud of me. I had done what I had to, what the situation dictated. But, then. . . ."

"But then, it all went to hell anyway, didn't it?" We both knew it.

"Yeah," she admitted. "The whole thing unraveled. I had to realize that I just didn't think it through. There were other options, other alternatives, I could have chosen."

I could see it then. "So, you made a mistake. A miscalculation."

Her eyes brightened a little. "Yeah." She liked those mechanical terms; she liked taking the humanity out of it. "A miscalculation."

I wanted her to have the best of excuses, but making mistakes didn't work. Making mistakes was too close to home. It's thinking that you have the right answers when you don't. It's thinking that you're good, good enough. It's like my father said; it's believing in the infallibility of yourself. "Somebody died," I reminded her.

Just as quickly as the brightness in her eyes came, it vanished, replaced by a dullness. "I know."

It was my turn to stare out at those hills. "I can't say I don't love you, Arlaine. I can't say that if you call me a month or a year from now, I won't come running to you. But, I can't forget that you suddenly had to go home after Hem and I discovered the flaw in Dounat's story. I can't forget that you went to him, sat next to him on that couch, and put the gun to his head, to the head of that kid that loved you so much. I can't forget that you pulled the trigger.

"The truth is a funny thing. It's something we all treasure, but something that can cut deeply when we find it. I can't deal with your truths right now, Arlaine. They're too much like my own."

"Things can't be the way they were anymore, can they?"

"No, not now. Every time I see you, I'll be reminded of too many things. Too many painful hurts. Too many sins we share."

"Will you tell Duvall?"

I laughed, but it didn't feel good. "Duvall knows, if I'm any judge of men. He knew back at Dounat's flat. He looked at the pamphlets on the table, too. But he had just enough pressure from above to end the affair cleanly. And he knew that the U.S. Embassy was taking potshots at me and Hem for a reason. He wanted the case closed, and he couldn't afford diplomatic entanglements. So, no, I won't tell Duvall that I figured it out. And he'll never tell me the truths that he knows."

"Will you ever change your mind?"

"Maybe later, but not now. Every time I look at you, I see my dream in living color; I see my mistakes walking beside me." I stood and picked up her bag. "I'll check your bag and get your ticket. Paris?"

She nodded and stared out at the hills again. The tears were no longer dammed, and they rolled down her cheeks.

It took a few minutes for me to buy the ticket and leave the bag with a porter. As I walked back across the street, I saw that she still looked across the valley.

"Are you okay?"

"I'm fine," she said, wiping an errant tear from her face. "I'm just fine." She stood. "What will you do?"

I shrugged. "Get drunk with Hadley and Hemingway. Try to forget you and Paul Dounat. Hope that the dreams don't start again."

"Have I ruined that for you too?"

"Maybe." But I knew she had. When I understood the truth, a shock, an electric shock, ran through my body, and all the strength she had given me, all of it, left. But I had beaten it once. Somehow, right then, I knew that I could beat it again.

"I can't say I won't call you," she said, stepping down from the sidewalk and starting towards the station.

"I hope I'll have the strength to ignore it."

And she was gone, disappearing inside the station.

And, it was then, as I watched her go, that I pulled the envelope from my pocket, read the first letter that my father had ever written me, and cried.

Epilogue

‘Y’ou were eavesdropping!"

"No, I was *observing*. There's a difference."

The sunlight flickered off the bouncing waves. The water was clean and blue like it always was off Key West. Hem was fishing, with no results. I was downing martinis to fight seasickness.

"Call it what you want, but you eavesdropped on me and Arlaine that day and turned it into this story." I waved a book at him.

"Papa?" A lean, tanned deckhand came from the cabin. "Time to head in, si?"

Hem nodded abruptly, scratching at his beard. "Yeah, I guess so, goddamnit. Can't make 'em bite when they don't want to."

Everybody was calling him "Papa" by then—he had a couple of bestsellers under his belt, and he'd completely eclipsed Gertrude Stein—but he'd always be "Hem" to me. He'd always be that young, amiable bear in Paris, poring over his stories and drinking everything in sight. The key to Hem, I think, was that he concentrated on his writing as hard as he did his drinking, and that made all the difference.

The boat came about and headed back towards the far distant pier. "And another thing, Hem. Arlaine and I *did* sleep together, and she was nothing like Duff Twysden. And, 'Jake,' Hem. Couldn't you have hidden me a little better than that?" It wasn't that I minded him appropriating my life, but he didn't have to let everybody know it was *my life*.

Ernest Hemingway unbuckled himself from his fishing seat and grinned that infectious grin. "Oh, hell, Jocko. Don't be so hard on me."

We moved to the upper deck and faced the bow, both drinking, both thinking. "You know, Hem," I said after a minute or two. "That day in the cafe, Arlaine and I *weren't* talking about abortion."

He shrugged. "I know."

In the distance, the shore came into view, and as we grew closer, a tiny dot on the pier became a man, a shawl covering his shoulders, sitting in a wheelchair.

"This Florida weather sure seems to sit well with your old man, Jack."

"Yeah," I said, watching as my father's wrinkled face loomed larger and more placid with each wave the boat vaulted. The stroke locked him in the wheelchair just after my mother died, just after I read his letter. "He needed me, and I guess I needed him."

A tiny figure slipped from behind the wheelchair and sat down on the edge of the pier, swinging his feet like seven year olds do.

"The kid looks a lot like you, Jocko. Kids are great to have, aren't they?"

I watched my son with pride. Time *does* heal *all* wounds. "Yeah, Hem, they are."

"Do you ever think about her, Jack?"

Turning my head a little, I saw that Hem was staring at me intently. I half expected him to get out his little, tattered notebook. "Sure. She was . . . well . . . special. I never heard from her again after that day in Spain, you know. And down deep, I really *did* want to see her again."

"You reminded each other of too many things, pal. You *can* know a person too well."

Silence covered us for a few more minutes. "You know, Hem," I began. "Sometimes those years in Paris seem like a big yoke around my neck. I used to see it as this wonderful sanctuary where you didn't have to worry about the rules. Hell, in Paris, there weren't any rules. But now the memories seem confining, claustrophobic, like a prison. Like I had to leave it, had to be released, before I could begin to live again. And then a part of me says that Paris was my release, the key to my sanity, the beginning and ending of my dreams. Oh, shit, Hem, I can't get it clear in my head." I paused and studied the small red alcoholic veins beginning to line Hem's nose as I tried to grip my feelings, my emotions. And, in my quest, I found myself back there, in that city of seductive smells and unbridled passions, and I saw again the faces—Frank, Mademoiselle

Mariette, Bob McAlmon, Ezra, Gertrude, Alice, Sylvia, Joyce, Duvall, and the rest. "Sometimes it seemed like heaven and hell all at the same time. And the funny thing is, I never knew which I preferred. But as dark as it seems now, I get the feeling that if it hadn't been for Paris, none of that," and I nodded to the dock, "would be possible."

"Jocko," Hem admonished, and those wonderful eyes, set above cheeks already plumping from excess, reflected the sparkle of that blue, blue water. "Paris was a great place to be young. I mean, I know that what she was to you was different than what she was to me, but that's part of her beauty. She changed as we changed." His eyes drifted out to sea, and a soft distant smile marked him. "She's the perfect mistress that molds herself to our pleasures, our hungers. She gave herself to each one of us completely. We were lucky to have been there, to have had her. She'll always be with us. And besides," the grin widened even further, and his eyes returned to lock me in their inescapable charm. "It was a hell of a fine time, wasn't it?"

And then we docked.

The End

Historical Notes

Expatriate Paris was one of the most colorful and exciting places a writer could be in the 1920s and 1930s. Almost every writer of consequence to American literature in that part of the century made at least a token appearance in Paris. To try to capture a hint of that milieu, a taste of that excitement, is almost beyond the abilities of any writer in the 1990s. But, for better or worse, that's what I've attempted in these pages. I've tried to remain faithful to the setting, and I've tried to paint the historical characters as true to life as my research and my skills allowed.

For the record, the novel takes place during late March and early April of 1922. Ernest and Hadley Hemingway had only been in Paris for a few months. Sylvia Beach did indeed publish *Ulysses* in March of 1922, and she did sink a great deal of her financial resources into that venture. *Ulysses* was banned from being published in the United States after a lawsuit filed by the Society for the Suppression of Vice. *The Little Review,* which had been publishing the novel in serial form, was ably represented by John Quinn of New York. Quinn failed, however, in his attempts. A favorable review by Sisley Huddleston in England during the middle of March had sparked a significant number of orders, and Joyce's fame was sealed despite the book's legal difficulties.

Hemingway himself spoke of the antics of the Communists and German Nationalists chasing each other through Paris. It seemed only natural to include them in the plot. And Joseph Stalin did object to the Soviet Union's participation in the Genoa Conference. And

German Foreign Minister Rathenau was not a favorite of the fledgling Nazi party. Indeed, shortly after the Genoa Conference, Rathenau was gunned down by two men described by at least one historian as young Nazis.

A plot against Lloyd George? It was not as implausible as it sounds. European stability was more a facade than anything real and lasting. The French and the English have always had something of a love/hate relationship. The Germans were quite unable to make their reparation payments as dictated by the Versailles Treaty. The Soviets, at least the Stalinist faction, were as anti-Western as the West was anti-Soviet. Rumors had been circulating for some weeks that Germany and Lenin were involved in secret negotiations aimed at giving Germany an opportunity to train military troops in violation of the peace treaty. Neither the Stalinists nor the Nazis would have looked on such an alliance, at that time, with favor. The assassination of Lloyd George, with a Frenchman as the fall guy, would have tumbled French and England into a major diplomatic crisis, potentially another war, one which would have quickly spread across the continent, so unsettled were the bulk of diplomatic relations.

As far as characters, I've made a valiant effort to paint the historical figures as close to life as possible. Have I made errors? Of course. No one, writing in 1993, can possibly do complete justice to describing people of 1922. Nor, might I add, could those same people have been accurate in describing their own movements and actions seventy-one years after the fact. So, the author strives for the essence of the person, while keeping in mind his ultimate goal of writing something intriguing and humorous, something entertaining.

Separating the real from the fictitious is often a problem. Inspector Duvall is, alas, a figment of my imagination as are Arlaine Watson, the right Reverend Quintin Karper, Frank O'Connor, Pierre Legrain, Heinrich Kopfmann, Paul Dounat, young Julien, Howard Brown, H. Winston Miller, and all the young ladies at Madame Mariette's La Panier Fleuri. However, the brothel itself and Madame Mariette indeed existed, and the laundry across the street where more discreet services could be provided was truly a Paris institution. Jimmy Charters, another unforgettable character, did wait bar at the Dingo, but I moved his tenure there up by a year merely so I could include him in the book. It seemed wrong to leave him out.

Joyce, Ezra Pound, Gertrude Stein, Alice Toklas, and the everpresent, but always unspeaking, Bob McAlmon were a part of the literary landscape in Paris. Others—Djuna Barnes, Andre Gide, Paul Valery— are mentioned in passing to give a hint of that fantastic melange of people that *was* Paris.

Of course, little of the book is true, but isn't it fine to think about?

About the Author

Tony Hays is a native of Madison and Murfreesboro, Tennessee. Holding degrees in History, Educational Psychology, and English, Hays has published extensively in the field of local history, and his short fiction has appeared in over ten different publications. He has raised goats, worked at a sawmill, been a veterinarian's assistant, served as foster-father to orphan cats, managed university residence halls, worked as a freelance writer, and taught English in Japan. A member of Mystery Writers of America, he teaches English at Motlow State Community College in Tullahoma, Tennessee and is married to his illustrator, Holly Lentz-Hays. Striper and Cleopatra Cat graciously share their home in Manchester with Holly and Tony.